My Sister's Fear

by

T.J. Jones

To my children,

for their love and support

of this, and all my projects.

My Sister's Fear

Chapter 1

Levi Davis claimed to be the husband of the great, great, granddaughter of the long-deceased Son of the south and President of the Confederacy. Putting aside the curious fact that he and his wife had started life with the same last name, that seemed like an extremely tenuous and convoluted relationship to assert when you were self-aggrandizing about your claim on destiny. But then Levi had accomplished very little in his thirty odd years and he probably felt the need to inflate his own ego. He didn't like when I pointed that out to him, or the crack about keeping it in the family. And for a guy his size, he couldn't throw a decent punch. I would have liked nothing better than to hit him back, but a couple of his good old boys had a hold on both of my arms, and a fourth was doing his best to pulverize my kidneys.

Levi was a few inches shorter than my six-three, and what some people called lanky. I called it scrawny, and he didn't like that either. He spent most of his days driving one of his father's paving trucks, smoking cigarettes and talking trash about things he knew nothing about. He spent most of his nights at the Outhouse, a remarkably descriptive name for the local bar and pool hall, doing his best to romance any woman who might not care that he was married, or foolish enough to be impressed by the fact that his father employed half the town. That's where our paths had first crossed.

Maggie and I had pulled into town and left our things at the motel, then walked across the street. The sign on the door of the bar said "The Outhouse: Where Shit Happens." It was on the south edge of town, roughly eight blocks from the north edge, if that tells you anything, and looked like the only place open to get a sandwich. Small towns can be charming and wonderful at times, like Mayberry RFD. Everybody knows everybody, or knows someone who does. Two, maybe three degrees of separation at most. Often as not, depending on the economy, they're happy to see strangers, and you'd think tourist dollars would be welcome everywhere.

But some little towns want to stay that way. They're content with the status quo. They want to keep their business local and make sure their sons and daughters marry their high school sweethearts, raise some grandkids, and get a job at the local mill. They have their own idea of a perfect life and it doesn't include people from out of town, or people that don't look like them. They don't care for outsiders, especially outsiders that are asking questions and learning their secrets.

It was a Thursday night and the bar was pretty busy, pool night for the ladies. There were eight or ten younger women circling the two pool tables in the back of the place, wearing cutoffs and sweatshirts, swilling beer and talking amongst themselves. They let out an exuberant shriek occasionally when someone made a tough shot and laughed loudly at jokes we couldn't hear. There were a group of guys sitting with them and another dozen scattered around the bar. We took a table right next to the kitchen and the waitress took our order. I went to the bathroom and when I came back found Levi Davis standing beside our table doing his best to cozy up to my girlfriend.

Maggie Jeffries, like her older sister, attracts a lot of attention everywhere we go. She's a couple inches shy of six feet with rust colored hair that cascades halfway down her back and brilliant blue eyes that take your breath away; or maybe that's just me. The girlfriend thing was new and still a little precarious, but even if I tended to be the jealous type I wouldn't have been worried about Levi Davis. He was doing his best to be charming, filled with the unfettered optimism that comes with intoxication and stupidity, weaving slightly as he talked.

Maggie made the introductions. "This is my boyfriend, Slater. Levi Davis, his Dad owns the local paving company."

"Not just local, we do most of the roads in all of south Georgia, three counties, all the way down to Tallahassee sometimes." He puffed up his chest a little. "Sometimes we have to get

6

subcontractors when we go out of state, we're that damn busy."

"Well, of course you are," Maggie said and I nodded, like we had a clue or cared.

"You folks just passing through? We're kind of off the beaten path and most people miss our little town heading down to the coast. Just fine by me, we don't need any of that riff-raff here."

"Hope we don't fit that description." I frowned up at him. "We're just going to be in town for a few days, visiting a sick friend."

"No, course I wasn't talking about you. Good people, you know, white folks are always welcome here. Here's a wild thought, being we just met, but do you think maybe I could borrow Maggie for a while Saturday night? They have a couples' pool night, if you're still going to be around." I had already formed an intense dislike for Levi and this wasn't helping.

"Thanks, but I'm not a pool player," Maggie said quickly. "We're going to be busy with that friend. Looks like they're plenty of extra women in here, I'll bet you could pick up a partner easy enough."

"Yeah, I partnered up with most of these gals already, if you get my meaning." He grinned at me like he wanted to be sure I appreciated the innuendo.

"Well good luck with that, it was nice to meet you Levi." I turned my back to him and after a minute he reluctantly wandered away.

Maggie sipped her beer. "He wanted to talk Slater. You could have asked about the girl."

"The only girl he wanted to talk about was you, and I think we need to find out a little more before we start asking the locals about her. For all we know she was a pool player. If she partnered up with that idiot, he probably has her tied up in his barn. He has some balls, asking you out with me sitting right here."

"Come on Slater, you two might end up being great friends." She laughed.

"Whatever we find out, I'm not going to be friends with Levi Davis." That turned out to be an understatement.

Despite what I'd said about his punches, Levi had managed to inflict some damage, and the guy behind me landed one on the side of my head that made me see stars.

"You get the message Slater? Take that sweet-assed redheaded girl of yours and get the hell out of our town."

Something witty would have been nice, but I was fighting to stay conscious. Someone hit me from behind again, and I went down. They had cornered me at the school in one of the ballfield dugouts near our client's house. My gun was locked in the pickup, and I wasn't sure if Maggie knew I was in trouble. I fell across the makeshift dugout bench, just a plank bolted to cinder blocks, and held onto it. I was sure that if I went to the ground, they would use their boots on me. Funny what comes into your mind, when you know you're about to take the beating of your life. I guess it was being in the dugout, but all I could think about was the one time in my life when I had played baseball.

When I was twelve or thirteen, I was the skinniest most uncoordinated string bean to ever step foot on a baseball diamond. Most of the time I was shunned when it came to any sports in the neighborhood, but on one Sunday afternoon half a dozen of the local kids were desperate for players and they let me join them. Their fears were well founded, because I was terrible. After considerable begging they let me try to hit. In my case, they let me swing until I finally connected, and it was a glorious feeling when I made solid contact six or seven swings in. One of the kids had a new aluminum Easton, and when I finally put the bat on a pitch it made the purest sound I'd ever heard and sent the ball out to the centerfield, just shy of the fence. I think I'll always remember that moment. It turns out a baseball and a kneecap make a similar sound when you hit the sweet spot.

As I fought to stay on the bench and cover my head, I heard the distinct ping of an aluminum bat striking a hard object, followed by the horrible shriek of a man in intense pain. One of the men holding me let go and I managed to stand and spin away from Levi Davis in time to see Maggie swing her bat again, catching her next victim on the arm, squarely in the elbow. Levi smashed me in the back of the head again and I went down, but I managed to grab at my third assailant's foot as he lunged at Maggie Jeffries. He tripped and fell forward with his arms flailing, and she quickly spun the bat around and drove the end of it into his forehead. He hit the ground hard, and I figured he was out of it.

I struggled to get to my feet as Levi rushed past me, trying to get to Maggie. The guy she had hit in the arm grabbed her from behind and while she was reaching back trying to gouge his eyes with one hand she held on with the other, using him for leverage to plant a good solid kick in Levi's face with those long, beautiful legs of hers. Levi was yelling, holding his nose and swearing, while trying to grab at Maggie while the poor guy that already had ahold of her was trying to push her away, undoubtedly concerned about his eyesight. She had driven a thumb into one of his eyes and she was going after the other one, all while doing her best to kick Levi in the face again.

I grabbed the bat from the ground, planning to do some real damage. Suddenly the man holding Maggie was plucked from his feet and tossed aside like a ragdoll, knocking Maggie forward onto the poor guy with the imprint of the Easton on his forehead. A massive hand came forward and pointed a meaty finger at Maggie, who had immediately started throwing punches again.

"Knock that shit off, right now!" Sheriff Alex Henderson bellowed at her and then pointed in my

10

general direction. I dropped the bat and stepped back. Maggie crawled over the top of her victim and scrambled to her feet next to me. The first guy was still clutching his knee, prostrate on the ground, and moaning loudly. Levi was the only one on his feet, relatively unscathed except for a nosebleed.

The Sheriff, all six-eight and three-fifty of him, looked around and shook his head. "Just what in the hell are you bunch of Goddamn idiots doing out here? You scared the shit out of old lady Johnson. She looks out her window and there's a free for all going on right in the fucking school yard. School just let out half an hour ago, little kids could see you morons acting like this."

"These two attacked us," Levi said quickly. "I want to press charges."

The Sheriff looked around. "They? He looks all beat to shit, but he and this pretty little girl attacked all four of you?"

"That bitch broke Jerry's knee with that bat," Levi yelled.

"Alright Levi, settle down." The giant pointed at my partner. "Maggie, right? You tell me what happened here."

"Four of them were beating on Slater. Some kid must have left his bat behind, so I grabbed it and I wasn't about to let them take it away from me."

"Levi?" Henderson turned and looked at him.

11

"They've been poking around, asking questions about Wally Weston, taking his side. They're saying he didn't kill Lilly."

"Weston hasn't been charged with anything, and as far as I know there's no reason he will be. You damn well better leave that business to me. I hope it wasn't you and your boys that gave him that beating, because if I find out it was, I don't care who your Daddy is, you're going to be sorry."

"Jerry's kneecap might be broke, I want to press charges."

"Yeah?" The Sheriff seemed to consider it. "Suppose I'll have to investigate the whole mess then. Tough to imagine how this one woman beat the hell out of all four of you, baseball bat or no. I got to say, it'll make for a good story at the coffee shop. Your Daddy ought to be real proud to hear about you fighting with a girl." Levi kicked the dirt and the Sheriff laughed. "How about you, Mr. Slater, want to press charges?"

"No, I'm good." I wasn't, but I'd heal. "We'll let it go if they do."

"Levi? You going to let this go, or should I tell everybody around town about how this woman kicked your ass?" Levi glowered, but nodded. The Sheriff motioned with a monstrous arm, dismissing the four of them like a grade school principal would dismiss a group of unruly third graders. "You boys need to listen really good for once in your miserable lives. You stay clear of these two until they leave town or so help me, I'll come looking for you, and I won't bother bringing a baseball bat. You get that?"

"This is bullshit," Levi mumbled, but he helped the guy with the sore knee to his feet. They started off across the ballfield and Levi looked back at us. "This isn't over, Slater."

"Bring it, Dickhead!" That was Maggie.

The Sheriff grinned at her. "Wow, you are quite the gal. Try not to assault any more of my citizens, okay? You two need to wrap up your business here. I don't think old Wally had anything to do with Lilly's disappearance either, but I'm not a big fan of outsiders sending my people to the hospital, or private investigators in general. Few more days, then you need to be on your way or I'm going to lose my patience. Long as old Wallace didn't hurt anyone, I'll be damn sure those boys leave him alone from now on. You okay, Mr. Slater?"

"I'll probably piss blood for a day or two, but I'll live."

"Okay then, you have my number."

I leaned on Maggie and we started back to Wally Weston's house.

"Sorry I got you into this mess, Slater." Maggie grimaced, looking at my face.

"Never a dull moment with you, Red. Remind me to stay on your good side. Do you teach baseball bat in those Karate classes of yours?"

"That's the advanced class. Sorry I said we should leave our guns in the truck."

13

"Not your fault. I could have said no to Tommy, but oh no, I had to show off! I should have gone to MacDonald's that night like I said I was going to."

Maybe I should back up and explain.

Chapter Two

Could you tighten your turn, Slater? I keep losing them behind the wingtip. Ever think about a Cessna or some other high winger?"

"That's blasphemy, woman." I banked harder and Maggie Jeffries put the binoculars back up to her face. "Can you see them, Jasmine?" I turned back to look at the girl in the back seat of my Piper. She appeared unimpressed. We were circling the St. Johns River, looking down at a group of Manatee that were feeding along the shoreline far below us.

"Yeah, very cool." She looked down quickly then dropped the field glasses onto her chest and looked up at me again. "When are we going to go back? I'm hungry, and if you keep tipping this damn airplane on its side, I'm going to hurl."

"Did you see the calves?" Maggie asked. "They're so cute."

"Cute? If potatoes could swim, that's what they'd look like. Fair warning, Slater, if I throw up, it's on you, and I do mean that literally."

"Alright, stop your whining, we'll head back. Weather coming in anyway." I glanced at Maggie. "Your new little sister is a pain in the butt. Tell me again why we rescued her from that meth-head biker?"

Jasmine Thatcher's grandmother was incredibly wealthy and she had sent Maggie and I to Atlanta to talk Jaz into leaving the middle-aged biker she had fallen in with. He wasn't happy about losing his teenage girlfriend and there had been a fight, some shooting, and Maggie had ended up with a nasty hole in one of her otherwise perfect legs. All things considered it could have been worse, but not much. At least Jasmine had reconsidered her life choices and returned to Jacksonville and her grandmother's mansion. Undoubtedly her affection for Maggie had a lot to do with that. They had bonded five minutes after they met and were still practically inseparable.

"I know, Slater, Saturday night, date night for you two lovebirds. I'm heading home right after we land so you can have Maggie all to yourself," she volunteered from the back seat.

"No you don't, Too Small. We're all having supper at the Jeffries' tonight and Angela is cooking. If I have to eat it, so do you."

Maggie grinned and glanced back at the tiny girl. "Slater used to call me Too Small when I was a kid too."

"She was as tall as you are now when she was ten." I added.

Jasmine blushed and smiled at me. "Alright, if you insist, I'll come to dinner."

If I was being honest, Jasmine Thatcher felt like my little sister too, or maybe my daughter since I had seven years on Maggie. Suffice it to say I had become extremely fond of the stubborn little wild child. At least she had let the shaved side of her head grow in so that the blue hair covered the tattoo. Nobody had asked, but I approved.

"Did Angela tell you about her dinner guest tonight?" Maggie asked. "It's your old buddy, Tommy Ackerman."

I snorted. "Have fun without me. Between Angela's cooking and that asshole, McDonald's is starting to sound pretty good."

"No way, PI, you're not bailing. Angie would think it really is because of her cooking, and Tommy is much more tolerable than he used to be. You won't need to knock him in the pool again. Besides, he's a lawyer now, and he'd probably sue you. I was going to wait to tell you but I figured a little warning might be nice. He wants to talk to us. He might have a job, an actual investigation job."

I had shared my teenage fascination for Magnum PI with Maggie, so now she had started call me PI. Eric Slater, PI, as if that was a thing. I hadn't decided if it was cute, or annoying.

"I have a job, and I really don't want to talk to him."

"He's married Slater, and you have a serious girlfriend, so there's no reason for you two to fight over Angela anymore. Besides, you're an adult now and you claim to be evolved."

"Really, I have a girlfriend? And it's serious?"

"You're not funny. We need a job. I'm tired of teaching overprivileged teenagers how to hurt

17

their friends. Tae-kwon-do is fun, but I want to investigate something. It's been weeks."

"Well, I like being a carpenter. This is the best shape I've been in for years. I kind of let myself go there for a while. Contrary to what you two may think, I'm not sure I would have won that fight with Cletus Johnson if you hadn't popped him on the head with that beer bottle."

Jaz snickered. "You didn't win that fight. As I remember we had to run for our lives."

"I'd be ready for him now, that's all I'm saying." That might have been a stretch, tough as Cletus Johnson was, but I had lost ten pounds and put on a lot of muscle in the last month. I looked over at Maggie. "Why don't you take us in, you need to get ready for your flight test."

"No, Daddy, don't let Mommy drive, she'll kill us all!" Jasmine pleaded from the back seat.

Maggie smiled over at me. "She is annoying at times, isn't she?"

Maggie took the controls and turned us north. Contrary to what Jasmine had hinted at, Maggie brought the Piper down without so much as a bump. She had been flying half her life, piloting her father down to Miami before his untimely death. That's what happens to people that are involved with kidnapping and child prostitution, they tend to die suddenly. Maggie didn't know all the details and she hadn't asked.

She didn't know about her uncle either, the man she knew as the Diablo Blanco. She and I had learned of his exploits from a young immigrant woman who had been brutalized at his hands. Little did we know at the time that the Diablo that had locked Rosalyn Cabello in a dog kennel and done unspeakable things to her, was in fact Gary Jeffries come back to life.

As far as Maggie and her sister knew their uncle Gary had died in a plane crash in the Everglades a little over four years ago. The truth was that he had faked his death and continued to terrorize young girls until he went into the witness protection program. There was a lot I hadn't told the sisters, and I couldn't see any reason to share some of the things I knew. There were too many bad memories as it was.

When I was a junior in high school, I had finally put on some muscle and used it to knock Tommy Ackerman into Angela's pool for calling Davey Templeton a name. Davey was gay and my best friend. Mostly I hit Tommy because he was an ass and I had gotten big enough to do it. I liked to think I had evolved in the last twenty years, but that didn't mean Tommy couldn't go back in the pool if he didn't behave himself.

Jasmine had driven us over to the airport and she dropped me off at my house, then she and Maggie headed over to Point Road and the Jeffries' house. Point Road was lined with big houses, Estates, and a few old plantations with structures that qualified as mansions in anyone's neighborhood. Most of the houses were on the Saint Johns River and had docks and boats and the occasional seaplane. I had spent some time on the water as a kid with Davey and quite a bit of it was in a seaplane. The remainder of my adolescence was spent desperately trying to have sex with Angela Jeffries, my current girlfriend's older sister.

Maggie had the PI bug, and a romanticized idea of what that meant. I had told her just enough about Davey's death to let her think that her half-brother had died a hero while trying to stop a group of child traffickers. It was mostly true, but I hadn't shared the fact that her father had been involved. Considering the abuse he had subjected her older sister to, Maggie wasn't likely to care that I had been part of the chain of events that led to his suicide. But she was nobody's fool and she had to know I had been right in the thick of things. For now, if she didn't ask, I wouldn't tell. I hoped she would never have to know everything her father had done.

Finding out the circumstances of Davey's death had been important, and it shed light on people who I knew should be spending their life in prison. Maybe someday I'd have a chance to even that score. If it was up to me, a one-way trip to the Everglades seemed like justice, considering the way Davey had died. Child-molesters make great alligator bait. I know thoughts like that aren't a sign of evolution, but I'm working on it.

Everyone has had the experience of seeing something you remember from childhood and thinking how small and unimpressive it looked once you were an adult. I was pretty sure Tommy Ackerman would look that way to me. The raucous teenager had repeatedly slammed me on the side of the head with his Geology book in middle school and had consequently landed in Angela's pool with a bloody nose our junior year. But Tommy wasn't intimidating anymore. I might have been smug about that fact had he not been sitting in that wheelchair. That was something my "serious girlfriend" hadn't bothered to mention to me.

"Eric Slater!" He spun his chair around when I walked into the dining room and greeted me like we were old friends, holding out a hand that I shook. "Been years and years."

"Yeah, high school, right?"

"Heard you got twenty in in the Navy, and Angela tells me now you and Maggie have started your own detective agency? But I'm being rude, this is my wife, Camille."

Camille was a tall, lithesome black woman that stood quickly and held out her hand, smiling warmly. "Tom was telling me stories about you, Mr. Slater. He said you gave him a much-needed attitude adjustment during high school." Tommy laughed the loudest, so I took that to mean he didn't hold a grudge.

I did my best to look sorry. "Too much testosterone at that age I'm afraid, not my finest moment. I never apologized Tommy, so, sorry about that."

He waved a hand. "I deserved it, I was a little prick back then. Just one more bump on the way to being a grownup. I got drunk and totaled my car a couple years after law school and landed in this chair, so that was a big life lesson. But Camille stuck by me and it woke me up to what's really important in life. I'm alive and healthy otherwise, so things could be a lot worse."

Angela Jeffries pointed at a chair and I sat down as she handed me a cold beer, then excused herself and went into the kitchen. Maggie and Jasmine came in and found their chairs, laughing at some private joke.

"Angela insisted that she's going to do the meal, and we can't help," Maggie explained. "Seems like she has things under control. Rosa helped her before she left, so at least we won't be poisoned."

"She was telling us a little bit about things, how difficult it's been, with Davey and Frank both passing away so close together," Tommy said cautiously. "I'm so sorry about your father, Maggie. How is your Mom handling it?"

"She's out, girls' night. She's really loosened up since Dad died and everything came to light," Maggie said. "I don't really want to talk about my dad, if that's alright."

"Of course, I've been helping Angela with the estate and we had a long talk about all that went on. I'm glad she's seeing a therapist and getting some help," Tommy said, then turned back to me. "So, Eric, I understand you and Maggie are working together, and you're licensed private investigators?"

"I'm his apprentice," Maggie said quickly. "He's the one with the license."

"I had some experience during my time in the Navy, and Maggie is really intuitive, so I guess we make a good team," I said. "But really, I can't say that it's more than a part-time thing. The business with Davey, that was important to me. But I'm not interested in catching cheating husbands or busting people trying to scam their insurance companies."

"Angela suggested I talk to you. I'm not looking for a detective for my law firm, Eric, it's more of a personal matter."

"Better call him Slater, Tommy," Angela said, carrying in trays of food. "He thinks it's terribly sexy, or maybe that's just my sister."

"Okay, Slater it is." Tommy grinned and glanced between us. "You and Maggie, you're more than just business partners?"

"Oh hell yes they are!" Jasmine jumped in.

"This is Jasmine, Maryanne Thatcher's granddaughter." Angela made the introductions. "Maggie and Slater rescued her from a situation and now she pretty much lives with us." She poked Jasmine's shoulder and laughed.

"Actually Angela, Jasmine and I have met a few times. She delivered some files to my office for her grandmother. I've done quite a bit of work for Maryanne and her charity. She's a very generous woman."

"She puts up with me, so she must be." Jasmine nodded. "I shouldn't talk about these two but they keep dancing around the good stuff, and I'm getting bored with it. Get a room already."

Maggie scowled in her direction. "Slater and I are going out, and that's all I'm saying about that. If Jasmine knows what's good for her, that's all she's saying too."

"And I don't get any of the details," Angela said. "I'm just the big sister."

I was tired of being talked about. "Alright, Tommy, Camille, is this something we can talk about over supper, or should we discuss it later, privately."

"It might be best if you and Maggie could come to my office, if that works for you. I have some files there that we could go over. But we need to do something soon, maybe as soon as Monday? I mostly just wanted Camille to meet you and Maggie and get a sense of who you are. It's a sensitive family issue, and we both want someone we can trust, and someone with an open mind. It's complicated."

"Complicated is our specialty," Maggie piped up. "That should be our slogan, Slater."

"Oh shit!" Jasmine blurted out suddenly, staring down at her phone.

"Come on, Blue," I admonished. "We're trying to act like professionals."

She looked up at Maggie and me. "Bad news guys, my Mom is coming to town."

Chapter Three

The next day Maggie and I drove down the manicured lane that lead to the Thatcher Estate. Given the opportunity, I would have been anywhere else, but Maggie insisted that as Jasmine's friends it was our obligation to be supportive. I'm not a big fan of being obligated to do things, I'd had enough of that in the Navy. There, obligations weren't something you knew you should do, they were something you did, or faced the consequences. This didn't feel that much different, but I had to admit I was curious about Jasmine's mother, the legendary Divine Thatcher, porn star turned internet investment guru.

A hundred feet from the huge white pillars that pretended to hold up the overhang of the Thatcher mansion was a small barn, bright red with white trim. A tall wooden fence wound its way across the small pasture where half a dozen horses were grazing, show-ponies for the idle rich to admire as they drove in. Jasmine was sitting on top of the fence with her toes hooked into the second row of the bright white boards. She waved at us listlessly, then turned her attention back to the horses.

We got out of the car and walked over to her as three of the horses trotted in our direction. I recognized the leader, a particularly nasty mare that had tried to rip my fingers off during a previous visit. I called out a warning. "Jasmine, that horse is a biter!"

She glanced back and grinned as the three horses crowded into the corner. "Slater, you're the one that told me I should learn to ride. Dolly just needed attention, she loves me."

"She loves human flesh." I said. As if aware that I was talking about her, the mare started fighting with the other two horses, biting and kicking at them until they relented and trotted off into the pasture. Then, surprisingly, she ran up to Jasmine and dropped her head between her knees. Maggie climbed up onto the fence and sat next to Jasmine and joined in stroking the mare. Convinced the nag had been domesticated, I started to climb onto the fence. I don't think horses can growl, but I swear that one did and reached out with her mouth open.

"Dolly, no!" Jasmine called loudly, and the silly horse actually listened, like a well-trained canine. I climbed carefully up on the fence and Dolly tucked her head back between Jasmine's knees again, willing to ignore me as long as the girl continued scratching her ears. Still, I kept a wary eye on the crowbait the whole time we talked and caught it glaring back at me more than once.

"What are you doing out here?" Maggie asked. "Isn't your Mom here?"

"We're still having brunch, right?" I asked. "I skipped breakfast." I was hungry.

"Mom's here with her dipshit boyfriend. She and Maryanne are having a discussion, or an argument, I guess. Mom has the idea that she's going to drag me back to New York, which isn't going to happen. I won't go and Maryanne isn't going to let her take me. I'll hit the road again before I ever move to New York with her."

"Don't think you'll find another idiot like Cletus, you better stick around." It was a poor joke.

"If I wanted to go, I sure as hell wouldn't need a man." Jasmine snapped.

"Of course not. You're all of seventeen. Lie about your age and join the Navy, I highly recommend it," I said seriously.

She slapped my shoulder and giggled, the anger quickly forgotten. Dolly's ears came forward and I couldn't tell if it was jealousy or maternal instinct; either way I kept one eye on her.

"Your grandmother isn't going to let her take you, and you have school coming up." Maggie interjected. "You're old enough to be emancipated if you have to."

"She wants me to meet my father."

"Really!" Maggie seemed surprised and I was confused.

"I didn't know you had one." I blurted out.

Jasmine laughed. "You see, Slater, there's this big cabbage patch, and..."

"Alright, I've heard that story. What I meant was, considering her lifestyle, and her job, you know."

"You mean, maybe my Mom was such a slut she didn't know who the father was?"

"That's not what I meant. Okay, it was. You've never met him before?"

"No. He lives in Los Angeles and he knew I existed and everything, but he married someone else and didn't want it to be weird. My Mom is a control freak and didn't want him being a bad influence on me."

"But she let you ride around with a thirty-six year old meth head?"

Maggie leaned forward and glared at me. "Slater, stop talking. So maybe that's all it is, Jaz, she thinks that you should meet this guy."

"Maybe, but if it goes well, she wants me to go to LA. Turns out I have a sister. I didn't expect to ever meet my father, now I find out I have a sister? My dad's wife is cool with me meeting her, but they want me to decide first, before they tell the girl about it. She's twelve, so they didn't want to tell her, then have me not show up."

"Jasmine, when did you find out about all this?" Maggie asked.

"My Mom and I talked last night, about the visit, not about me moving to New York. I think she figured I'd get all excited about the sister thing and then spring the move on me. She said it this morning, like it was a done deal. I'd love to meet my half-sister but I don't care either way about my dad. He could have come to see me anytime, right? I'm not living in New York, that is for sure. I like it here. I have you guys, Gram, Dolly." The horse's ears came forward and she sighed comfortably when Jasmine renewed her scratching. "And I even met a guy."

"Oh man, I knew this was going to happen." I grimaced. "That sounds like trouble."

Jasmine laughed again. "He works at the Safeway as a bagboy and he's sweet. More importantly, he's my age. In case you've forgotten, Slater, I spent six weeks with a middle-aged biker, I'm not some innocent virgin. I've been around the block a time or two."

"I'm not talking about any of this, and I don't want to hear any more about it." I crossed my arms for effect. She made a face at me, and I continued. "When will you find time to date, you're always with us?"

"See, if I spend time with Jessie, you and Maggie can have some much needed alone time."

"We're taking it slow, like I told you," Maggie said.

"Slow? It's been a month, aren't you getting horny?" Jasmine shook her head. "You're both healthy adults. I know you're old as dirt Slater, but Maggie is hot, you have to get after it already!"

I didn't need any convincing, but it wasn't that simple. "Hey, I'm not that old and slow is good. You're seventeen, you should be taking it slow with this Jessie guy, too. Very, very, slow."

She rolled her eyes. "You two are ridiculous. Let's go in and you can meet my Mom. Lucky her boyfriend went into town, he's disgusting."

Divine Thatcher wasn't what I expected. During long deployments I will admit to watching an occasional erotic movie. Okay, it was porn. Fortunately, Divine had never been featured in any of them, but I was aware of her reputation, both as a porn star and as an internet blogger with hundreds of thousands of followers. There was talk of a television show. I'd seen pictures, publicity shots that were obviously trying to take advantage of her notoriety to promote her current gig. In those, she just looked like a porn star with glasses, sometimes sitting in front of a computer with a low-cut dress that showed too much cleavage and plenty of leg.

The real woman was plain looking at first glance. She wore a plaid cotton shirt, blue jeans and sneakers, pretty standard wear for Florida in the winter. She stood and reached out a hand when Jasmine introduced us. When I got close, I was struck by how tiny she was, and by the fact that I could have ever thought she was plain looking.

Close up, her face looked like an artist's rendition of beauty. Her cheekbones were impossibly high, her jaw angular and sharp, her lips full and sensual, made more so by a delicate nose and eyes that were an undefinable shade of green.

31

The baggy clothes did little to hide a perfect figure or disguise the vague scent of some intoxicating perfume that I realized may have simply been pheromones. It occurred to me that I was staring and I glanced nervously at Maggie, but she was staring too.

"Jasmine has told me so many wonderful things about you both, and about that horrible Cletus person shooting at you and wounding you, Maggie. I had no idea he was such an ass. You must think I'm a terrible mother for allowing her to ride with him. My god, I'm so glad you're alright. Is it healed?"

"I'm fine, no permanent damage, just some muscle pain and a bit of a scar. I'm back to running ten miles every morning."

"Really, I'd love to go with you while I'm here. But you have those wonderfully long legs, no doubt you'd leave me in the dust."

"It would be one way to get Slater to show up." Okay, she had noticed me staring. "He's been skipping out on our morning runs lately."

She raised a brow. "You might need to let him sleep at night, but that's no fun, right?"

"Mom! One minute and you're already talking about sex, give it a rest." Jasmine complained.

"Sex and money, Jasmine, that's what makes the world go around." She threw her head back and laughed. "I'm considered an expert in both fields."

"I don't know if I'd brag about that." Jasmine put in.

"Good one, Jaz." Divine laughed loudly again, but it was quick and her eyes narrowed a little. She was putting on a show for us and that had hurt her.

"Divine, cut the crap, it's all decided." Maryanne Thatcher took over, dismissing the chit-chat with a wave of her hand. She looked every bit the powerful woman who had built a fracking company from scratch and owned sizable chunks of North and South Dakota. She was used to calling the shots, and she wasn't about to let that change.

She pulled her glasses off and slid them into her silver blond hair, then pushed a small stack of papers across the mahogany surface and tossed a pen on top of them. "This is what we talked about this morning. I had it drawn up last week because I saw this coming, sign it."

"Really, Mom, now, when we have company?"

"I wanted them here, Divine. I need it witnessed. These two risked their lives for Jasmine, and since then they've been like family to her, so I wanted them to know what's going on. I'm done fighting about this. Jasmine is staying here and you can go back to New York or LA or wherever the next reprobate that catches your eye drags you. You're my daughter and I love you, but I won't let you drag Jasmine around the country and be exposed to the riffraff you surround yourself with.

Cletus Johnson was completely your fault, not Jasmine's. She's a child and you're her mother, it's supposed to be you that protects her. But starting today, I'm going to be her legal guardian until she turns eighteen."

"Jasmine, is this really what you want?" Tears slid down Divine's beautiful chiseled cheekbones, and I couldn't help feeling bad for her.

"Yeah, Mom, this is home. It's steady and there's no craziness. I love you, but I really want to stay here. You can visit whenever you want, but I won't go to New York or anywhere else."

"But what about your dad? He wants to meet you. He was planning on flying to New York, or down here if need be."

"Maybe sometime. Maybe I'll come for a visit after a while or he can come here. Just sign the papers, please?"

There were several pages, and she went through them quickly, scratching out her signature and sniffing through tears occasionally. When she finished, she stood and put her arms around Jasmine, clinging to her. "I'm only doing this for you, Jasmine, you know that, right?"

"Sure, Mom, thank you, really. Want to go meet my horse? Maggie, you want to come too?"

I stood there awkwardly and watched the three of them walk out the door, then turned back to Maryanne.

"Don't worry about signing anything for now, Eric." She waved a hand. "My lawyers will deal with it. I'll say one thing, that daughter of mine is a good actress. Too bad she had to do it with her legs in the air, she might have amounted to something."

"Sorry, Maryanne, not really sure what to say about that one."

"Anything happens to me in the next year, Slater, and you and Maggie will be Jasmine's legal guardians, presuming you're willing. My granddaughter loves you both and Divine doesn't want anything to do with her, not really.

"I offered her a pile of cash, and she just signed all her rights away, didn't bat an eye or have to think about it. Don't waste your time feeling bad for her, those tears weren't real. I don't know where I went wrong with her, but she's just a beautiful empty vessel without a soul as far as I can tell. Jasmine is a good person, and I want her to be around good people."

"Why would anything happen to you?" I asked nervously.

She laughed. "Don't worry, I have no intention of leaving you with an obstinate seventeen-year old girl if I can help it. I'm not sick, I don't have cancer or any terminal disease. I plan to be around for another thirty, forty years. But I didn't get where I am by not preparing for the unexpected. If I had the big one tomorrow, Divine would get half of my money, but the rest would go to Jasmine.

"I trust you and my lawyers a hell of a lot more than that irresponsible daughter of mine to take care of my granddaughter and my business should something happen to me. Divine is bad enough, but she continually surrounds herself with drug addicts and greedy men. I don't think she's quite the successful business woman she claims to be. She jumped on my offer of money pretty quickly."

"I'll talk to Maggie, but I'm sure we could work it out, heaven forbid, anything happened to you."

Maryanne smiled mischievously. "How's that going? You and Maggie?"

"She's holding back, says she wants to be sure. I'm sure, but I've got nothing but time and she's worth waiting for. She says it's about her divorce, but I think the thing with her dad messed her up more than she wants to admit."

"She's an incredible woman."

"That she is, Maryanne, and so are you. You have to know Jasmine knows that."

"Thanks, Slater, she's a good girl. I'll get the paperwork together for you and Maggie to sign and then I'll call you. I need to get back to work, say Hi to Dolly for me."

"I hate that stupid horse." I shared as I left her office.

36

Chapter Four

Tommy Ackerman's office was in downtown Jacksonville, and Maggie and I managed to get there twenty minutes late. I didn't believe the GPS on Maggie's phone and got us a little lost; a guy thing I'm told. His office was on the ground floor of a small commercial building in a renovated district of the downtown area, very plush, spacious and expensive if I had to guess.

His receptionist, or legal-aid according to the plaque on his desk, was a tall gawky looking young man that asked us to take a seat. Maggie sat down and I wandered around the office a little, looking at some of the paintings on the wall and the pair of sculptures that stood on either side of the entry door. Both were half high wood-carved statues of women, black women, depicted in different types of labor. One carried a jug on her shoulder, and the other had a bundle of sticks strapped to her back. I had seen similar depictions before, but the statuettes were intricate beyond belief, undoubtedly carved from the dark mahogany by some patient craftsman with a tiny chisel and mallet. Even the dark eyes, somehow carefully gouged into the wood, managed to be full of expression, imparting a sense of haunting sorrow and weariness.

I'm no art critic. I never understood Picasso, and I always thought Monet painted fuzzy pictures because it was easier. And there's the Mona Lisa. That's it, that's all I know about art; but those statues blew me away. After a few weeks of playing carpenter I was developing an appreciation for anything wood, and I couldn't fathom the patience it must have taken to create something so perfect. When I knelt down to look closer, Maggie walked over and I started explaining to her how difficult it must have been to make the statues without fracturing the wood. We were both crouching in front of the depiction of the woman with the bundle on her back, when Camille Ackerman walked in.

"I'm sorry, I'm really late. You must think I'm rude, or scatterbrained." She apologized.

"We were late too, we just got here. Slater doesn't trust technology so we drove around the block a few times."

"She picks on me continually, but I don't take it personally," I assured Camille.

"He knows how much I love him, he just puts on a show," the redhead said, chuckling.

"These statues are unbelievable," I said as I stood up.

"My uncle did those, and he's the reason we wanted to talk to you." She turned to the receptionist. "Jarrod, tell Tom I'm here, and that we're coming back, okay?"

"Will do, Mrs. Ackerman." He hesitated. "Mister Slater, would you please tell Jasmine I said hello?"

"Sure, Jarrod is it?"

"Yes, sir, Jarrod Kinsley."

"I'll tell her." Maggie poked me as we walked back to Tommy's office, and snickered. I shrugged. "Beats the bag boy at Safeway."

Tommy Ackerman sat behind his desk and shook our hands again. "Hi guys, I'm glad you could meet us here. I didn't want to discuss this in front of Angela, considering everything. Maggie, if anything we're talking about makes you uncomfortable just say so."

"Everyone's been tiptoeing around what my father did, Tommy. I'd prefer it wasn't common knowledge, not to protect him, but to protect Angela. He was a sick bastard, plain and simple. But Angela shouldn't have to suffer through being looked at and talked about because her father molested her. I appreciate your discretion where she's concerned, but I'm fine. You can tell us whatever this is about and it won't upset me or drum up memories of my dad. He's gone, good riddance."

I knew it wasn't that simple, but there was a time and place for everything. "So, your uncle, Camille? How can we help you with that?"

"Alright, kind of a long story. My uncle's name is Wallace, Wallace Weston. He's always been a little odd, and maybe that's why he's artistic. My Mom swears that he couldn't have done anything to that girl, and there's no evidence, but it looks bad. Let me start from the beginning.

"Uncle Wally had one girlfriend his whole life, then he got drafted and went to Vietnam. He was wounded and lost his leg, most of it anyway, well above the knee, and by the time he came back, his girlfriend had married someone else and moved away. He's never even looked at another woman since. Our family is from over north of Tallahassee, a little town just across the Georgia line. Not an area known for its progressive politics. Racism is still alive and well there."

"Just to be clear, we don't know for sure that racism played a part in what happened." Tommy put in. "Granted, it does seem likely."

Camille continued. "After Vietnam, Wally went home, stayed in the same town and still lives in the house where he grew up. My grandparents died years ago, so he inherited their house, and he refuses to leave it, says it's the only home he's ever known. The house is right across the road from a middle school, and there's a high school just down the block. That's how he got to know Lilly."

"This part is why I thought it best to talk here, without Angela around. The circumstances of the allegations are similar enough that I thought it might be a trigger of sorts for her. Are you sure you're okay with this, Maggie?" Tommy interjected.

"I can imagine where this is headed." Maggie nodded. "Don't worry, I'm fine."

40

"My uncle is on a pension, and with the house and everything, he's been able to make a living with his carvings. He got kind of a reputation as an artist in the area, so he would work on his carvings in the garage with the door open to the street, since he didn't have a car and the light was good. People would come all the way from Pensacola to buy his carvings, so he usually kept the garage door open so they could find the place.

"I don't really know the whole story, just what my mom told me. Being the middle school was right there, the kids coming and going would wave and some would stop to watch him carve. Lilly Franklin walked by every day and she must have been an art nut, because before long she was there a lot and they became friends. Granted, old guy and a young girl, I'm sure people's tongues were wagging. If she'd been a white girl, someone would have put a stop to it right away, that's just the mentality around there. But she's black, and her home life wasn't great, so my uncle let her hang around. At least he always kept the garage door open when she was over there, he had that much presence of mind."

"Middle school? How old?" I asked.

"She was fourteen when it started. I mean her hanging around, there was never anything inappropriate. She came by every day and watched, then he started letting her help, and she just kept showing up. My mom went up there to help him out and check on things about a year ago, and she met Lilly. Lilly would have been seventeen then. Mom said Wally adored Lilly, but like a father or a mentor because of the sculpting. That was the impression my mom got, and I'm fairly sure that was all there was to it."

"Fairly sure?" I asked.

"My uncle has always been a little odd, and when he got hurt in Vietnam and lost part of his leg we think there might have been some brain damage, too. Of course, I wasn't alive yet. My mother was the youngest in the family and Wally is a lot older than her. But my mother and grandmother both said that he was never the same after he came back. The VA could never diagnose anything, but he's always had these episodes. There are times when he talks about random things that don't make sense, like he's somewhere else or has forgotten where he is and is trying to make sense of it. He is very smart, but something is off. Sometimes he loses big stretches of time."

"And you think, during one of these stretches, that he may have done something to this young girl?"

"He called my mother a couple months ago. He was in a shelter in Charleston, South Carolina, no money and no recollection of how he got there."

"So, if he did something to her, he might not remember it?"

"That's why I said fairly sure, I can't be positive that he didn't do something. When the

42

trouble started, my mom and I went up there, and he denied knowing anything about what had happened to Lilly, but it was weird. I felt like he was holding something back. I couldn't be sure he wasn't having one of those episodes. Now things have only gotten worse, after the beating." Camille drew a breath, near tears. "He refuses to leave. He says Lilly may come back and that he needs to be there for her. Sometimes, when he's confused, he calls her Lainey. Elaine was his girlfriend's name before Vietnam."

"Take it easy, Camille, I can tell them the rest." Tommy leaned forward and Camille took his hand. "About two, two and a half weeks ago, Lilly disappeared. Apparently, she lived with her father and he drinks a lot and didn't report it at first. Finally, when the Sheriff gets wind of it, he starts asking questions and it comes out that the girl has been hanging around at Wallace's place a lot. The Sheriff asked Wally what he knows and he clams up, says he doesn't know anything. Then the Sheriff asks if he can look around the place."

"Needed his lawyer about then, right?" I said.

"Yes and no. Sheriff Henderson is a good guy, but when a possible suspect says sure come on in and look around, he isn't about to turn down the invitation. First thing he finds is a long note from the girl, sitting right there on the end table next to Wally's reading lamp. It says Lilly is sorry and she loves Wally more than she can say, but that she has to leave town. The Sheriff pointed out the fact that it went into some lengths detailing her affections for Wally and that it was obvious they were very close."

"And now no one can find her?" Maggie asked.

"She's eighteen, legally she can go wherever she wants. I talked to the Sheriff and there were no signs of foul play. With no reason to think otherwise, the Sheriff would have just dropped it. Eighteen-year old girls strike out on their own all the time, but her dad started making a stink. He claimed Wally had been molesting her for years and that she had finally told him about it and that Wally had killed her to shut her up."

"And the note?"

"Wally would have made her write it of course, right before he killed her and buried her in the backyard," Tommy said sarcastically.

"Okay, so do you want us to find this girl, or do you think it's remotely possible that Wally did something to her?" Maggie asked.

"No way he hurt her, absolutely not." Camille jumped back in. "But her father ran around town spreading rumors, saying Uncle Wally was molesting her the whole time she was helping him sculpt. Pretty soon all the school kids going by are throwing stuff and calling him a pervert, breaking his heart. A few days ago, some guys caught him in his garage in the evening and beat the hell out of him, put him in the hospital for two days. My mother went up there, but she can't stay and he refuses to come home with her. Like I said, he still thinks Lilly might need him. He hasn't even been sculpting much, he just sits there and waves at the kids that walk by and call him names. That's what hurts him the most. He loved that those kids used to watch him sculpt, and now they all hate him because of something he didn't do. All he wants is to work on his art and to be able to die in the house he grew up in, it's not fair."

Tommy looked at me solemnly. "Bottom line, Slater, we can't say with a hundred percent certainty that something didn't happen to this girl. It's remotely possible that Wallace had one of his memory lapses and something bad happened, maybe he did do something to the girl. That seems unlikely, but right now he's presumed guilty by everyone in that little town until we can prove differently. He won't talk to us, and if he knows where Lilly is, he won't tell the Sheriff. The girl's father is an ass and he keeps throwing around wild accusations and stirring up the town. The guy should be thanking Wally, he basically kept an eye on his daughter for the last four years while he sat in the bar. And Wally taught her to sculpt to boot."

"Just sounds like a girl sick of her old man and hometown to me. She's eighteen, she can come and go as she wants. Was she still in school?"

"She was supposed to graduate this spring. The Sheriff did say he thought it was suspicious that her cellphone went completely dead, so he did check that much out at least."

Camille spoke up again. "I just want my uncle to be able to sell his art and be left in peace. Unless we can prove he didn't do anything to Lilly, the whole town is going to continue hating him and something worse is going to happen. It still isn't easy being a black man in Georgia, no matter what they say on the six o'clock news. There are people that hate him just for the color of his skin, much less thinking he's a child molester or a murderer."

Tommy leaned forward. "We want you to go up there as soon as possible, you and Maggie. The Sheriff doesn't think Wallace did anything to her and he just wants to move on, but that might not save Camille's uncle from another beating or worse if this doesn't get straightened out. Ideally, you find Lilly, prove to the town that Wally didn't do anything bad to her, and he can go on with his life. The whole deal just seems odd, her leaving suddenly without telling her father or Wally where she was going. There has to be more to it."

"There's always more to it, especially when there's a teenager involved." I said.

Maggie poked me with an elbow and laughed. "He almost said teenage girl, but he's evolving."

We worked out the details: the town, the Sheriff's phone number, and Wally's address. As soon as possible would be later that day. We both had things to take care of before leaving town, and we weren't sure how long we would be gone.

"I'll call and explain that you're coming. My mom had to come back today, but I'll explain it all to him." Camille said as she held the door open for us. "Hopefully he'll remember and be willing to talk to you."

We walked out into the outer office and I looked at the sculptures again. The lanky young man behind the desk waved as we opened the door to leave.

"Don't forget to tell Jasmine I said Hi, okay?"

I pulled the door shut and gave Maggie a smile. "Teenagers, they're all trouble."

I dropped Maggie off at home, then went to the construction site to talk to Luis. As was usually the case, he had everything under control, so I went home to pack some clothes and do some laundry. Half an hour after I got home my phone chimed, and I picked it up, expecting a text from Maggie.

Susan Foster? *'Slater, need to talk to you, soon!'*

I texted back. *'Can you call?'*

'No, in person.'

Short and direct, what I would expect from a government employee. I replied.

'Heading out of town on a case for a few days, can't delay. Can it wait?'

'Call me ASAP when you get back, we need to meet.'

Susan Foster had been the woman working undercover with David Templeton when he was killed. She had a fake job as the receptionist at the talent agency that Davey ran. The agency was part of a larger network, a network that traded in the misery of young women, girls as young as thirteen that were often abducted and forced into prostitution. Davey Templeton had been pulled in, duped into thinking the agency was legitimate by Maggie's uncle, the man we knew as the Diablo Blanco.

Susan Foster had been working, with Davey's help, to expose the individuals at the top of the organization. She wasn't FBI or a US Marshall, and she claimed to work for Homeland Security. Whatever the agency, she worked closely with the Feds and had no trouble calling in the local police when it became necessary. We had formed an uneasy alliance predicated on our shared hatred of the people responsible for Davey's death. Some of those people were still at large, connected to organized crime and a couple of movers and shakers in Washington and beyond.

Frank Jeffries, Maggie's father, had gotten in too deep financially and otherwise, and it cost him his life. Maggie knew about some of it, and soon I would have to tell her everything, including the fact that her Uncle Gary was still very much alive. I wasn't sure how that was going to go, but I knew it was too big a secret to keep from her for very long. Meeting with Susan would give me a chance to talk to her about that. Gary Jeffries was a protected federal witness, but Maggie had a right to know her uncle was alive.

Chapter Five

What is it, three hours?" Maggie asked as she tossed her bag in the back of my truck. I had opted to drive my old pickup.

"This late there won't be much traffic. You found us a room, right?"

"Yeah, but no bets on how nice it will be. It's a pretty small town."

"Who's covering for you at the gym?"

"No classes this week. Luis is running your crew?"

"It's his crew, he just lets me help. It isn't like they're going to miss me." We wound through the evening traffic in silence for a few blocks then hit the on-ramp of the Interstate that would take us west. Maggie seemed excited.

"This is great PI, just like our first case, hitting the road together. Like old times."

"That was just a few weeks ago, Red. Why did you start calling me PI all of a sudden?"

"Why did you start calling me Red?" She shot back.

"If I stop, will you?"

"Probably not." I watched her auburn hair sway as she laughed and shook her head from side to side.

"Alright, but if it's going to be Eric Slater PI all the time, I'm growing a huge cheesy mustache, just like Tom Selleck."

"Yeah, maybe I'll have to find a new nickname. I'm not kissing you if your top lip gets any hairier."

"I notice you haven't been kissing me much anyway," I said cautiously.

"Sorry." She slumped down in the seat frowning.

"I don't want you to be sorry, it's fine." I didn't want to be a whiner. "I'm not trying to guilt you into anything, I just want to know that we're alright."

"Of course we are. I've just got a lot going on in my head. With Dad dying and then finding out Davey was my half-brother, it's a lot to process. I'm getting there. You didn't even hear what I said to Camille yesterday, did you?"

"What, you think I don't listen?" I tried to sound surprised.

"No, as a matter of fact I don't."

"Well I do, listen. You said you were madly in love with me."

"I did not say that." She eyed me skeptically.

"It was implied, we all knew what you meant."

"You're comfortable, like an old shoe, that's what I meant." She grinned and closed her eyes and I thought she might have fallen asleep. Then she asked the question I'd been dreading. "Slater?"

"Yeah?"

"Was my Dad the Diablo Blanco?"

No, your uncle was. But I couldn't say that. "No, but he knew about what was going on."

"Why do you think he killed himself?" Her eyes were still shut and I was glad she couldn't see the emotion on my face.

"You knew about his girlfriend down in Lauderdale, right? Your Dad got mixed up with some very heavy hitters, organized crime, and he was in over his head. He screwed up somehow, and they gave him a choice as a reminder of who was running the show, or a punishment of some sort. Someone had to die, Maria and her son, or you and Angela. He came home to Jacksonville that night thinking an assassin was going to kill Maria and her little boy. I don't know if it was that guilt, the terrible things he'd done to Angela, or just the fact that you and she would always be at risk as long as he was alive that made him hang himself. With Frank dead, there was no reason for them to come after you."

"Maria and her son, they were murdered?" She asked, wide-eyed.

"They sent an assassin, but I shot him. They're both fine, the babysitter too." She just stared at me, putting the pieces together, pieces that had to hurt. "If I'd realized what your dad would do, killing himself that way, I would have tried to stop him, called or something. I'm sorry."

The truth was that I expected Frank Jeffries to go on with his miserable life even if he thought he was responsible for the death of his young girlfriend and her child. That was the kind of narcissistic, miserable bastard he had been. Had I suspected what he was going to do, I couldn't say with any certainty I would have tried to stop him. Cold, but I had witnessed some of the destruction he and his brother had wrought on a young woman's soul, and he deserved whatever Hell there was available as far as I was concerned. The remainder of the trip was quiet.

One motel room, two beds. It's what I was expecting, so it wasn't hard to hide my disappointment. We tossed our suitcases on the beds and walked across to the Outhouse and our first encounter with Levi Davis.

Later, we climbed into our respective beds and turned off the light. Maggie hadn't said much after the bar and I could tell she was deep in thought. I was waiting for the second shoe to drop. My eyes were heavy and I was close to nodding off before she spoke.

"Slater, you awake?"

"I'm awake."

"I do, you know."

"You do what, Red?"

"Love you, a lot."

"I love you too, a lot." Good to hear and good to finally say it.

She was quiet for a long time. "That bastard tried with me once."

"Your father?" There it was.

"Mom and Angie were gone somewhere, and he came into my room. I was eleven. I had just started wearing a bra, and he must have noticed. He came in and sat on my bed and asked me to show it to him. He said it was a right of passage, a girl needing a bra, and that he wanted to see it. I thought it was odd, but bras are no different than a bikini top, so I opened my shirt and showed him. He said he wanted to see the back, so I took my shirt down and turned around." She stopped for a long minute. "He came up behind me, telling me how pretty it looked and started touching my neck. When he slid the straps off my shoulders I freaked out. I knew that wasn't right, or normal."

"Did he try to force you?" I don't think I ever hated anyone more in my life than Frank Jeffries in that moment.

"No, I started crying and yelling. He pushed me against the wall, and maybe he would have kept going, but I kept fighting him and screaming as loud as I could. He finally left, but not before telling me that if I said anything to my mom, he would make me regret it. After that, anytime I had to be alone with him I was terrified it might happen again. I hated flying with him, but I went anyway. A small part of me was still jealous of Angela, which seems really sick."

"None of that was your fault, Maggie. Something was very wrong with him. I don't know what made him that way, but it wasn't anything you did." She was up suddenly and pulled the covers of the small bed back, sliding against me and wrapping her arms around my neck.

"Can you just hold onto me?" she said through tears. I held her as she sobbed against my neck for a good long time, then kept her from falling off the bed when she leaned back to look into my face. "Do you know the worst part?"

"I can't imagine what could be worse." I admitted.

"I was so afraid of him that I never said anything, not to Angela, or to my mom. I should have told someone, a friend or a counselor at school. Angie was sixteen then, and he'd been raping her for years. I could have said something. I should have told, I could have made him stop!" She buried her face against my chest and started sobbing again.

"Maggie, you were a little girl. Eleven years old isn't mature enough to deal with anything like that. It isn't a child's job to be responsible for her parents, and you weren't responsible for what happened to Angela. You were the little sister, Too Small, remember?"

She laughed a little through her tears. After another minute she kissed me softly before going back to her own bed. "Thanks Slater, I'll be okay." It was another five minutes before she spoke again. "Maybe I'll talk to that shrink Angela is seeing, couldn't hurt right?"

"Sounds like a good idea to me. Goodnight, Red."

The next morning, we asked the guy at the front desk where we could get breakfast and he directed us to Maryetta's Diner in the middle of town. Maryetta was the original proprietor, apparently deceased and enshrined in a series of large pictures scattered around the place. There were four pictures of just her, and two with a bespectacled thirty-something man with a large nose and shock of curly brown hair that was all plastered to one side. I guessed him to be her son, same nose. Judging by the photos, she had been a matronly, robust woman; undoubtedly smelling of pancakes and piecrusts, capable of encircling her son and the patrons of her establishment in a warm embrace while she doled out fresh coffee and wry wisdom with a gentle smile.

"I worked for her for five years," the grizzled waitress with the tattoos and assortment of hardware in her lip commented when I asked her about the pictures. "Meanest bitch ever walked the face of the earth. My guess is her kid photoshopped that smile on her face, because I never saw one. You can make anybody look good with computer technology. My boyfriend, he's the cook in the back, he bought the place from her kid this fall. He was the one that hung all the pictures up and we just never got around to taking them down.

"He's some sort of a highfalutin photographer somewhere, but he come back last summer to wait for the old lady to die and sell this dump to my old man. Don't know how he ever pried the cigarette out of the old bat's mouth long enough to take those pictures." She stared angrily up at the nearest framed photo for a minute, then threw her pad down on the table between us. "What'll it be, I don't got all day."

"Nice place." Maggie smiled as she sipped her coffee. "Quaint, plenty of local charm."

I grimaced. "I thought it would be a step up from the Outhouse, now I'm not so sure."

We'd gotten up early and the Diner was bustling with locals, most of whom appeared to be on their way to work. Levi Davis and another young guy had been sitting at the counter and must have finished their breakfast. They stood, and while his friend paid, Levi swaggered over.

"Morning you two." He stared at Maggie. "Ya'll are looking lovely this morning."

"Thank you." I winked at the redhead. "Or were you just talking to her?"

"Nice, Mr. Slater." Levi laughed. "Who knew a Yankee would have a sense of humor."

"Born and raised in Jacksonville, but yeah, we kind of sound like Yankees over that way. Twenty years in the Navy probably changed the way I talk."

"Yeah? Well, thank you for your service. Makes you pretty long in the tooth, don't it?"

"He keeps up just fine." Maggie smirked. "I thank him for his service every night."

Levi laughed cautiously, confused by the double entendre, then seemed to catch on. "Well, that makes him the luckiest man in Georgia, that is for sure. Still need a pool partner for Saturday night, just in case you change your mind, Maggie. You can bring Grandpa along if you want."

Alright, that was a little funny even if it was at my expense. I went along. "Us old guys hit the rack pretty early, and I'm scared of the dark. Maggie hates to see me sleep alone."

He leered at Maggie again. "Luckiest man in Georgia, like I said. Ya'll have a good day. Me and my brother Kyle here got to get to work."

Kyle nodded, touched his cowboy hat and smiled shyly at Maggie as they left.

"That wasn't so bad," Maggie said. "I wonder if he knows Wallace?"

"Riff-raff, since he's not white. Odds are if he does know him, he's not a fan of his art. Probably can't spell art." The Grandpa crack was wearing on me.

"Wow, why don't you like my pool partner?" That didn't even deserve a response. Our food came and we started eating.

"Best hash in Georgia, right?" One of the extra chairs at our table slid back, and a small giant of a man sat down without being invited. Maybe a real giant, there was nothing small about him. He extended a frying pan paw. "Sorry to interrupt, but I figured you must be Eric Slater and Maggie Jeffries. We don't get many strangers around here, and you look fresh off the boat. Early, and I'm officially off duty today, but I thought I'd introduce myself. Sheriff Alex Henderson. County seat is up the road, but I live here in town."

We shook hands and I put down my fork. "Nice of you to stop by to say hello, or is this more of a business call."

"Little of both." He shrugged. "I talked to Wallace Weston's niece yesterday and she said you'd be coming up this way to see what you could find out. Real polite gal, she made it clear you just want to clear his name, not like ya'll think we're incompetent here or anything."

"Not that at all. You're a busy guy, and eighteen-year old girls can move away anytime they want, right? Nobody expects you to spend a ton of time looking for her."

"That's good." He looked at the coffee the waitress tried to hand him and waved her away with a nod. She scowled, but didn't say anything.

"I'm sympathetic to your cause, Mr. Slater. Seems unlikely old Wallace did anything to that girl. Peculiar though, she just didn't show up for school one day. Good student and none of her friends knew about her going off, or if they did, they're not talking to me. Kids see me, sometimes they clam up. But you'd think she would have stuck around long enough to graduate. Might be she just got sick of her Daddy ripping on her all the time. Evert's an asshole. He drives a roller for Davis Paving when he's not too hungover. He's the one been carrying on about Wally doing something to Lilly and got the whole town stirred up."

"Perhaps he doth protest too much?" Maggie asked.

The big man got the reference and smiled. "Lilly's Dad doesn't have the stones to kill anybody, but I think it bothered him she liked Wallace so much. If he had stayed home once in a while, she might have cared more what he thought. I can try to protect Wallace, but the best thing would be if he went to live with his sister in Jacksonville until this all blows over, or Lilly comes back."

"Free country though, right?"

"Sure, people are free to live where they want or hate who they want, even when there's no sense to either one. But a girl disappears and it gives people an excuse to be nasty and think the worst. Bottom line, all I know is that her cellphone is inactive and if she was planning to run off, she never said anything about it to anyone except for the note to Wallace. It comes off as a little weird that she would leave him that note, but I had someone look at the handwriting and it checks out, most likely hers. I kept it for evidence, just in case. I can put her name and picture in the database and hope I get a hit, but she didn't even have a driver's license, much less a credit card. Without some evidence of foul play, I'm as far as I can go."

"Any thoughts for us?"

"Yeah, take Wallace and go back to Jacksonville." He chuckled. "Lilly worked here last summer waitressing part time, maybe Bonnie can tell you something. Good luck with that one, she can be mean as a snake some days." He stood and nodded to us.

"What'd Mr. Bigshot want?" Bonnie the waitress asked when she circled around with the coffee pot. "Comes in here expecting free coffee all the time. Lousy tipper to boot."

"He wanted to talk to us about Lilly Franklin, we're kind of looking for her," Maggie said.

"Might want to look in the Ochlockonee, plenty of rain and she's running high; high enough to carry a body away. Then again, old man Weston might have just buried her somewhere."

"Wally Weston, he's seventy-something, isn't he?" I tried. "Doesn't see so good, doesn't drive, and he's only got one leg. Hard to imagine him overpowering a healthy eighteen-year old girl, much less disposing of her body without getting caught."

"He's lucky Leo Davis isn't around here, he'd have got more than a beating."

"Who's Leo Davis?" Maggie tried to keep her talking. "I met Levi Davis, seems like a nice guy. Are they related?"

"Brothers. Leo, everybody just calls him Lee cause of Robert E Lee. Anyway, he and Lilly were going out kind of on the sly, her being black and all. But she was a really good kid. I worked with her most of last summer. Her and Lee, Christ those two used to fight! Young love, you know how that crap goes. Lee kinda flipped out last summer. Got so damn mad he went and got a job in the oil fields in the Dakotas, just to get away from her and get her out of his system, or so I'm told. Course, there was that trouble with his brother, but according to Levi, Lee and Lilly kept talking and Facetiming, so I was betting they would get back together. Been months though, so maybe not."

"Funny he wouldn't come back if he cared that much, her disappearing and all."

Bonnie leaned in and lowered her voice. "Makes me wonder if she snuck up there to be with him. Lee's Daddy didn't like him dating a black girl, even though her old man works for them. I heard tell there were some horrible fights, Lee and his Daddy. I hear a lot of what goes on in this town, 'cause of me working here."

"I'll bet you do." Maggie nodded emphatically. "Wouldn't the Sheriff know about all that?"

"He's too damn lazy to care. I think he figures old Wallace did something to her and is just waiting for him to slip up. I asked Levi and he says she isn't up there, that he thinks Wally did something to her too. Course if she ran off with Lee, they wouldn't be likely to tell anyone."

"And Wallace, how'd Lilly know him?"

"She always walked by his place coming and going to school and just felt really bad for him, him being old and living all alone. She claimed he was a savant, like a genius in his head, but it all came out in his sculptures. I warned her, old or not, the man had eyes. Creepy old guy like that and a pretty young girl, something bad was bound to happen. If she didn't run off with Leo, my guess is old Wally tossed her in the river. Her Daddy sure thinks so."

"Sounds like a lot of guessing without any evidence." I put in. Maggie had Bonnie talking and if I had any sense, I would have kept my mouth shut.

"You taking his side?" Bonnie straightened up and eyed the two of us. "How do you know Lilly anyway? You said you're looking for her, why is that?"

"We represent someone who is interested in knowing what became of her, that wants to know that she's alright." Maggie explained.

Her eyes narrowed and her tongue flicked across the gold in her lip. "Say it plain, Honey, it's really old Wally your looking after, isn't it?"

I spoke up again. "He was beaten up, Bonnie, convicted by public opinion when he didn't do anything except be nice to a lonely girl who wanted to learn about sculpting."

Bonnie tended to talk with her hands, which became somewhat concerning, given that she was holding a pot of hot coffee. A few drops flipped onto the table and the waitress in her had enough presence of mind to back up, but she got upset in a hurry. "Are you two lawyers, or reporters of some

63

kind? CNN showed up in town last year asking me questions about our school board, which was none of their business. You Goddamn liberals don't need to come around here and stick your nose in things that don't concern you."

Maggie kept smiling even though the situation had taken an ugly turn. "Bonnie, we're not reporters. We work for Wally's niece, and she just wants to clear her uncle's name."

"If I was guessing, I'd say he killed Lilly and he got the beating he deserved." She spun around, throwing a good amount of coffee on the tile, and disappeared into the kitchen.

I glanced at Maggie. "Don't let me talk anymore. You get information out of people and then I piss them off."

"She would have caught on sooner or later."

"By the way, I like your lips." I shared.

"That was random, and I was just thinking about a piercing."

As suddenly as she had stormed off, Bonnie returned with our check. She put it down, then pulled another stub from her book and scribbled on it quickly and handed it to Maggie.

"What's this?" The redhead asked.

"Couple of names, friends of Lilly's. Maybe they know something they aren't telling the Sheriff. Sorry I went off like that, I got a short fuse. But nobody in this town likes outsiders showing up and telling us how to live, me included. Honest truth is old Wally probably didn't kill her. He's been in here and he's polite and nice enough. He don't seem like the type to hurt anyone, and like you said he's old and not very spry. Lilly's big boned, not fat mind you, but pretty tall and athletic like. I doubt an old fart like Wallace with one leg could get the best of her unless he conked her on the head with a club or something. Lilly liked him, so I guess I should give him the benefit of the doubt. I shouldn't listen to all the gossip around here, it's rottin' my brain. I'd like to know that Lilly's alright too, so let me know what you find out."

"Thank you, Bonnie." I risked a comment. "Are these girls that Lilly went to school with?"

"Clara did. She probably walks by Wally's house every day. You can't miss her. She's a really skinny black girl with bright orange hair. Teenagers, they've got some weird ideas about fashion, don't they?" That, as her tongue hooked momentarily on the aggregation of metal in her lip. "Jane's a year older, a white gal, and she works at the Shell station as a cashier. Normal hair and she's there most afternoons."

"Thank you again, this is really helpful." That was Maggie.

"Like I said, sorry I blew my cork. Sometimes I got a big mouth. I hope nothing happened to that girl." She walked away and we sat finishing our coffee.

"Could it be that easy, that Lilly's shacked up with an old boyfriend in North Dakota?" Maggie suggested.

65

"If Cletus Johnson is typical of the people in North Dakota, I'm not going up there." I assured her. "Tommy can hire someone local to check on Leo and see if she's with him. Meanwhile, we'll see what we can find out here."

Chapter Six

It was time to meet Wallace Weston.

The middle and high school that Camille had mentioned were on the north edge of town, on opposite ends of a large block, both modest buildings in the days of school consolidation. The buildings were older brick structures that looked clean and well maintained. The Weston house was half a block down and across the street from the middle school, situated so that most of the kids that didn't ride a bus would walk right in front of it coming and going to the rest of the town.

Wallace Weston's house was a tiny two story with a rickety porch surrounded by a broken lattice fence once meant to keep the largest of animals out. A giant Tabby cat let out a moaning growl and jumped through a large hole in the lattice, then spun and raced away around the corner of the building as we approached. The hardwood floor of the porch was uneven from years of disregarded maintenance, buckled and warped sufficiently in spots to stub an unprotected toe. The whole front half of the structure had started to sink, and we leaned precariously as we made our way to the front door.

The interior door was open but there was a screen door, latched from the inside. I wrapped on the door frame and waited. We heard some movement, then a faint thumping, and Wallace

Weston came limping into view. The bump-bump of his cane matched his cadence. He walked to the door and popped the latch, then turned and walked back into the kitchen without comment. I pulled the door open and held it for Maggie.

"Wallace?" She called loudly as we walked into the room.

"I got a limp, and I'm a little worse for wear, but my ears work fine. No need to yell."

He was a tall slender man, bent over slightly, with a scraggly beard and short hair the color of wood smoke. He eased himself onto a kitchen chair and pointed at two others with the end of his cane. Maggie took the closet one and extended her hand. "I'm Maggie Jeffries, and this is Eric Slater, your niece sent us."

"She called, bunch of nonsense you coming here." He had a large bandage over one eye and several stitches in the corner of his mouth. He paused, pulled his pantleg up and adjusted a strap on his artificial leg, then dropped it back into place. "I threw this damn thing on too quick when I heard Jasper making a fuss. Better than a watchdog, that old stray cat. He's been living under my deck for three years on leftovers I toss out for him." He smiled about the cat and seemed to have lost his train of thought. Maggie and I waited quietly until he started talking again. "People get something in their head, there's no changing it. Don't care what most folks think, but the same kids used to watch me and Lilly carve, they yell at me and throw things, call me dirty names. Lilly went away, but she'll stop back and visit, sure as we're sitting here. She'll tell them how it is."

"Where did she go?" Maggie asked gently.

"Don't know, somewhere away from all the trouble I expect. What is it my niece thinks you can do to help me?"

"Maybe we can find Lilly, then everyone would realize you didn't do anything to her."

"Four years, three, four days a week the whole town seen us out in my garage making my statues, seeing she was like my daughter. Now they think I would hurt her?"

"Can you tell us about the men that beat you up?"

"White men. It was dark and there was three of them. I'm an old man and I don't walk so good, so I sure as hell couldn't outrun them." He chuckled at that. "Don't matter, the law ain't gonna' go after them, not in this town."

"We met Sheriff Henderson this morning at Maryetta's, he seems like a really good guy." I commented.

"White man. He's not going to try too hard to arrest them what put the boots to an old black man like me, especially when he thinks maybe I hurt a young girl."

"White or black, Wally, I'm sure he'd like to arrest them. These days, people like Sheriff Henderson watch out for everyone, no matter what color they are," Maggie said.

He put his head down and cackled briefly, then winced and rubbed the stitches in his lip. "Not in this part of Georgia, Miss Maggie. Lilly, she worked at Maryetta's for a spell. Good food in there. I got no problem with those kinds of people, but some folks do."

I looked at Maggie and shrugged. The reason for the observation wasn't clear. There was a sharp rap on the wall, then another. Wallace eyed the door sadly. "School's starting. Sometimes the kids throw rocks when they walk by."

"I'll go see about that." I said and left them sitting there. I walked out of the porch and sat on the front step. It was thirty feet from the sidewalk to the front of Wally's house, and I saw a couple young kids toss their rocks into the street when they saw me come out. The high school must have started a few minutes after the middle school, because the age of the passersby went up shortly after I heard the first bell ringing from down the street. Two boys and a girl slowed and gawked when they saw me, then stopped and started a conversation.

"You a cop?" The girl asked.

"Yeah, rock patrol. Hope you don't plan on throwing any."

They seemed to think that was funny. The boy spoke up. "Most of the older kids know old Wally wouldn't ever hurt Lilly. Besides, she liked older guys." They all snickered.

"So what do you suppose became of Lilly, if you were to guess." I was stalling, hoping Maggie would come out. The two boys were sixteen or seventeen. One look at her and they'd skip first hour and happily tell us everything they knew.

"If somebody killed her, I'd say it was her Daddy." One of the boys said quickly.

"Or Leo Davis. That guy isn't wrapped too tight, and they were always tearing into each other." The girl said.

"No way." The second boy got into it. "She ran off, left her Daddy a note and everything."

"Bullshit, I heard she left Wally the note, a suicide note." That was the first one again.

"You're high, asshole." The girl laughed and pushed on her friend's shoulder, then turned back to me. "You tell Wally we don't think he killed Lilly, she never had anything but good to say about him. She said he was just old and mixed up. I bet wherever she is, she really misses him."

"Probably in heaven, 'cause he killed her." The second boy quipped. They walked off laughing. Teenagers.

The screen door creaked and Maggie held it open as Wallace stepped carefully down the three steps to the yard. He held a door opener in his hand, and he used it to lift the garage door and expose his work space. He pointed listlessly to a beautiful figurine lying on its side on a table next to his work bench. "Night they came after me they smashed a lot of my stuff. That one was Lilly's favorite. I didn't have the heart to throw it away even though it's cracked right down the middle."

"No idea who the men were though?" I asked again.

"Like I said, don't matter, they were white boys."

"Things are changing Wallace, if you know, you need to tell us." I tried.

"Don't need to do anything but eat and sleep, carve once in a while until Lainey comes back." Maggie glanced at me and raised a brow, but Wally realized his mistake. "Lilly, I meant Lilly. She'll come back and check on me, and I ain't stirring up any trouble in the meantime."

"When do you think she'll come back, Wally?" Maggie asked.

"Lainey isn't coming back, married a man and went to Carolina."

It was hard to know if he was talking to us, or himself. "Lainey, or Lilly?" I asked.

"Lainey didn't wait. I come back from 'Nam all shot to shit and find out she run off to Charleston and married up with some salesman."

"That had to be hard." Maggie sympathized. "Is that why you went to Charleston a while ago, to try to find Lainey?"

"Lainey? Hell no." He frowned at her and you could see him trying to work it out. "I never been to Charleston, and I think maybe Lainey is dead. She is dead, isn't she? I remember something about that. She died, or got herself killed somehow best I recall. I'm sorry, I don't remember things so good sometimes."

"Lainey's husband, what was his name?" I wanted a last name.

"She was a damn fool, running off like that. I'd have made sure she was okay."

"No idea about his name though?"

"There's some damn fools think she went with that Davis kid."

"Lilly broke up with him, didn't she?" Maggie picked up the shift right away. Wally shrugged, and I realized he was having trouble separating the two young girls; the one gone a lifetime, and the one just weeks ago.

The old man coughed and seemed to choke up. "She would lie down with me in the bed sometimes, just hold onto me and sing gentle like, till I fell asleep."

"Lainey did that?" The redhead asked him softly.

"No." Wallace muttered as he picked up his small hammer and a carving tool. "Wasn't Lainey." He appeared lost in thought or his sculpting, and when Maggie looked my way, I tipped my head toward the front yard.

We sat down at the small picnic table half way between the house and the garage and talked quietly. "Did I hear what I thought?" I asked.

Maggie shrugged. "It sounded like he was talking about Lilly, but it's hard to be sure. Poor guy seems to confuse the two of them a lot."

73

I pulled my phone out. "Curious about this Lainey woman, and her getting killed. I'm going to call Tommy, see if he knows her last name and if he can hire someone up north to look in on Leo Davis."

Surprisingly, the dopey kid with the crush on Jasmine put me right through and I got the details. I told Maggie the name and she started Googling the Charleston newspaper's obituaries while I finished explaining to Tommy why he needed to hire someone to go to Williston to track down the youngest Davis brother.

"Elaine Johnston passed away seven weeks ago from unknown causes. There was an obit, but also an article about her death being investigated by the police as suspicious. No follow up, just that. Not good, considering that was about the same time Wallace ended up in a homeless shelter up there."

"Well, we may have to go to North Dakota, Tommy says he doesn't trust anyone else."

"No way. Do you know how cold it is there this time of year?"

"Freeze the balls off a brass monkey."

"God, you're a Neanderthal. Let me try something." She punched at her phone for a few minutes while I sat there enjoying the fact that there wasn't a snow drift in sight. Finally, she looked at me triumphantly. "Yes, thank-you Facebook. Looking at Levi, I wasn't sure his brother would be on social media, but he is. His account says he's in a relationship, and it has a picture of him with a blond girl. Her profile lists him as her boyfriend and there are even cute pictures."

"Well that proves it, no way Lilly could be up there. The Internet wouldn't lie to us." I have to admit, I hate Facebook.

"Alright, granted it doesn't prove anything for sure, but it lists the bar the girl works at. That would be easy to verify and someone could ask around there and get eyeballs on Leo."

"Hopefully not us. Maybe that would be enough for Tommy. It's silly for both of us to go up there just to find out she isn't there. If they fought as much as Bonnie says it's not likely he'd let her stay with him just as friends, even if he had a place of his own. Guys don't normally let old girlfriends hang around, especially if he found some new talent."

That was a poor way to put it. I have to blame it on the fact that I'd been hanging around with construction workers all day, for a month. As a group, we all talk like fifth grade boys.

I thought Maggie had missed it, but then she showed me a picture of Leo's new girlfriend. "What do you think, she has to be an eight, eight and a half, don't you think?"

Alarm bells sounded somewhere in my Neanderthal brain. I feigned shock. "That would be sexist, me giving her a number based on her appearance!"

She laughed, well aware that I'd caught on. "There may be hope for you yet, Slater. I'd say she's a hard nine, all day long. I'll text Camille about the girlfriend and tell her we don't have time to go to North Dakota."

The morning had been cold, but the sun had started to warm the yard and it felt good to just sit there and listen to the tapping of Wally Weston's hammer. There wasn't much traffic, and it was hard to miss the Davis Paving truck when it crept slowly by. There were three people in the front seat and the two on my side were unfamiliar, but it looked like Levi Davis in the driver's seat. The men closest to us glared, and as they drove away the passenger offered a middle finger. So much for southern hospitality.

"Nice bunch of guys working for that outfit. Are we going to go talk to Lilly's Dad? He's supposed to be the one that got everyone at Davis Paving mad at Wally, right?" Maggie asked.

"Yeah, I'm guessing he won't be thrilled to help us. That's probably not going to go well. It's not like he's going to confess if he killed her, but maybe he knows something about her and the Davis kid. I say we hang around here for the day, maybe talk to some of the kids when they walk by, see if we can't find that girl with the orange hair, Clara. I hope having orange hair isn't a thing now, or is blue still in?"

"Neanderthal."

"I think we need to go to Charleston and talk to whoever looked into Lainey's death. If we go up there, maybe we can see if someone at that shelter remembers Wally and the particulars of his visit."

"If we time it right, we could swing through Jacksonville and spend the night at home. I'm not a fan of the bed at that fleabag motel we're in. But we're kind of going off script, aren't we? If the goal is to find Lilly and prove Wallace didn't do anything to her, how do we explain going to Charleston to Tommy and Camille? And what if we find out he might have killed Lainey, what then?"

"If it turns out he did something to Lainey, wouldn't it make it more likely that he could have killed Lilly? He confuses them so often, maybe he killed them both." I could hear the soft tapping of his hammer, and imagined the haunting eyes of the figurine in Tommy's office. "I don't really believe that old man is capable of murder, but we have to follow whatever leads we have. Sometimes you find what you were afraid you'd find, but sometimes the surprises are good ones."

"Is that what happened with my dad? You found what you were afraid you'd find? There sure as hell weren't any good surprises there."

The pain was hiding behind the smile she kept painted on her face, showing occasionally in the moments when she let her guard down and I caught her staring off into the distance, imagining the worst. There wasn't anything she could have imagined that was worse than the truth, and I was sure I knew only a small percentage of the carnage her father and uncle had wrought in countless young girls' lives. It was almost unbelievable that Frank Jeffries had spawned three such wonderful children, fragile and broken as two of them had been. Maggie was the strongest of them, the least broken, and the one that had suffered the least at the hands of their father. I wasn't about to let him continue hurting her from the grave, and if that meant lying to her, that's what I would do.

"Like I said, Maggie, he got in over his head with some really bad people."

She sighed and looked at me. "I know there's more to it, Slater, you don't have to protect him, or me."

"I'm not protecting him, but I'll always protect you whenever I can, that's what people do that love each other, right?"

"Thanks, Slater." She cocked her head. "That's what Wally is doing, just protecting Lilly because he loves her. I bet he knows where she is. Maybe the way he loves her is a little mixed up with the way he loved Lainey, and maybe what he feels for her is a little inappropriate, but at least it really is love."

Not like my father, the words unsaid. Some wounds take a long time to heal, and it occurred to me that maybe I was wrong, maybe Maggie was as broken as her sister and half-brother had been.

Being a Neanderthal, it hurt me to realize that it wasn't something I could fix for her or protect her from, that it was beyond my abilities. I could do acrobatics with an airplane or stack up bullets in a bullseye from twenty-five yards, but those talents wouldn't help my partner with this. All I could do was be there and try to be supportive. Some things can't be fixed or undone, but broken hearts are like missing legs; the pain becomes bearable and you learn to live with it. I stood and reached down for Maggie's hand.

"Come on, let's go watch him work for a while. Maybe we can talk him into having lunch with us."

Chapter Seven

It was well after noon before the thought of a piece of Maryetta's apple pie managed to pry Wally away from his work. He closed the garage door and we squeezed into my pickup and made the short trip to the Diner. Heads turned when we walked into the place and took a seat in the corner. A couple people gave Wallace a nod, but most of the patrons shook their heads at us and went back to their food. I could see tongues wagging and furtive glances in our direction as the locals tried to deduce what this new development meant.

Maggie ignored them and helped Wally into the booth, then sat beside him. "The board said the special is roasted chicken, Wally, sounds good doesn't it? Lunch is on us today."

"Not often I get out for lunch, and I never have company pretty as you, Miss Maggie. When Lilly worked here, she'd buy me pie sometimes."

Bonnie scurried up with three cups, slopped some coffee in their general direction, then shared some more local charm. "Here's coffee, I'll try to get back in a minute and take your orders. Why in the fuck does everybody have to eat at the same Goddamn time?"

"It is lunchtime, that's what people do." I made sure she was out of earshot before sharing that. "Was Lilly a good waitress, Wally?"

"Lilly was good at everything, and she didn't cuss like Bonnie."

"She's outspoken, that's for sure." Maggie looked over my shoulder and frowned. "Incoming."

I shifted in my chair slightly and looked up at Levi Davis. He wasn't smiling.

"Wallace, you feeling all right? Looks like you took a bad fall. Best to mind where your walking. I'd be sticking close to home if I was you."

"I'm just going to have some chicken." Wally didn't meet his eyes, and he rolled his spoon nervously in his hand.

Levi turned his attention to Maggie and me. "Wally Weston, he's your sick friend? Might pay to be careful around him, he's accident prone. Could be what he's got is catching. If I was you, I'd head on back to Jacksonville."

"Darn, Levi, does this mean you don't want me to be your pool partner after all?" Maggie taunted him. "Maybe best if you and I don't hang around together. We wouldn't want you catching something."

"Yeah." He leaned forward and sneered at her. "Don't guess I'd want any of the bugs you might have."

A diner is a poor place for an altercation, but I stood up quickly and got in his face. I had six inches and at least forty pounds on him and he stepped back quickly. "You need to walk away right now, Levi, while you still can. You talk to her like that again and I will beat your hillbilly ass until they

81

have to carry you out of here." His brother Kyle, stuck with the check again, looked over from the cash register.

Levi backed up a step or two and glanced in Kyle's direction. "Two of us."

"Two of us," Maggie said quickly, sliding to the edge of the booth. "But I doubt he'd need my help."

"This isn't over, I'll be seeing you around, Slater." He backed away, then turned and hurried out of the restaurant with his brother at his heels.

"He's not likely to forget that." Bonnie said glancing around the diner as she walked over. "He won't take kindly to you running him off like that in front of people."

I didn't like losing my temper, it never helped and made me feel stupid. But that wouldn't have stopped me from breaking something if he hadn't left. "Tough, he would have liked the alternative a whole lot less."

She nodded up at me. "Yeah, no doubt. But he'll make trouble for you if he can, that's all I'm saying." I sat down and Bonnie took our order and headed back to the kitchen.

Maggie grinned at me. "Wow, Slater, you actually defended my honor, that was kind of hot!" Wally was still fidgeting uncomfortably, and Maggie noticed. "Wally, was Levi one of the men that hurt you the other night?"

"Don't know, it was dark." His hand was shaking noticeably. "Don't know why they care what became of Lilly. She's fine. When I came back from 'Nam, she was gone and married off, didn't want a man with a bum leg is all."

"Lainey missed out, Wally. She should have waited for you." Probably the stress of the near altercation or maybe it was that he was getting tired, but he started rambling on and on about Lainey and Lilly. He confused the two girls, jumping from the past to the present, Lainey to Lilly, without distinguishing one from the other until it was clear to us that they were one and the same in his mind, just a young woman that he loved deeply.

The thing that struck me was that there was no anger. He would talk about Lilly not wanting a man with one leg, and say that he just wanted her to be happy. The fact that I was fairly sure he was talking about Lainey, was confusing. When I reminded him that it was Lainey not Lilly who had married someone else, he just smiled and shrugged, said she needed to be happy. Didn't sound like a killer, or someone who would hold a grudge and go all the way to Charleston to even a score.

I tried again, to either jar his memory or trick him into telling me what I wanted to know. "What did Lainey say when you went to see her, Wally?"

He gave me an odd look. "Couldn't say anything, her being dead, Mr. Slater. Besides, I told you, I never been to Charleston."

83

After lunch we took Wally home. He admitted to being tired and went in to nap while Maggie and I tried to come up with a plan.

"We need to go to Charleston and talk to the cops there. I can't imagine Wally ever hurting anyone, but he's so confused sometimes it worries me. We need to be sure he wasn't involved in whatever happened to Lainey. My PI license is worthless up there, but maybe we can get someone to talk to us."

"Much as I hate to, I could call Richie and see if he can grease some wheels for us. He did call and offer his condolences when my dad hung himself."

"I know he's a lawyer in Charleston, but does he have some pull with the cops up there?"

"He's the assistant DA, so I'm thinking he does."

"Wow. No doubt that would open some doors. Maybe he could even look into it, save us a trip?"

"He and I are on speaking terms, Slater, but it doesn't mean we're buddies. He did cheat on me with his twenty-year old secretary and that didn't go over so well. I'll call him, but let's not push it."

"I don't like the idea of leaving Wallace here alone. Maybe you should just go."

"We're a team Slater. Hard to say what kind of trouble you'd get in around here without me. He's been fine so far, and it'll only take the day. Maybe we could leave your vehicle here. I don't think Levi wants to mess with you after the thing at Maryetta's."

"You think there's a car rental in this little town?"

"You make sure Tommy found somebody to check on Leo, and I'll call Jasmine. She's always begging to help with a case, she can bring us my car."

Maggie stayed at Wally's house, afraid he might be confused if he woke up and we were gone. I drove out to the edge of town, to the Shell station. Jane, the cashier Bonnie had described was behind the counter with another employee, a man in his mid-sixties with a face that sagged on the right side and an eye that didn't work quite right. He limped up to the counter and I realized he must have had a stroke at some point. Bernie, his name tag said.

"What can I do for ya?" He mumbled.

"Actually, I was hoping to have a word with Jane if I can. Bonnie at the Diner said she might be able to help me with some information."

"Bonnie? I didn't even know that old bitch knew my name." The chubby little blonde offered. "She used to run me out of the restaurant if I didn't order something. That was even before they bought the place. What's the deal?"

"Alright if we step outside?"

Her eyes narrowed. "You a cop? How do I know you aren't a pervert, wanting to kidnap me?"

"Not a cop, a private investigator. If I wanted to kidnap you, I wouldn't stand in front of this camera in the middle of the day."

"Yeah, I guess that's true. I'm due for a cigarette anyway. Okay if I step out, Bernie?" He nodded and we walked outside. She lit up right away.

"Those things are bad for you," I offered. "I bet Bernie was a smoker."

"Jesus mister, it's bad when a total stranger thinks he can complain about your smoking. Fish with your own bobber, asshole." Outspoken young lady, but I was used to that.

"Sorry, but my mom died young, the cigarettes are what killed her."

She took a long drag, then flipped the cigarette out into the grass. "Alright, happy now? What's this about? You're screwing up my break and I still don't know why."

"I understand you were a good friend of Lilly Franklin's."

"Were? You know something I don't?" She looked scared for a moment, then covered her tracks. "Far as I know she ran off to find herself or some shit like that. What's your deal, and what business is it of yours what happened to Lilly?"

"Wally Weston's family hired me to try to find her, to prove that he didn't kill her or abuse her like most of the town seems to think. I don't know if you heard, but he got beat up pretty badly, and the kids all yell at him when they walk by, call him a pervert and worse."

"Most of the town are idiots if they think that. Old Wally wouldn't hurt a fly, and he loved Lilly. She told me before she left that she was thinking about going. Nothing for sure, just that she'd like to get the hell out of here and away from her daddy. She never said goodbye, but if something bad happened to her it would be more likely it was that old man of hers. He had big plans, and she screwed them up."

"How's that?"

"When she started going out with Leo Davis, right away Evert had them married off in his head because then he would have it made at work, being family and all. But Leo was a dick, slapped Lilly a couple times, told her what she could do and what she couldn't do, and he didn't want to let her go. It got really ugly there for a while, and Evert was on her to get back with him all the time, wouldn't even stick up for his own kid. Lilly kept saying one day she was going to just run off and not tell anyone where she'd gone, even Wally."

"You think she might have told him, even though she didn't tell you?"

"Clara maybe before me, but if she told anyone, it would have been Wally."

"She left him a note, but it didn't say where she was going. The Sheriff has it, and he said as far as he's concerned it's a done deal, she probably just wanted out of this town."

"That's what I thought all along. I'm hoping sooner or later she'll call."

"Any chance she's up north with Leo?"

"No damn way! She hates that prick."

"If he didn't want to let her go, why did he take a job up in Williston?"

"Good money, maybe. I heard him and his brother got in one hell of a fight and Lee took a proper ass kicking. Guess he ran off to lick his wounds. Didn't want any more of that shit."

"Really? Levi must be a lot tougher than he looks."

"Wasn't Levi did it, it was Kyle. Levi talks a lot of shit, but he'd run like a little girl if Kyle was to come after him."

"Huh, always the quiet ones, isn't it? But no idea where Lilly might have gone?"

"Wish I knew, but if anybody does, it would be Wally."

"He talks a lot about her, confuses her with his childhood sweetheart sometimes."

"Don't know if it's that." The young woman laughed. "That old guy had it bad for Lilly. Not that he would have ever tried anything, but he had it bad. They never had sex or anything, but Lilly did shit she shouldn't have; danced with him and kissed him on the lips sometimes. I'm not too damn sure she didn't sleep overnight there, like in his bed." The look on my face spoke volumes, and she continued quickly. "It wasn't like they were screwing! She probably would have if he'd wanted it bad enough or was capable, she cared that much about him. But I know for a fact, she would have told me about that." Jane's eyes teared, and she choked up a little, like she was telling me about a sad movie and this was the part where somebody had just died. "She said she would just hold onto him sometimes and sing to him like his old fiancée had done fifty years ago, and he would fall asleep thinking that it was her. It was really sweet, that's all it was."

Tears were streaming down her face, and Bernie stuck his head out of the door.

"Everything okay out here, Jane?"

She laughed. "I'm fine, Bernie, I'm just worried about Lilly and being stupid." He gave me a dour look, but went back into the convenience store.

"Did you tell the Sheriff any of this? Any kind of inappropriate relationship like that would make him wonder. It makes me wonder, and I really like Wally."

"No way, I knew he would have taken it wrong, just like you're doing. I know it sounds bizarre, but Lilly told me once about Picasso, how he had muses, and she said she was like that for Wally. Bottom line, if she contacts anybody, it will be Wally."

"What about Clara, can you ask her if she's heard anything?"

"You better talk to her. She might tell me, but it isn't my business to be telling you if she does."

"I really have to thank you, this has been very helpful." I extended my hand.

She laughed and shook it. "Are you a real Private Eye? I never met one before."

"Private investigator." I corrected her. "PI for short."

When I got back to Wally's house, he was in the garage carving and Maggie was sitting on a lawn chair in the front area of the garage. Not surprisingly, several teenage boys were standing around, watching Wally carve and Maggie sit. The two boys and the girl I had seen that morning were there as well as three or four more guys that looked younger yet. For the most part they seemed more interested in Maggie than Wally's art, but he was smiling and talking to some of the group, thrilled not to have to dodge rocks and insults.

As I walked up, the girl had bent down next to a figurine and Wally was telling her how he made the hair look real, or something artistic sounding. I stood aside and listened. The girl was really interested and you could see Wally was in his element talking about art.

Then she brought up Lilly. "Bet you miss Lilly, huh Mr. Weston?" She asked.

"Sure I do, but everybody has to find their share of happiness. Hers wasn't here, that's all it was."

"Nobody in the high school thinks bad things about you. Maybe a few, but they're just jerks and everybody knows that. The younger kids, they're just being stupid."

"I know, they're just being kids. They hear things at home and don't know any better."

That was generous, considering the front of his house had been peppered with rocks and tomatoes, half his work had been damaged beyond repair, and his face looked like he'd returned from the war yesterday, not fifty years ago. The small group of teenagers hung around for fifteen minutes, then started wandering away. The girl and her two friends lingered, talking to Maggie and me.

"I was talking to Bo and Jimmy, and we're going to walk over a little early the rest of the week, make sure the kids from the middle school don't throw stuff anymore."

"That's so sweet. Thank-you guys, Wally will really appreciate that," Maggie said happily.

"So, are you going to be around in the morning, Maggie?" That was Bo, not surprisingly.

Maggie smiled. "Not tomorrow, we have to run back to Jacksonville overnight, but we'll be back. We'll see you then."

I was pretty sure Bo didn't care if he ever saw me again, but the main thing was that Wally would have some degree of protection from the meaner little kids, and the not so little ones. Between the high schoolers and the presence of my pickup, maybe Levi Davis and his posse would keep their distance until we got back.

"You're a big hit with the high school boys. Learn anything useful?" I asked Maggie.

"Just that Clara wasn't in school today, flu bug or something. How about you?"

"Quite a bit. Some of it was kind of odd." I watched Wally tapping away. Did he know where his Muse was, and would he eventually slip up and tell us? "I'll tell you about it on the way back to Jacksonville."

Jasmine pulled into town at six-thirty with Maggie's convertible. We left our things at the motel since we planned to be back the next night. It would be a short night's sleep because we hoped to be in Charleston by nine the next morning. Jasmine was wound up, happy to be included.

"What a shit hole." She commented as we drove out of town. "How did Camille ever manage to get out of this mess. Tommy said she was the class valedictorian, but I'm guessing that was no big deal, considering."

"People are people, Blue, don't be so judgmental." I groused from the back seat. "Good ones and bad ones everywhere."

She actually seemed to think about that. "Yeah, your right I guess." She finally admitted.

I leaned forward. "What? Did you just say that I might be right? Maggie, you're my witness, write this down or something."

Jasmine laughed. "Alright, don't get carried away. But look at my mom. All the advantages in the world, and look what she's done with it. Pretty sure Maryanne paid her off because she's already gone again. So much for maternal instinct."

"On a positive note, you're stuck with us." I reminded her. "Just saying, I'm old and wise, you should listen to me. Everybody has stuff to deal with and they all deal with it differently. Sometimes there are reasons people do things that we don't understand. We can stew about it and hate them for it, or just learn from them and try and do it better." I was feeling pretty smug, almost forty and all.

Maggie spun around in her seat. I couldn't see her clearly in the dark car, but from the tone of her voice she was clearly angry. "Was that little lecture for my benefit, Slater? Talk about being judgmental! Are you trying to say I shouldn't hate my father? Jesus!"

Talking always got me into trouble, even when I had the best intentions. "That's not what I meant, Maggie. I really was talking about Divine. She's not your Dad, and I didn't mean to compare the two. I understand why you'd hate Frank, because I hate him too. I guess I'm not that evolved, because I can't forget about what he did and I probably never will."

93

The anger in her voice turned to sadness. "I guess that makes us a good pair, Slater, because I'll never forgive that lousy bastard either."

We drove through the night for several miles in dead silence until Jasmine spoke up. "And here I thought we were talking about me and my problems." It helped to laugh.

Chapter Eight

I hadn't been to Charleston in eight years. I'd been stationed there for eighteen months, and it was probably the best duty I had during my twenty years in the Navy. Most of the time I lived off ship in the barracks, worked short days while we waited for deployment, and drove home on the weekends.

While most of my single friends were out chasing the local girls, I was still stuck obsessing over Maggie's older sister, Angela. I kept telling myself I was working on getting over her, but that wasn't really true. By then she had married Charlie, a man forty years her senior that had leveraged a hedge fund into a considerable fortune rumored to be worth seventy-five million dollars when he sold his share. Tongues wagged, but looking back, I had never known Angela to be happier, and the reason never dawned on me. It had probably put a stop to her father's abuse.

At the time, I held out hope for his early demise, leaving me to pick up the beautiful pieces. That was a selfish fantasy, but it kept me from dating seriously, always pining for the day Angela would be single again. Looking back, it seems nuts, and it probably was.

But had I not been obsessed with Angela, stayed in Charleston and joined my buddies pursuing the local girls, I just might have found one. Then what? Every little step we take, every tiny decision we make as we stumble through life, good or horribly bad, brings us to today. And when I looked over at the redhead driving us into the city, today was definitely where I wanted to be.

She glanced over at me and smiled. "Penny for your thoughts."

"I was thinking that it's not so bad turning forty, maybe I'm getting things figured out. Have you noticed a change? Do I seem especially wise to you lately?"

"I don't know if that was wisdom or bull-hockey you were throwing around last night, but I'm sorry I yelled at you."

"I would never tell you how to feel about your father."

"I say it doesn't matter, but of course it does. Someday you need to tell me everything. I know there's a lot I don't know, but at some point, your not telling me will start to feel like lying, and that's not okay. Being honest with each other, that has to come first."

"No argument there. But for now, let's work on making sure Wally didn't do something to his old flame."

Deflection, it works for some people.

"My ex made a couple of phone calls. I have the name of the detective we're supposed to talk to. He wasn't sure, but he thought the case went through their office."

Charleston is a beautiful city, a mix of the old and the new. Shimmering glass towers, scientifically engineered by men with complicated computer systems to weather the worst of hurricanes and global warming stand a hundred feet from stone and brick structures designed with common sense, sweat, and the misery of slave labor long before the Civil War. Both are beautiful and functional for the most part. The building that housed the team that we needed to talk to was functional, and that was about all I could say for it.

Charleston's police force is compartmentalized and crimes such as murder, or any death considered suspicious are handled by special investigators. They are housed in a two-story mundane looking building that is part of a city services complex that includes a jail and fire department.

Detective David Harrison looked like the building; serviceable, mundane, and not likely to be moved easily. He was probably due for retirement soon, too heavy to walk a beat, and didn't seem especially interested in detective work or our problems.

"Really isn't right me even talking to you, and if not for the higher ups I wouldn't be," he said after the introductions had been made. "We work with PI's some when we have to, but they're all local guys. With valid licenses. In this state." Having made his point, he leaned forward and punched away on his computer board with two pudgy fingers. "This is a new system, top of the line. I can't run it for shit yet, but I'm learning."

"Elaine Johnston, died about two months ago. The obit said the death was under investigation as suspicious, but there was no follow up." Maggie explained patiently.

"Kind of remember something about that. I was out there." He must have found what he was looking for, and sat reading for a moment. He finally looked up. "Knew I could find it. Seventy-two. Went down the stairs of her apartment the hard way. Died from head trauma before the ambulance arrived."

"It was just a fall, an accident?"

"Coming back to me now. Neighbor claimed there was an argument, and that she heard yelling. Someone found the old lady at the bottom of the steps a couple hours later, but it wasn't clear when she fell. It was late and most of the people in that building are elderly. The old gal that heard her, she said it wasn't the first time they'd made a ruckus. The husband claimed he was in bed and asleep the whole time."

"No cameras? No security?" I asked.

"Not the Ritz, Mr. Slater. Buildings in that area don't have security doors. Poor lighting and there was no railing on the steps. The building owner is ass deep in trouble, but without any evidence of foul play we couldn't bring charges. Those two fighting all the time, maybe the husband pushed her down the stairs, maybe she went out for a smoke after the fight and just fell. That age, people's balance isn't great."

"The neighbor, she was sure that Mrs. Johnston was fighting with her husband, not someone else?"

"She's eighty and doesn't hear great, but that's what it sounded like." He wasn't totally useless as a detective, because he did ask the obvious question. "Something makes you think there was someone else there? Who is it your representing?"

We could have claimed client privilege, but that would have been the end of his cooperation. He would have had us out the door in half a minute. I explained as much as I dared. "The man we're representing, he knew Lainey a long, long time ago. He just wanted to be sure she died of natural causes, because the newspaper made it sound like it might have been something else."

"Old flame? How long ago did he know her?"

"Fifty years, give or take."

He whistled softly and showed some interest. "Long time to hold onto a crush, almost unnatural. You think that might have been him arguing with her that night instead of her husband?"

"No. Just covering the bases. He's four hundred miles from here, doesn't have a car, and I know for a fact he hasn't left his little town in years. War veteran, seventy-four, and he can barely walk."

Harrison leaned back in his chair. "Well there you have it, case closed far as I'm concerned. Your guy didn't do it, and I can't prove the husband did either. She took a tumble and it killed her."

"Yeah, that's probably all there is to it. Okay if we go chat with that old lady and the husband? It would help if you could give us the address, save us some time."

"Alright, just don't piss off the old fart any more than he is already. He's threatening to sue the city because the code violation wasn't caught in the last inspection. What's your email? I can send the whole file to you with two clicks, coolest thing you ever saw."

"Well, that wasn't what we wanted to hear," Maggie said as she put the car in gear.

"No, but it's still a stretch to think Wally would push her down the steps. According to this file, that was a Saturday night, and the funeral was on the following Tuesday. Camille picked him up from the shelter on Wednesday afternoon. That's five days, probably four nights. Where did he stay during that time?"

"You're presuming he was here on Saturday and that it was Wallace that she was arguing with. Maybe he found out she died somehow and got a ride up here with someone to go to the funeral. Maybe Lilly brought him."

"Lilly doesn't have a car or a driver's license according to the Sheriff," I reasoned.

"Well, who else would have brought him all the way up here? He didn't hitchhike."

"If someone brought him, how did he end up at the shelter?" All good questions we could ask Wally, but given the state of his memory he was an unreliable witness to the crime even if he was the perpetrator. "Do you think Wally's memory is as bad as it seems? I get the impression sometimes that he remembers things but just doesn't want to tell us."

"I would bet anything that he knows where Lilly is." Maggie agreed. "But I think the times when he seems to confuse the two of them, I think that's real. I'd say he definitely has a degree of dementia and he shouldn't be living alone."

"He's not going to thank us for telling Camille that, but I'd say you're right."

The apartment building was a rundown fourplex, two apartments up, two down. We knocked on both of the lower doors and got no answer, then went up the stairs. There was a railing now, but it wasn't even close to code height. I'd spent a few sleepless nights studying for my Contractor's License and I had managed to retain that much. The steps weren't code either, too narrow and steep, undoubtedly built before Charleston had building codes. There was one dim light bulb, and tumbling down the steps looked

101

more likely than not. We knocked on the door of Alfred Johnston.

After a moment he came to the door, older than Wallace by at least five years, but with clear eyes and a strong voice. He opened the door a crack, but left the two security chains in place. He wasn't happy to see us at first.

"What'd you want? You from the insurance company?"

Maggie gave him a big smile. "No, but we heard about your trouble. We're representing a law firm from Jacksonville, and we'd like to talk to you." Okay, we were working for Tommy Ackerman and his wife, so what she said was true, technically. It's a known fact that doors open more easily for attractive people, and Maggie Jeffries fits that description. I'm pretty sure he would have told me to go to hell, but he swung the door open for her as fast as he could unlatch the chains.

"I don't like ambulance chasers," he said as he waved us in. "But the attorney I've got talks like I should settle for next to nothing, and that ain't right. How the hell did you hear about this all the way down in Jacksonville?"

"We had to come to town on another matter, and we read about your wife's death. Looking at those steps, I would think you have a case." She was on a roll, that was mostly true, technically. "I am so sorry for your loss. Can you tell us what happened?"

"Like you said, damn steps are too steep and there was no railing. I gave her hell if she smoked in the apartment, so I guess she snuck out for a cig after I went to bed. I told her smoking would kill her, just turned out to be quicker than I thought." I could see he thought that was funny, but when we didn't laugh, he didn't either.

"The police report intimated that you two might have been fighting."

"Yeah? Fifty-two years of marriage, who doesn't fight? They saying I shoved her down the stairs? I went to bed at ten, and the neighbor downstairs came home at two because he works in a bar, and he found her in a pile down there. I got sleep apnea, and that damn machine is so noisy they could drop an A-bomb and I wouldn't know it. My poor Elaine could've been down there screaming for help and I'd never have known it." He drew a breath, seemingly overcome by emotion. "Thinking about it about breaks my heart. Isn't that emotional distress? I deserve compensation for that, don't I?"

"So, back to the facts. You were in bed by ten, never heard a thing after that?"

"Damn apnea, like I said."

Maggie stood and I followed her lead. She extended a hand which he grabbed and held on to. "We have your contact information, Mr. Johnston. I'll talk to our team about the possibility of representing you." Not one thing was true in that statement.

103

"Thank you. You be sure they send you back, I don't want to talk to nobody else!"

"You'll be hearing from us very soon."

The door closed and we heard the chain locks and deadbolt falling into place. The door across the hall creaked open slowly and a tiny, wrinkled face looked up at me. She narrowed her eyes and studied me, then spoke. "You the cops?"

"No. We're friends of an old friend of Elaine's, from years ago."

She closed the door quietly, unchained it, and pulled it open another six inches. She was tiny, four feet seven or eight inches tall, with very dark skin and very white hair. She eyed us both again without saying a word, then seemed to make up her mind and pulled the door open all the way. She put a finger to her lips to silence us, then motioned for us to follow her. We walked down a short hallway into the main room of the apartment, living, dining, and kitchen all in one room. There was a bathroom where I could see a rusty tub and one other door I presumed led into the bedroom. It was tidy, but smelled a little funky if I'm being honest. There was a monstrous old couch and she told us to sit down.

"I don't want that old prick next door overhearing what I got to say. Would you like some coffee?"

"We're fine, right, Slater?" I nodded and Maggie started asking questions. "You knew Elaine well, Mrs. Lewis?"

"How'd you know my last name?" She asked shrewdly.

"It's on your mailbox in the entry." And in the police report, I thought to myself. As usual, Maggie's instincts were spot on. The old lady was no fan of the police.

"I liked Elaine, when I could get her away from Al. He ran her ragged and barely let her out of his sight, always chewing on her for something. I still say he shoved her down those steps."

"We've been told those two fought a lot."

"I'll say they did, yelling all the time. I told that idiot detective from the police about it, but he didn't pay no mind. Said there weren't any laws against fighting with your wife. Damn fool just wanted to go on his way and track down another donut by the looks of him."

Maggie smiled at that. "Our friend, did Elaine ever mention Wallace Weston to you?"

"Sure. I thought more than once over the years living across from them, Elaine was going to leave Alfred and run off to find Wally. She always said she was a damn fool for marrying the man she did, and I always agreed with her. Wally would have to have been pretty God awful to be worse than that asshole she was married to. I seen him that night, that Wally, talking with her out in the hall, and he didn't seem so awful. Handsome, too. If she had a brain in her head she would have just walked off and got in the car with him, left that prick Al in the rearview mirror. Scared to leave him

I guess after fifty-some years, and too proud to admit she'd made a mistake."

"You're sure it was Wallace Weston? Were they fighting?"

"It got a little loud, him begging her to go with him and her telling him to just go away, that it was too late." She shrugged and smiled timidly. "I may have been listening by the door. I stuck my head out once and she about bit it off, so I didn't stick my nose in any further. Makes me wish I had now. I could have pushed the both of them down those stairs."

"What?" I asked without thinking.

She laughed at my expression. "Not down the stairs in a pile, down the stairs and away from Al. All she had to do was screw up her courage a little and climb in that car. Her life would've been different." She snorted. "Least she'd have one!"

"You said there was a car, and you saw Wally get in it?" Maggie asked.

"Yeah, window in my bedroom, I can see the street. After she sent him away, he climbed in that car and went away."

"Could you see who was driving or what kind of car it was?"

"Wrong side to see the driver. It was a car; four wheels and a dark color. I don't see so good from that far away."

"And that was it, you went to bed?"

"I heard her go inside, and her fighting with Al some, then it was quiet and I fell asleep."

"What time do you think that was?"

"I never miss Fallon and they were still yelling when it ended. Must have been one by the time they were done. Can't hear words, but I hear the noise."

"So Al is lying," I stated the obvious. "He wasn't asleep by ten, and he must have known she talked to Wally."

"And you told the investigator about all of this?" Maggie reiterated.

"Not about Wally, I ain't stupid. The cops made up their minds and they're probably right. Even if Al did shove her down those steps, nobody seen it and there's no way to prove it."

"Unfortunately, you're probably right about that. Did you see Wally again? Did he come back and try to talk to her, after the fall?"

"No, but he found out some way, 'cause I saw him at the funeral. He was in a bad way, crying and carrying on. I was wanting to talk to him, but afterwards he just disappeared."

"Was he alone?"

"People all crowded together, I couldn't say. Wasn't anybody hanging on him like family would."

We all stood up and Maggie wrapped the old woman in a hug. "I'm sorry you lost your friend Mrs. Lewis, and I hope it was just a fall. I'm afraid we'll never know."

The old woman wiped at her eyes. "She's in a better place, that is for sure."

We had the address and contact name for the shelter where Wallace's sister had picked him up. It was a solemn ride. When we pulled up to the shelter, Maggie finally spoke.

"The Wheels of Justice don't always work, do they?"

"We can't be sure what happened. But you're right, it didn't get looked into like it should have."

"Is that because she was a poor black woman, or because Harrison was just too damn lazy to get out of his chair?"

"Some of both I would imagine."

"Do you think the cops at home would have done a better job investigating if Davey hadn't been gay? It wouldn't have changed anything for him, but it makes me wonder. If they had taken it seriously, maybe Sam would still be alive, or my dad."

"Considering the people involved, I don't think those things would have changed, Maggie. Susan Foster and the group she works with are better cops than Harrison or the bunch of losers that ignored your brother's murder. Sooner or later they are going to get the people responsible for what happened to Davey."

"And my dad?"

"I wish I could say he didn't deserve what happened to him, but you said you want me to be honest with you."

She shook it off and smiled. "The good news is it doesn't seem likely Wally killed Lainey. Maybe the woman here can tell us something helpful."

"I remember Wallace very clearly." The homeless shelter that Wally had stayed at wasn't very large: two dozen beds, a small kitchen, and a couple bathrooms with stall showers. The smiling woman walked over to a post and lifted a clipboard from it. She flipped back several pages and ran her pen down a list. "We sign people in, even if we're not sure if the names they give us are real. You said the twenty-third, right? Here's Wally right here. Came in about nine o'clock in the evening and called his sister the next morning bright and early. He was on a suicide watch because he was so distraught, cried himself to sleep, poor thing."

"And he just walked in off the street, nobody dropped him off?"

She shrugged and looked at her notes. "No. Most of the people that come in here don't have somebody to call like Wallace did. They come alone and leave alone."

"We really appreciate your help."

Chapter Nine

I called Detective Harrison on the way out of town and gave him a piece of my mind. It was a futile gesture but it made Maggie and I both feel a little better. It was early so we decided to drive straight back to Georgia and check on Wally. He was parked on his couch watching television in an old pair of ragged pajamas when we arrived.

"No problems today. Older kids came by and gave the younger ones a talking to. Good kids, those three. Bo, he was asking after you, Maggie." The old man chuckled and raised an eyebrow. "You get your business done in Jacksonville?"

Maggie was abrupt. "Some of it. Our lives would be easier if you just told us where Lilly is, Wally. We're sure you know."

"Note said she had to run off, cause of her Daddy. Why don't you ask him what become of her? Note said she would call when she could, and I'm still waiting. Y'all don't need to be hanging around if you don't want, I'll be fine here. Sheriff was by today and said he'll keep an eye on me. I ain't complaining mind you, I like the company."

"Camille wants us to keep trying to find Lilly." Maggie touched his shoulder. "You don't remember the car ride you took? The time you went to Charleston?"

He frowned at her and huffed out a reply. "I said, I ain't never been there! Why you keep asking? I'm plumb beat, time I go to bed."

"Okay, will we see you in the morning?" Maggie asked.

"Suit yourself, I'll be here." He mumbled and shuffled toward his bedroom. "Lock the door on your way out."

We left my truck there and drove back toward the motel. "I made him mad by asking again, but it's hard to believe he doesn't remember being there for five days, especially after seeing Lainey and then going to her funeral three days later."

"People lie, even nice old guys like Wally." I said. "He thinks he's doing it for a good cause and that Lilly will thank him. It seemed like she led him on some. Maybe he was giving her money."

"They were both getting something out of the friendship, she learned to sculpt and he had company. Doesn't mean that he gave her money, but if he did, would that be so horrible?" Maggie asked.

I chose my words carefully. "I guess, during the times Wally's mind isn't playing tricks on him, they're both consenting adults. But after what we saw in Miami, and the thing with your dad, I'm surprised you aren't a little cynical about the age difference."

"Rosalyn Cabello was fourteen when the White Devil locked her in a dog kennel and raped

111

her, it's not even close to the same thing. You were running around Miami without me, shooting people, why didn't you shoot him?" She was suddenly angry and I lashed back without thinking.

"I could have, and believe me, I thought about it. I had to go to Miami myself because Cletus Johnson had shot a hole in your leg, remember? And you're the one that insisted we go to Atlanta. Was that my fault too?" We were both tired and it could have escalated into our first real fight, but she stopped it.

"You could have shot the Diablo?" She asked quietly. "Why didn't you?"

How was I ever going to tell her that the Diablo was her uncle, still alive and well? "Because, he was unarmed and helpless at the time. I'm not going to kill someone in cold blood, even someone I know deserves it."

"Did he kill my brother, my brother Davey?" She whispered, blue eyes staring through me.

"No. But he was in business with the people that did. A lot of people were." We had rushed into dangerous territory and I wasn't ready for that conversation. "Maggie, it's complicated. Diablo, your dad, Davey, they were all involved one way or another in something much bigger than they knew. International, people protected at the highest levels of several governments, and organized crime. There's a lot I have to tell you and I will, but this isn't the time or place. Can we just focus on what we're doing here, because the rest of it is out of our hands. I will tell you everything I know, but I need some time. And please trust me on this, so do you. Okay?"

I was afraid to tell her how deeply her father and uncle had been involved, and maybe she was afraid to hear it, because she let it go.

"I'm starved, want to stop at the Outhouse and eat?"

I laughed. "Doesn't sound very appetizing when you say it like that, but I am hungry."

If I'd known Levi Davis was in the bar, I might not have gone in there. Then again, I might have. Maggie and I took our table near the kitchen again and each ordered a beer and burger. The bar was quiet, just one other couple and three men sitting at the bar. Levi, Kyle Davis, and a third man, an older black man. I nodded in their direction.

"You whip the Davis brothers, I'll take the old guy."

Maggie snickered. "Behave yourself. We start a fight and the Sheriff will run us out of town. I know you don't want to argue with that guy."

"He is impressively huge, that's for sure. What does your Sensei say about fighting a guy that big?"

"Don't!" Maggie giggled. "But I don't need a wise old Japanese man to tell me that. Fighting any guy is hard, because pound for pound they're usually stronger. You can be faster and use their weight against them, but if someone like the

Sheriff or your buddy Cletus lands a solid punch, it's game over. I teach the girls in my classes to avoid situations where they have to fight, but if they have to, then fight dirty."

Levi Davis had glanced in our direction once or twice, and now he seemed embroiled in an argument with his brother. The third man was tending to his beer, but he looked at us repeatedly as well.

"Think that might be Lilly's dad?" I asked the redhead. "Right age, and he works with those guys. I don't imagine it would be a good time to ask about his daughter's whereabouts."

"You go up there and I'm leaving. I'll pick up the pieces at the jail tomorrow morning. You're about to be forty, act your age."

"I was kidding. I don't think old Evert knows where she is either. Sounded to me like she wanted out of this town to get away from him as much as anything. Hope we can find the girl with the orange hair tomorrow, she's about our last hope. Jane swore she doesn't know, and she said Clara probably didn't either, but it won't hurt to ask. We'll have to feed Wally more pie. I think he's getting tired of our company."

The Davis brothers had lowered their voices, but I could see they were still disagreeing about something. I was speculating that Levi wanted to resume our quarrel. If all three of them came over, it would get ugly. Our food came and we had just started eating when suddenly Levi slammed his beer bottle on the counter and walked out the door, giving Maggie and I a scathing look as he went by. Half a minute later, the older man that I was sure was Evert Franklin, sauntered on past and followed him out the door. Kyle glanced in our direction, then returned to his beer and the game that was on the big screen. I may be a Neanderthal, but I breathed a sigh of relief. One Davis brother, even the toughest one, wasn't nearly as worrying as three men to deal with.

We had just finished eating when Kyle Davis walked over to our table. I expected the worst. Instead he walked up to the table and smiled, pulled his cowboy hat off and nodded to me, then spoke to Maggie.

"I heard there was a problem at the diner yesterday morning, Ma'am, and that Levi was disrespectful to you. I want to apologize for him, 'cause he's too stupid and mean to do it for himself. Our daddy, he's a hard man sometimes, but he always taught us to respect a lady. Levi gives you any more trouble, no disrespect to you, Mr. Slater, but I'll have to have a chat with him."

"Thank you, Kyle, that's very sweet." Maggie extended her hand and he shook it briefly then put his hat on, preparing to leave.

I spoke up. "All we want is to find Lilly and prove Wally didn't have anything to do with her disappearing. Is there anything you can tell us that would help with that?"

"Old Evert, he wasn't any kind of a father after his wife died, and now he's a drunk. I think he figured if Lilly stayed with Lee things would work out better for her, and for him. But Lee's like Levi, he gets an idea in his head and there's no changing it. He was bound and determined him and Lilly were meant to be together, and she was bound and determined they weren't It got ugly, and didn't end well.

"Lee and I got into a pretty good scrap over it and that's mostly why Levi wants to make trouble for Wallace. Evert's just stirring the pot, sticking with Levi. They don't believe that old man did anything to her any more than I do, but like I said, Levi is stubborn. He didn't like that I gave Lee a beating, but he had it coming and then some. I got word he slapped Lilly around, and I wasn't about to let that stand."

"Where do you suppose she is?" I asked.

"Anywhere but here, I guess, happier for it most likely. Levi gives you any more trouble, Miss Maggie, I'll have that chat with him. Night folks."

Maggie stared after him. "Is have a chat, hillbilly for an ass whupping?" She looked at me and laughed. "Wow, Slater, I am crushing on that boy, so bad."

Okay, now I was a little jealous.

Somehow, we missed Clara the next morning. Wally was his cheerful self, happy to see us again, and all seemed forgiven from the night before. He was in his garage early, chiseling away on a different figurine. It was one I hadn't seen, not a figurine exactly, but a bust of a beautiful girl. He grinned from ear to ear when the three high-schoolers walked into the garage and recognized his depiction of Lilly.

"That is so beautiful." The young girl exclaimed. "And it looks so real, except maybe it's even prettier than Lilly. What do you think, Bo?"

"I don't know, Lilly is pretty hot. Looks just like her to me."

"Do you have any pictures of her, Wally?" Maggie asked him.

"No need, I see her up here." He pointed at his head. Obviously, the neurons that connected her memory to his hands worked very well, because the face of the girl he had produced in the wood seemed to be staring out at us, a wistful look in her eye and a shyness in the curve of her full lips. He had managed to make the block of wood do everything but draw breath.

It dawned on me that we hadn't seen any photographic evidence of the girl. Maggie pulled out her phone and took a picture of the carving, so that was something. There had to be yearbook pictures, and I made a mental note to find one. But all the pictures in the world wouldn't do us any good if we didn't have a flesh and blood girl to compare them to. If Wally knew where she was, he was being very stubborn about telling us. We needed Clara.

117

Rose, the girl in the little trio of our high school friends wasn't sure about Clara.

"She's kind of a loner, like Lilly was. When either one of them hung out, it was usually with each other, you know?" I admitted I knew nothing about high school girls, but Rosie promised to look for her in school. "I'll tell her you're looking for her, but I can't promise you that will help. Her Daddy's been in some trouble and she's likely to run, thinking you're the law. She doesn't care for the Sheriff any, that's for sure. I'll tell her you want to talk to her if I can find her between classes, but best bet is to catch her walking by. Have Maggie do it, she sees you, she'll think you're a cop for sure."

It wasn't clear to me if I should be offended by that.

We took Wally to lunch again. It was a cheap trick, trying to bribe him with a pork chop and Apple pie, but we were getting desperate. The hope was that as he became more comfortable with us, he might trust us with Lilly's location. Bonnie waited on us, dispensing coffee and gossip in equal doses.

"I hear Levi and Kyle about got into it last night at The Shit-shack." She shared.

"Bonnie, come on, we have to eat." I groaned.

She blinked. "I'm the waitress, ain't I? You think I just come over here to chat?"

"We were at the bar last night." Maggie put in. "They argued a little, but there wasn't much to it."

"Don't encourage her." I looked up at Bonnie. "How could you possibly know anything about that? We were the only ones in there."

"I hear things, Smarty-butt, like I said. Bartender was already in for his grits. Call me when you're ready to order." She put her nose in the air and stomped away.

"Why would anyone in their right mind call their bar the Outhouse? It's like they're asking for it." I fumed and picked up the menu.

"Lilly, run off and married someone else." Wally said glumly.

Maggie looked at him sadly. "I'm sorry Wally. I know you miss her, but it was Lainey that married someone else, remember? That was a long time ago."

"Wasn't all that long ago, just a bit." His eyes were glazed over, and I noticed he was shaking again, like the day we had the encounter with Levi. Beads of sweat dotted his face.

"Wally, are you feeling okay?" I asked, and Maggie put a hand on his forehead.

He jerked away and looked around the restaurant as if he were lost, then his eyes came to rest on one of the pictures of Maryetta hanging on the wall over the counter and he sat staring at it. He reached for his water and I could see his hand was shaking even more than before. "Damn, that

Lainey," He shouted, suddenly loud and aggressive. "Black girl can't be no Jew. Damn Lainey, and damn Lilly too."

"It's okay Wally. Nobody's a Jew." Maggie shook her head at me, wide-eyed as she rubbed his shoulder. I reached for my phone, thinking about calling for an ambulance. I was no medic, but it seemed like more than dementia, possibly a stroke.

Bonnie appeared suddenly with a glass of orange juice. She slammed it down in front of Wally, then snapped her fingers loudly and waved them in front of his face. "Wallace, drink this orange juice, right now." He reached out a shaky hand and hoisted the glass as she watched. She looked over at me. "Seen him like this before. He's a diabetic you know. Damn fool is too proud to use a pill box, so sometimes he takes too many pills. Late lunch like this, his blood sugar drops too low and he gets all wonky. Couple minutes, he'll be fine. Lilly used to tend to those pills for him, now he has to figure it out for himself. So order your food, I don't have all day."

"Wonky?" Maggie snickered after she walked away. "Takes all kinds, but that Bonnie is amazing."

"Now I'm the one crushing on somebody," I admitted.

"Swears too Goddamn much," Wally mumbled and drank the last swallow of his juice. "Lilly never swore like that."

When school ended, we took our posts, sitting on lawn chairs in front of Wally's garage waiting for Clara to come by. How many skinny black girls with orange hair could there be? Rose walked up and told us that she had talked to Clara, but that it sounded like she wasn't wild about the idea of talking to us. I was afraid we would miss her and that she might take another route home to avoid us.

"I'm going to walk over to the other side of the ballfield and see if she comes down the backstreet over there. We need to find her."

"I'll wait here, maybe she's just running late," Maggie said.

I walked across the open field to one of the two baseball dugouts and leaned against the block structure, hanging back a little, so if she did come by, she wouldn't see me until the last minute. If she ran, I would have to let her go. No matter how badly I wanted to talk to her, it wouldn't look good for a thirty-nine-year old man to be chasing a high school girl down the street. Besides, there was always the chance that I wouldn't be able to catch her, and I'd never hear the end of that.

I heard a scuff and had started to turn when someone hit me from behind. I fell forward into Levi Davis's fist as he stepped around the corner of the short wall in front of me. Before I had time to react, two sets of hands grabbed me from behind and Levi and his three accomplices began taking their frustrations out on me.

But you've heard that part of the story.

After the Sheriff left, Maggie and I walked back to Wally's house. I was hurting, I'm not going to lie. I used Wally's bathroom to clean up while Maggie explained to him what had happened, then we got in Maggie's car and drove back to the motel.

"Seriously, Slater, should we take you to the doctor?"

"I'm just banged up, nothing broken. Some ice from the fridge and I'll be fine."

"Can I get you anything else, maybe a backrub?"

"Now? Now, you want to give me a backrub?"

"A backrub is not code for sex, Slater."

"You don't know me at all."

She chuckled. "Suit yourself, a hot shower would probably help. Do you think Wally's memory problems are just because of his medication? He shouldn't be living by himself. I'm going to call Camille and talk to her about it."

"Wally isn't going to thank you for that."

"I don't know what you think, but we're about out of options here, aren't we?"

"Another day or two and the Sheriff will give us the boot. I'm not arguing with him, one butt-kicking is enough for a while."

"It already looks better." She kissed me gingerly on the cheek.

"Good enough for a backrub?"

We were late for breakfast. Nothing to do with a backrub, it just hurt to move very fast. Another hot shower had helped and I was beginning to feel human. I had a wisp of a black eye and a couple cuts, but all in all it wasn't too bad. It was just before eight when we got to Maryetta's. Bonnie came up with coffee, grabbed my chin and inspected the damage.

"Four of them," Maggie volunteered.

"Heard all about it. Kyle was in here, but no sign of Levi. He's asking for it and Kyle's likely to give it to him, that's all I'm saying." But of course, it wasn't. "News is Levi is going to be looking for a new job if he doesn't get his act together. Old man Davis heard about Levi lifting his fist to a woman and he's likely to kick his ass if Kyle don't."

"Odd mix of chivalry and redneck you have in this town," Maggie said.

"Thank-you," Bonnie said and walked away. I had no idea if she was serious.

We'd only been there a few minutes when Clara, the orange-haired black girl walked in. Couldn't be too many of those. She spotted us and walked right over to our table. "Heard you were looking for me."

"We are, Clara, right?" Maggie asked her and held out her hand.

She ignored it and backed up half a step. "I don't know anything about Lilly. Don't know where she went, or who she went with."

"She went with someone? And you're sure she's not dead?"

You could see it in her face, the realization that she had already given too much away. "I never said she was dead. Henderson asked me, and I told him she probably just ran off. I'm sorry, but it wasn't my fault what happened to old Wally. Haters gonna' hate, they don't need a reason."

"What about Leo Davis? Any chance she went up north with him?"

She scowled. "Hell no! He's a dick. Too young for her anyway."

"Young? He's a couple years older than she is, isn't he?"

A smile crossed her lips. "Lilly always went for older guys, like, a lot older. Claimed she was an old soul, because of the art, or some shit. Maybe that's why she got along with Wallace so well. But a girl's got needs, and Wally wasn't much help there."

High school girls have sure changed in the last twenty years. I was glad when Maggie jumped in. "So, you're sure, not Leo Davis. Hooking up with some older guy just to get out of town could be dangerous."

"Maybe so, but she was desperate. I'm not saying she went for creepy old, just not Leo. Look, I don't know where she is, and I wouldn't tell you if I did. Lilly was afraid that no matter what, her Daddy would find her and try to drag her back here. I'm sorry for what happened to old Wally, and I'm sure Lilly didn't intend for her leaving to bring that trouble down on him, but she hasn't called me and her phone is out of service. That's all I got, and I have to go to school. Don't bother me anymore." She turned and left. It seemed like our last chance to find Lilly had just walked out the door.

"Maggie, why do so many people in the south call their father, Daddy? I never had one, so it never came up. Did you call Frank, Daddy?"

"Right up until the day he tried to touch my boob."

We ate in silence. It was depressing to think that we had been stumped. After we had finished, Bonnie came back to our table to chat.

"Slow day." She shared. "I guess I can get some cleaning done. Maybe I'll pull those ugly-assed pictures of Maryetta down and put them away."

Maggie studied the photos. "Didn't you say her son took those pictures, and that he has a gallery in Charleston?"

"Up that way, not sure where exactly."

Maggie seemed interested suddenly. "Maryetta. What did you say her last name was?"

"Cuff something. No, Kaufman. It was Kaufman. Danny, he hung around some last summer, like I said. Waiting for his inheritance, I reckon. Your face don't look so good, Mr. Slater."

"In general, or just this morning?" While Bonnie and I exchanged jabs, Maggie was busy punching buttons on her phone. After Bonnie walked away, she grinned at me and I could see she was excited. "Alright, Red, what is it?"

"Drink your coffee, you can sleep some more in the car. We have a long drive ahead of us, and we need to go right now."

"Where are we going?"

"Sheldon, South Carolina. It's a little town about an hour this side of Charleston."

"And why would we go there?"

"To get Lilly Franklin."

Chapter Ten

The Kaufman Gallery was an old barn that had been fixed up and divided into viewing rooms. It appeared that Daniel Kaufman leased spaces to several local artists, as well as showing his own work and advertising for senior, wedding, and Bar Mitzvah pictures. One of the rooms was filled with photos, one with pottery, one with paintings, and one with wooden sculptures. It was the newest of his galleries, according to the banner we saw hanging below the main sign when we pulled in.

Lilly liked older men, we had heard that repeated more than once. When Wally Weston had muttered about a black Jewish girl during his glucose deprived rant, the pieces had started to fall into place for Maggie, and Clara had given them a final shake. The internet provided quick verification. Her theory was that during Maryetta's extended illness, Danny Kaufman and Lilly had spent time together at the diner, maybe became friends, or maybe more. When Leo Davis became too controlling and abusive, and her father kept trying to push them together, leaving town was Lilly's only choice. She had needed a place to run, and Daniel Kaufman's gallery was her best option.

The website said only that a new artist had joined the Gallery; a sculptor of extraordinary talent, trained by a genius mentor unnamed. It had to be Lilly. We walked in the front door and recognized Danny Kaufman from his pictures in the diner. In person he looked older, closer to forty than thirty. It made me uneasy, but we weren't sure the relationship was anything more than a professional one.

"Hello folks, feel free to look around. I'm the resident photographer and we have three other artists here, creating their art as we speak."

We were in a hurry. It was a six-hour drive, and we hoped to take Lilly with us. Maggie gave Danny her best smile. "We've heard so much about the new sculptor. Could we see her work, and I'd love to meet her, if that's possible."

"Of course. As I said, all our talented artists do their work onsite. Just walk through the door there and take a right, then walk down the hall. We each have our own space here."

We followed his instructions and saw an open door that led into a well-lit room that smelled of wood shavings and scented candles. There was a small sign at the entrance: L A Kaufman, Sculptor in Residence.

Lilly Franklin was wearing a smock and safety glasses, hunched over the beginnings of a figurine that was almost three feet high. Wally's bust had captured her perfectly and there was no need to look at the high school picture I had managed to find online. We stood there watching her for a minute, not sure if we were being ignored or if she was just so immersed in her work that she didn't see us. Suddenly she glanced in our direction and quickly put down her tools and pulled the glasses off.

"I'm so sorry, I didn't see you there. I am struggling a little, starting is always the hardest part of a piece."

"What you've done is exceptional, you must have had a good teacher," Maggie said circling the room.

"The best." She smiled. "A kindly old man that was nice enough to share his gifts with me."

I wasn't sure if Maggie had noticed the ring, so I asked. "L A Kaufman, what does the L A stand for?"

She hesitated for a beat. "Lainey, Lainey Alice Kaufman. My husband thought it was catchy."

I couldn't see any point in continuing the charade of being customers. I shrugged at Maggie.

She spoke up. "Lainey? Fitting, since Wally calls you that half the time anyway."

"Oh shit." She backed away from us, eyes wide, like she thought we might drag her out of there physically. "Did my dad send you? I'm eighteen, and I'm married. That asshole has got no say over me anymore."

Maggie raised a hand. "No, Lilly, that's not it. But Wally needs you, just for a day if you can spare it."

"What? He needs to get over me. I love the old guy, but he thinks it's something that it's not. I wanted to call him, but I didn't want to stir him up.

He hated that I was going to marry Danny. Did something happen to him?"

"I'm Maggie, and this is Slater. Wally's niece hired us to find you. The rumor around town was that Wally may have abused you, and that he might have killed you. Lilly, you disappeared without a trace, without telling anyone except for the note to Wally."

"Clara knew! But Clara being Clara, I suppose she didn't trust anyone to not tell my Daddy."

"Someone, probably Levi Davis and a couple of his buddies went over and beat Wally up pretty badly. Some of the people in town still think he did something to you, and we're afraid it might happen again. His niece and sister both want him to move to Jacksonville, but he won't leave, mostly because he's waiting for you to come back to him."

"Well, obviously I'm not doing that. They beat him up? My God, that's my fault! Should I call somebody, like the Sheriff? I can tell him I'm up here, alive and well. So help me, if my old man comes up here, I'll shoot him myself."

"Lilly, is there any way you could come back with us? Just for a day? I'll drive you back tomorrow if you want, but you need to show up to talk to Wally as much as anything. Like you said, you're eighteen and your father can't tell you what to do. Slater and I will be there to make sure those idiots that work with your dad don't try something."

"I can watch the shop, Lilly." The noise must have attracted Danny's attention, he stood in the doorway. "You could give Wally a proper goodbye and confront your Dad like you say you want to. If you want, we can shut down the shop and I'll come along."

"No, thank you Danny, but I'm the one that needs to tell him off, and say goodbye to Wallace. Maybe someday Wally could come up and see my work?"

"Yeah, that would be nice." I have to say, they looked pretty good together, the middle-aged Jewish guy and the young black girl. It was...evolved.

Within fifteen minutes we were back on the road. How we didn't get stopped for speeding, I'll never know. While we tore south on 95, Maggie and I took turns quizzing Lilly, filling in the blanks.

"Danny and I hit it off right away, right after I started at the diner. I was only seventeen then, and he didn't want any part of it at first. But he was stressed about his mom and I wouldn't take no for an answer." She laughed a little nervously and I wasn't sure if she was embarrassed or if Maggie's driving scared her as much as it did me. "I kept following him into the walk-in cooler and more or less jumping on him. Guy can only turn it down so long, right?"

"Statutory rape in Florida, perfectly legal in Georgia. Technically there's nothing wrong with it," I said without much conviction.

"Most people think like you, Mr. Slater." She shrugged. "After my Mom died, my Dad started drinking heavy and was never around. I was out sleeping with guys by the time I was fourteen, so I knew what was what long before Danny came along. If it wasn't for Wally and him teaching me about art, I would have lost my way completely and been a druggy on top of being a slut. He always talked about Lainey, and it kind of helped me figure out how things were supposed to be, love and stuff like that. Sex is fun and everything, but really caring about somebody is where it's at. I have that now."

"Wow." Maggie put in. "Pretty smart for being eighteen."

"I'm an old soul."

Old soul or not, fourteen? "You and Wally, you never..." I had to ask.

"Oh, hell no. There was a time when I first started going over there when I thought it would be romantic, like the misunderstood artist and his ingenue muse that have this forbidden affair. But he wouldn't have any part of that shit, fortunately." She bit her lip, uncertain of how much to say. "The last couple years he would get confused sometimes and call me Lainey, and really believe I was her. I'd play along, kiss him, and dance with him, let him be happy for a little while. Everybody deserves that, right?"

"But he didn't want to give that up." Maggie nodded. "When did you decide to leave?"

"A couple months ago, when I turned eighteen, I told Danny I couldn't stand it at home anymore. Being all noble and shit, he insisted we get married. I figured, what the hell, it was probably going to happen sooner or later. I explained it all to Wally and it broke his heart, but he said he was just worried about me. So Danny came down and got us both and took us back to his place and we got married. Strange I know. I wanted to, because I'm crazy about Danny, but part of it was that I thought it might help Wally let go. I knew he was kind of in love with me, or maybe me and the memories of Lainey that were all messed up in his head."

"That must have been when he went to see her?"

She laughed. "Yeah, that was my idea. What a fucking disaster. She told him she had married the wrong guy, but here it was fifty years too late and she wasn't about to start over. What the hell, Bitch? Next day we went back so he could try again and there's police tape everywhere. I wouldn't let him go in but I talked to the downstairs neighbor, the guy that found her."

"That must have broken Wally's heart!"

"No kidding. We took him to the funeral, and I should have gone in with him, but like a dumbass, I waited outside. He must have gotten confused and wandered out a side door or something. He has times where he gets really mixed up and he was a mess because of her dying. We looked all day, and called the jails and the shelters. He had a cellphone but he wouldn't answer it and I thought sure as hell he'd been murdered or something, and it was my fault."

"He was in a shelter, we talked to them."

"We missed him somehow, but he called me the next day, right after he talked to his sister to get a ride. He didn't want her to know how he'd gotten to Charleston and wouldn't tell us where he was, but he begged me not to stay with Danny. He said Lainey had left him and that if I did, he might as well just die. So I gave in and went back home, for me as much as for him. The marriage thing was too sudden, I was scared and confused, and figured it would give me some time to think. I thought I'd graduate, make sure it was what I wanted, and maybe by then Wally would calm down enough to understand. Danny was amazing. Most guys would have had the marriage annulled, but he waited for me to get it figured out."

"But the plan changed?"

"My dad and Levi, they kept saying I needed to get back with Leo. He's moved on, has a girl in North Dakota, but they kept saying he'd be back and I better damn well wait for him. Jesus, it's not the eighteenth century, I get to choose. I couldn't take it and I couldn't face Wally. I left him a note and Danny came down and got me."

"And you destroyed your phone?"

"They can track you anywhere with those damn things. I didn't want my Dad going to the Sheriff and finding out where I was. I had planned to call Wally after a few days from Danny's phone, but then I convinced myself it would be better if he just forgot about me."

"He clung to Lainey for fifty years." I pointed out.

"That isn't right, or normal."

"Your Dad and Levi went around telling everyone Wally had killed you, and that he'd been molesting you for years. The junior high kids were throwing rocks and calling him all kinds of names."

"Oh my God, I'm so sorry. I just didn't want my dad knowing where I was. Not that I care, but me marrying a Jew won't go over very well with him. You don't have to be white to be prejudiced. I'd be okay with never seeing my dad again."

"Yeah, I know that feeling," Maggie said grimly and drove even faster.

Thanks to Maggie's penchant for speed, we reached Lilly's hometown by nine-thirty that evening. Before we made the final turn a block from Wally's house, we knew there was trouble. It was pitch dark, but the street was lit brightly with emergency lights and the stench of smoke and burnt shingles filled the air. We pulled up behind the firetrucks and jumped out of the car. Sheriff Henderson walked out from behind the first truck, saw us, and walked over.

"Well, Lilly Franklin, alive and well it looks like. Don't worry, it was just the garage. Wallace is over by the front of the house. Next time you decide to run off, tell somebody young lady. You get everybody all riled up thinking Wally did something to you and stuff like this happens."

Lilly wasn't listening, she was running through the group of onlookers to find Wally.

Maggie wasn't happy. "Don't blame Lilly for this, Sheriff. What happened to keeping an eye on Wally? Do your job and go find the redneck bastards that did this!"

"Yes Ma'am, I plan to do that, real soon." He tipped his hat and backed away grinning. Maggie and I walked over to where Wally and Lilly were standing. The old man was wrapped in a blanket with one arm around Lilly.

He turned to us, his eyes wet. "Worst of it is they killed old Jasper. That damn cat never did them no harm. Found him dead, by the front step when I came out. Fire was already so big it lit up the whole yard."

"Did you see who did this Wally?" I asked.

"Not for sure, but I thought I seen Levi Davis's truck tearing off down the road. This time I told the Sheriff who it was. What kind of a miserable bastard would kill a cat?"

"All your art, Wally. I'm so sorry," Maggie said looking at the rubble.

"Just blocks of wood, but I wanted to give Lilly that piece I was doing for her. I told y'all she

136

would come back when she was ready." He smiled at the young woman and pulled her closer.

We stood there in the eerie shadows of the firetrucks LED lights, watching them put out the remnants of the smoking garage and talking to everyone who came up to quiz Lilly about her disappearance and whereabouts. Some were her friends, and some were just nosy or surprised to find her above ground. It was midnight before Maggie and I went home, but I called Camille and told her what had happened, and about Wally's trouble with his medication and our concern for his ability to be on his own going forward. Lilly spent the night at his house. She said they had a lot to talk about.

We all met for breakfast the next morning, Maggie and I, Wallace and Lilly. Bonnie came up to the table and greeted us like it was just another day, although she did acknowledge Lilly's presence.

"How's life up north. Heard you're shacked up with Maryetta's boy. Hope he don't get mean in his old age, like his Momma did." Lilly extended her left hand, showing off the small wedding band. The grizzled waitress smiled. "Nice, does that make you Jewish?"

"It makes me happy, Bonnie."

"Well, ain't that something? Pretty good thing, ain't it, Wally?"

By now I was a pretty big Bonnie fan. She didn't always say it well, but she always knew what needed to be said.

"I been saying she had to go find her own happiness, and she'd come back to say goodbye, but nobody believed me." Wally smiled, but there was some sadness.

Bonnie looked at me. "So, Slater, you and Red here, you leaving our little town? Probably tired of getting beat up."

"It was just the one time, Bonnie. And you know you're going to miss me."

"Yeah, maybe. For a Yankee, you're not so bad."

Half way through breakfast Kyle Davis walked in, pulled his hat off and walked over to our table. "Lilly, nice to see you, healthy and all. Glad you could shake loose of the Davis family."

She smiled up at him. "If your brothers were more like you Kyle, maybe I would have stuck around."

He hesitated, then turned to Wally. "Mr. Weston, there's no replacing your art, but my daddy and me talked, and we'd like to rebuild your garage for you. Levi, he's locked up for a bit where he can't cause anyone trouble. I'd like to think he'll learn his lesson, but there's no excuse for his kind of meanness. Maybe it taught my daddy something, too. Times change and we have to change with them. If it takes beating some sense into my brother, I reckon I'll have to do that."

138

"Thanks." The old man looked into his coffee cup, then back up at Kyle Davis. "I guess maybe it's time I go live with my sister, like Lilly and everyone's been saying. I'm old and forgetful. I forget to take my medicine or take too much sometimes. My legs don't work the way I want and I don't see so good. I thought I'd die here, but it don't feel much like home anymore."

"Sorry to hear that. This town will miss you, even if it doesn't know it yet. But we can still rebuild that garage for you. It'll make the property easier to sell." He reached out and shook my hand. "It was good to meet you, Mr. Slater, Maggie. If y'all get up this way again stop in here and I'll buy you breakfast. Have a good day."

Maggie poked me as he walked away. "If you and I don't work out, I'm moving here and getting a job at this diner."

I wasn't really worried. "Kyle Davis can find his own partner, I'm keeping you."

Camille and her mother arrived in town around noon and we all went back to Maryetta's again for lunch. It was settled. Wally would move to Jacksonville and live with his sister. Maggie would take Lilly Kaufman back to her husband, where she could be happy and practice the craft that Wally had taught her. It wasn't a perfect solution, but the best it could be. I checked us out of the hotel and threw everything in my pickup, then went back to the little house by the school to say goodbye to Wallace Weston. He gave me a big hug and told me to come visit in Jacksonville, then I got in my pickup because I didn't want to watch Lilly say goodbye to the old man. I was afraid there would be a lot of crying and I didn't want some of it to be me.

Lilly and Maggie walked over when I started the truck. "Thanks for coming to find me, Mr. Slater, and I'm sorry you got beat up on my account," Lilly said.

"Thank Maggie, she figured it all out, and kept me from getting a worse pounding than I did. You have a happy life, okay? Red, I'll see you back in Jacksonville."

"I might stay at Lilly's tonight, it'll be late."

"Good idea. Could you maybe slow down a little bit? You drive like a maniac."

"Yes dear," She mocked, then leaned in to kiss me. "Good job, Slater, the bad guys are in jail and nobody got killed. We make a hell of a team."

"That we do," I admitted. "See you at home."

Chapter Eleven

Forty was coming in a hurry, and I wasn't sure how I felt about that. The thing is, you don't have a lot of choice, not any good ones. There had been a few times in my life when I wondered if I was going to make it to forty, but luck, quick reflexes, and my natural abilities with a handgun had gotten me out of some tough spots.

I've always been a natural when it comes to shooting. I have good eyesight, steady hands, and learned good technique when I was in the Navy. I practiced long hours with my favorite gun, a Sig Sauer 226 9mm, until I was winning most of the base competitions. I had been issued the Sig when I went to work alongside NCIS and I fell in love with it instantly. When I mustered out, I had to leave the gun behind, but I had since picked one up at a local gun store. Most recently I had used it to kill the man hired to assassinate Frank Jeffries' girlfriend.

Maggie knew some of that story, and since returning from Georgia she hadn't quizzed me any more about what had transpired while she was laid up with her own bullet wound. It was coming sooner or later, and it wasn't a conversation I was looking forward to.

Frank Jeffries had been a sick individual on so many levels it was hard to categorize his brand of evil. Early in his marriage he had crossed the line of infidelity, literally, sneaking across Point Road for a one-night stand with Edith Templeton. Davey, the fruit of that union, became my best friend as a young boy and we spent many days swimming with Angela and sometimes Maggie, never dreaming that he was their half-brother. Davey was gay, and considering how close he and Angela were, it was probably a good thing, or the situation would have been even more convoluted.

I had it bad for Angela Jeffries back then, and arguably well into my thirties. If I'm being honest, it was probably my rediscovery of the younger Jeffries sister grown into a woman that saved me from the kind of life Wallace Weston had lived, always pining for someone he could never have, because it was never in the cards for Angela and me. I had a good feeling about Maggie, despite the fact that she couldn't shoot for shit.

"I'm doing everything you said, why do I suck at this?" She complained, pulling off her ear protection.

"You're good at practically everything you do, just relax. Extend your arms a little more, and stop anticipating the shot, you're flinching."

"I'm tired, maybe I need a lighter gun."

"Maggie, you're the strongest woman I know. It's because you're all tensed up, you have a death grip on that gun, and that makes you yank the trigger."

"My hands aren't as big as yours are, maybe that's the difference."

"Hopefully we never get into a situation where people are shooting at us. If you think you can't shoot now, try it with someone shooting back at you. Forget I said that, we are sticking to less dangerous cases from now on. After you whacked his buddy with that bat, Levi could have really hurt you."

Maggie slid her gun into its holster and snapped the cover, glowering in my direction. "You have a short memory. It was you that got his ass kicked, I was doing just fine. I've been punched and kicked in competitions a lot harder than that skinny turd Levi Davis could hit, and I picked myself up and kept going. My bruises heal, too, Slater, same as yours. Quit protecting me. Anytime you don't think I can pull my weight, you let me know."

I cased my gun and put my tongue in my cheek. "You know I don't want that, but maybe you should leave the gun at home and just carry a club, you're good with those."

She shrugged and smiled coyly. "If you're going to pick on me, maybe I'll cancel your birthday party."

"Not a surprise party, I'm guessing."

"Forty is a pretty big deal, you had to know we were planning something. Jasmine and Angela are all over it. It's good those two are finally getting to be friends."

"Jasmine's seventeen and acts thirty, your sister's thirty-eight and she acts twelve. Match made in heaven."

"Don't be mean." Maggie snickered. "Angela is getting things figured out. She's not nearly as self-involved as she used to be before the therapy. And Jasmine is good for her, she doesn't cut her any slack and makes her behave. It's upside down, but Jasmine's so incredibly smart and mature she's like the mother Angie never had."

"Except she did, have a mother."

"Don't get me started on my mom, Slater, just be happy Jaz and my sister stopped fighting."

"Good for me, I get to spend more time with you."

We climbed in my old pickup and she slid across the seat next to me. Maggie is normally a very practical woman, not a sit next to you as you drive kind of girl. It seemed like an odd place and time to make-out, but I was okay with it.

"Thanks for trying to teach me how to shoot. Hopefully I'm better at being a pilot, my certification is next week."

"Piece of cake, you're every bit as good a pilot as I am."

"I don't know about that, I don't have the feel you do."

"I've logged hundreds of hours in that Piper, that's the difference. What do you hear from Camille?"

"She wants us to stop by with a bill. She said to come in, not email it, and to let her know when we're coming. She has something she wants to give us. Oh, and Tommy wants to talk to us about possibly working for him some more, for his law firm."

"I hope he doesn't want us to chase ambulances. I made it clear I won't stoop to that."

"That would be safe. You wouldn't have to worry about me chipping a nail."

"Alright, I'm sorry I said that. I'm sure you could kick Levi Davis's ass in a fight."

She grinned at me. "Probably not Kyle though. If he wanted to wrestle, I wouldn't bother fighting back."

"Is this how it's going to be? Kyle this, Kyle that? How long is this going to last?"

"Until I don't think it's funny anymore." She leaned over to kiss me again. "You know I'm kidding. Forty, anything special you want for your birthday?"

"Other than the obvious?" We were teasing, couldn't hurt to drop a hint.

"Hmmm, what would be obvious?" She knitted a brow. "Angela is baking a cake, and we're going to decorate around the pool. We do have something special planned, but we're going to wait until after the party to give it to you." The teasing had turned physical, she was biting my ear.

"Forty is just a number, and it's only a few days away. Maybe we should celebrate early." I suggested. She laughed, then slid over to the other side of the truck and buckled her seat belt.

"No early birthday presents. Besides, Jasmine and Maryanne want to be there." She laughed at my expression. "That's not what I meant, pervert. But Jasmine was right the other day."

"Jasmine was right about what?"

"I am getting pretty horny."

It was just after lunch the next day when we walked into the Ackerman law office and took our spot in the waiting area. Jarrod brought us coffee and tried to make small talk.

"I met Jasmine's mom the other day, she's very pretty. I saw Jasmine, too, and she said you never said Hi for me."

"I thought I did, I don't remember," I said absent mindedly paging through a magazine.

Maggie had slipped away to the bathroom, and Jarrod must have thought I was lonely. He was a tall guy, unnaturally pale with blotchy skin that might have been freckles or psoriasis and had curly brown hair that hung down over one eye. He kept tossing his head, trying to rid himself of the obstruction, but it kept falling back into the same spot.

"Is it true that Jasmine's mom was in the movies? I mean, the erotic kind? Not judging, but Jasmine doesn't seem like that kind of girl to me."

"The kind to be in a porno? She's only seventeen, and I don't believe it's genetic."

"We handled the transaction with Maryanne, and she seems normal. Sad, when you have to pay your daughter just so she won't drag your granddaughter off and expose her to that kind of thing."

"Pretty sure Devine doesn't bring Jasmine on the set."

"Still, nice that Maryanne would keep Jasmine. Of course, she has more money than she can spend, what with all those oil wells."

The kid was getting on my nerves. "Do you generally discuss your clients with strangers, Jarrod? I would think that would be something lawyers aren't supposed to do."

"Sorry. Yeah, it's not. It's just that I know you and Maggie know the whole family so I didn't think it would matter. But, sorry, you're right." He was quiet for a minute while I sat there hoping Maggie would come back soon. "It's just that I really like her, you know?"

"Who, Devine?" I thought that was funny, he didn't.

"God no! Jasmine. Do you think she would go out on a date with me?"

"I think she's seeing someone, but I'm not sure. Call her up, and ask her out. I'm betting you have her number in your files, since you obviously snooped through everything else. Worst she could do would be to say no."

"You really think she would go out with me? And I wasn't snooping, Mr. Slater, it's my job to proofread the contracts. What if she laughs at me?"

"She wouldn't. Okay, she might, but she wouldn't be mean about it. She's a really great girl, Jarrod, but I can't play Cupid for you. I'm twice your age and women are still a complete mystery to me. Screw up your courage and ask her, that's all you can do. But keep in mind that she's only seventeen."

"She'll be eighteen soon, a few months. Maybe I can ask her then."

"You read that in those contracts?"

"How else would I find out?"

"I was going to ask the same thing. Jarrod, the best way to get to know a girl is to talk to her, not by reading her file."

"I'm too dorky to ever have a chance, I better not even call her."

"Nobody was a bigger dork than me, and look who I ended up with."

"What are we talking about?" Maggie slid into the chair next to me.

"How lucky I am." I winked at the kid. "Jarrod is going to ask Jasmine out."

Jarrod turned a very deep shade of red and stared down at the papers on his desk. "I don't know, maybe."

Maggie gave me her disapproving look. "I think she might be seeing someone, Jarrod."

"The bag boy at Safeway?" Jarrod wasn't any prize, but the Safeway kid struck me as a little too slick, and he had a brand new Mustang. Slick and spoiled. I didn't trust him and Maggie knew it.

"Jaz is a big girl, Slater."

"Exactly, call her up Jarrod, couldn't hurt." I was surprised when Maggie agreed with me.

"Sure, Jarrod, I don't mean to discourage you, give her a call. She said she doesn't want to get serious with anyone, so give it a try. Worst she can say is no thank you."

"There, see? That's exactly what I just said." I got the look again.

"Maybe I'll call her, I'll see," Jarrod said. He didn't look too confident, and if I was going to guess, I was stuck with the Safeway guy. Okay, Jasmine was stuck with the Safeway guy, not me. She had pointed out, painfully, that she had been around the block; her way of telling me, "I'm a teenager, stay out of my business." Still, I didn't trust the slick kid with the new car, and this was Jasmine. I worried.

Ten minutes later Tommy's door opened and he came rolling out of his office, followed by a man about my height, dressed in a brightly colored jacket that didn't quite fit around his middle. It must have taken half a bottle of gel to plaster his graying hair back over his head and he sported a tiny mustache that completed the impression that he might well be selling snake-oil. I eased myself down in the chair and lifted my magazine up slightly, trying my best to hide behind it.

149

"Eric? Eric Slater?" Randall Jenkins stepped across the room and held out his hand. I heard a quiet groan from Maggie when she recognized him.

"Hey RJ." I shook his hand quickly, hoping he hadn't run it through his hair recently. "How've you been?"

"You know me, never a dull moment, always in the middle of things. Tommy is helping me with a deal. Well, this is like old times! You're Maggie, right? I think you were probably ten years old when all us guys were hanging out at your house trying to get in Angela's britches. I knew back then you were going to grow up and be a hottie. I should have been nicer to you."

Maggie had never liked RJ, but she smiled. "That wouldn't have been creepy at all, and I'd have a Me-Too story to tell. I knew there was something missing in my life."

"Ouch! Take it easy on a guy, would you? Careful, Slater, this one has teeth."

"Good to see you, Randy," I hinted and picked my magazine up.

"What are you doing now? I heard you were in the Navy. Get the boot, or did you retire? I've heard it's hard to stay in if you don't make rank."

"I made rank, but I retired. I just thought it was time to have more say in my own life."

"And now this one tells you what to do, am I right?" He motioned to the redhead. Her eyes were narrow angry slits, but Randy didn't seem to notice. "How's Angela doing, Maggie? I heard her husband died a while back. He had one foot in the grave when she married him, didn't he? What the hell did she see in a guy that old? Had to be the money. Old Charlie was swimming in it from what I heard."

"Are you fucking kidding me?" Maggie finally bristled, throwing up her hands.

Tommy tried to come to our rescue. "Maggie, Slater, we need to have our meeting, I'm really running behind." Maggie was seething, but Randy was too full of himself to even realize it.

"I just got divorced you know, no more ball and chain. Maybe I should give Angela a call for old times' sake, she if she wants to go out sometime."

Maggie smiled coldly up at him. "I'll be sure and warn her."

He chuckled and tried again to get his jacket buttoned as he opened the door. "She's a pistol, Slater, good luck with that one."

I glanced over at Jarrod who had taken it all in. "Jarrod, if you want my advice about girls, just don't act like that idiot."

"I'm really sorry about that Maggie," Tommy said as we settled into chairs across his desk from him. "I shudder to think I ever was friends with that guy. RJ always has some get rich scheme, and it usually involves someone else's money. He just got out of his third marriage and I don't think any of those poor women had much left by the time he was through. I would caution Angela if he comes knocking, chances are it will cost her money. I get paid upfront for anything I do for him."

"My sister is lonely, Tommy, but I don't think she's that stupid."

"He has a gift for bilking people out of money. He's a client so I won't say more, but I'm aware Angela is at a particularly vulnerable place in her life and I wouldn't want RJ trying to take advantage of her."

"That wouldn't be good for his health, not at all." That was Maggie.

"Is Camille going to join us?" I changed the subject and slid the bill they had requested across the table. "I itemized our expenses and kept the time down as best I could. I don't expect you to pay us for sleeping."

"I'm sure you were fair, and I'm sure Camille will insist on a bonus. She tells me Wallace is very fond of you both, and you went above and beyond, shedding light on the trouble he was having with his medications. It wasn't the outcome he was hoping for, but it was the right one. He isn't able to live on his own, especially in that town. It's sad, the fact that people were willing to believe the worst, just because he's a black man."

"It wasn't the whole town, just a few of the worst, so there's that." I shrugged, but it wasn't that simple and I wasn't really that optimistic.

I was continually surprised by people's ability to be terrible to each other, be it Levi Davis or Frank and Gary Jeffries. Sometimes the motivation was simple ignorance and hate, ginned up by like-minded individuals until beating up a helpless old black man seemed reasonable; and sometimes it was greed or an even baser instinct, the need to dominate someone weaker than you, be it sexually or by brute force. Just because you could. Frank couldn't do that anymore, and hopefully Gary was somewhere where he couldn't hurt anyone either. I was going to have to find that out.

Maggie's voice brought me back to the moment. "Slater, did you hear what Tommy said?"

"Sorry, not a word. I was thinking about Wally."

"I was saying how Lilly is going to let him help at the gallery from time to time, so he gets to see her and do some of his art. Best possible outcome. You two seem really good at finding people. I think you could really make a go of this PI thing, maybe even specialize in missing persons cases."

"All things considered, Tommy, we were really lucky this time. Often as not, missing people get found in a ditch somewhere by a passerby and identified by DNA evidence. And I'm not interested in hiding in the bushes, taking pictures of somebody's cheating husband."

"I get calls from time to time, people looking for their runaway kids and wondering what their legal options are, if and when they find them.

Next time something like that comes up I could give out your name. You got Jasmine out of a bad situation, and you found Lilly. Good feeling, helping people and getting paid for it, isn't it?"

"I'm all in, Slater, you know that." Maggie smiled at me. "If we helped one kid, or even just gave a family closure, it's worth doing. I know we're not going to solve every case, but it's like you said, we don't want to chase ambulances or take pictures of cheating spouses. Trying to find missing people would be a good use of our talents."

"So is pounding nails, I like being a carpenter."

"From what I've heard, you're a much better PI than a carpenter," She pointed out awkwardly.

"Have you been talking to Luis? He told me I'm getting better. At least they aren't spending all their time fixing my screw ups."

"You'd probably make more money turning houses by just letting them do the work Slater. And you can always help them when we're not on a case."

That hurt a little, but I knew it was true. I usually broke more than I fixed. "So that's it? Slater and Jeffries, Private Eyes. It does sound kind of cool."

"We'll work on the name, but since you have the license, I suppose your name should come first." She was kidding, I think.

It was kind of a big moment.

"What about our other deal, Tommy, the offer on the Lauderdale office." Maggie asked. He glanced at me, then back at Maggie who waved her hand. "You can talk in front of Slater, he's not after my money. Until just recently, I didn't have any."

"Alright, I do have those papers ready for you to sign. Let me know when that works."

"My mom needs to sign them too, right? She's already booked her trip to Spain."

"Yeah, let me know and I'll sit down with you both and go through them. Pretty basic real estate deal, all things considered."

"I'll explain it all to you later, Slater," she said to me. "Turns out my dad's building is worth more than we thought and I have an inheritance."

There was a noise and Camille came bustling into the room, apologizing. "Why am I always late? Did you bring that bill?" Tommy handed her the paperwork, and she sat down behind his desk.

"You can just mail it to us." Maggie volunteered.

If there was one thing I had learned in the construction business, it's that when people offer to pay you, you take the money. "Make it out to S and M Investigations," I said, not really thinking it through.

"Say what?" Camille asked.

"Slater and Maggie, S and M Investigations, sounds catchy doesn't it?"

Maggie laughed. "Sounds like one of Devine's movies, Slater. Just make it out to Eric Slater for now, we'll keep working on the name. Wait, what about Slater and Partners?"

"There's only one of you." I stated the obvious.

"For now, but we might have to hire help, you never know."

"Alright, Slater and Partners it is," Camille said. "I know a good lawyer that can help you set up your LLC or a corporation. I added a little bonus and I have something else for you." She handed me the check and motioned for us to follow her. She insisted that we take the two statuettes from the outer office.

"I saw you looking at them, and Jarrod said you checked them out every time you came in. I already told Uncle Wally I wanted another set. He's happy to have something to do."

I was blown away. From the first moment I saw them, I had fallen in love with the figurines. "Which one do you want, Maggie?"

"But they're a set," Camille complained. "They're for when you two get your own place. I heard you were moving in together."

Maggie and I looked blankly at each other, then back at Camille.

"That's what Jasmine told us," Jarrod volunteered.

"Oh really!" Maggie laughed. "It sounds like something she would say. Thank you, Camille, we'll find a nice place for them, one way or the other."

I didn't say another word.

Chapter Twelve

Jasmine Thatcher bit her lip nervously and looked across the table at Maggie and me. "Thanks guys, for coming along. My mom bailed, as usual. My dad called her and said that Tiffany isn't coming, and that her mother wanted to meet me first."

"Tiffany?" I couldn't help myself. "Who picks these names?"

"Tiffany is a pretty name," Maggie said.

"If you're a stripper." Jasmine giggled. "I've seen pictures. If all goes well with her mother, I'm going to call her. It would be kind of cool to have a sister, someone I can hit up for a kidney if the time comes."

"Do you even know what your dad looks like?" I looked around the restaurant. There were two or three couples. "Could it be any of these people?"

"He said he'd be wearing a straw hat and sunglasses. That looks like them coming in now." Jasmine flipped her hand at the entry and motioned to the young couple that had just walked in.

The guy looked thirty-two, maybe thirty-five on the outside. Too young to have a daughter Jasmine's age. Divine must have been into younger guys back then. He looked like he had just walked off a California beach, stuck his board in the sand, and was ready for a game of beach volleyball. He had a floppy light-colored straw hat and dark sunglasses with yellow frames, a brightly colored Hawaiian shirt, and the best suntan I'd ever seen. His companion looked to have a couple years on Jasmine.

"Jasmine?" He asked as he walked up. "Bring it in!" She stood up hesitantly and he grabbed her and swept her into a hug, spinning her off the ground. "This is so cool."

When he released her, she stepped back quickly and pointed at us. I slid out of the booth and extended a hand. "Eric Slater, and this is Maggie. We're friends of Jasmine's and her grandmother."

"Derrick Longfellow, and this is Honey."

I had to bite my cheek. Were they all in the business? "Really good to meet you, Honey."

Honey looked over at Derrick. "I thought it was just going to be the three of us."

"I asked them to come," Jasmine volunteered. "Honestly, I was nervous, and I don't get nervous very easily. Sorry Tiffany couldn't make it."

"Yeah, she's with her mom," Honey commented. "Not like that woman would ever let her spend time with me." They slid into the booth. "We have a gig lined up in Daytona so we were in the area."

"You aren't Tiffany's mom?"

"Do I look like a mom? How old do you think I am, go ahead guess. How old?"

"Twenty-six," Maggie said quickly. It was clear she was supposed to guess younger from the hard look Honey pointed her direction. Maggie just smiled at her. "I'm really good at guessing people's age."

"Well, I'm twenty-nine, but a lot of people say nineteen or twenty. No stretch marks for this girl."

"But, Derrick, I thought you wanted me to meet Tiffany's mom? That's what my mother said." Jasmine did a poor job of hiding her disappointment. "I thought this get-together was so your wife could get to know me."

"You can call me Dad, Little One. Yeah, I don't get what Divine was thinking. I haven't been with Tiffany's mom for, like, years. That's messed up, am I right?" The waitress came and asked about our order. Derrick fumbled around then looked my way. "Dude, I left my wallet back at the place."

"We've got lunch, no worries, Dude." Maggie kicked me under the table and we all ordered.

Jasmine was still trying to get an answer. "Is there a chance I'll get to meet my sister sometime? Kind of why I'm here."

"Wow, sorry, Babe." Surfer Dude mumbled. "I was hoping we could hang out, maybe have, like, a bonding experience."

"Yeah, way to kill the vibe," Honey muttered.

160

"I guess my mom gave me the wrong impression, or just plain lied. So, you're in Florida on business?"

"Honey's dancing in Daytona, then we're going down to Lauderdale, then Miami. East coast tour. All the big names are doing it."

"The big names?" I kept a straight face, but it was hard.

"All the best exotic dancers." Derrick nodded seriously. "Money is tight on the West Coast, so we decided to expand our horizons. Florida needs our kind of entertainment, am I right?" That expression was getting annoying. I was pretty sure he wasn't right.

"And what is it you do?" Maggie asked.

"Management. It's a fulltime job lining up gigs for the little lady here. When the money's tight I pick up a dancing gig myself. Been a while since I've done a movie, but my agent is working on it. Money's always tight in this business."

"Yeah," Honey said dryly. "We can't all be Divine Thatcher. Better stake out your share, Kitten, before your mom gets it all from the old lady."

"It's Jasmine, not Kitten," Jasmine growled. I could see that she was holding back. "And what goes on between my mom and grandmother is none of your business, Honey."

"Woah, harsh!" Derrick held up his hands. "Honey didn't mean anything bad, did you, Honey? Let's just all chill. I get that your disappointed about not seeing Tiffany. Maybe we could work something out and we could all go out there. We could rent a motorhome, or does Maryanne have one we could borrow? Road trip. That would be a great way to get to know one another."

"Nothing my mom said was true," Jasmine said, as much to herself as to her alleged biological father. "She's always been a liar."

"Now, I know I haven't been much of a Dad, but it's not cool to say that about your mom, it's bad Karma." He looked to me for support. "Am I right?"

"Yeah, you are right," Jasmine said sadly. "You haven't been much of a father. This is all a big mistake."

"Aw, come on, Little One, that's harsh. I haven't had it easy like your mom. Not my business, but having a mother worth billions kind of takes the pressure off."

"Maryanne isn't worth billions, and she's worked really hard for what she has. But you're right about Mom getting money from her, she just hit her up again. Maryanne pretty much paid her off to get custody of me."

"Well at least my daughter's rich, glad you don't have to pinch pennies like me."

"Maybe the old broad would pay you to go away, too," Honey joked. Nobody laughed. Our food came and we all started eating. Derrick and Jasmine talked and Maggie and I stayed out of it. It seemed clear that Jasmine wasn't going to get to meet her sister anytime soon. I was beginning to wonder if she existed.

We all sat around after lunch and tried to make small talk, but it was awkward. The Surfer Dude and his Honey seemed desperate to hold onto their youth, and wanted us to all go to Daytona and party with them. Derrick kept complaining about the business, and how the money wasn't good. Honey bemoaned the fact that the younger girls got most of the tips. Finally, Jasmine laid it out for them.

"Maybe you two should look for real jobs."

"I'll be damned if I'm going to let Honey be a waitress." Derrick announced.

"You'd rather she gets up on a stage and takes her clothes off?"

"Rich people never get it," Honey said, looking back at Jasmine. "You'd think being family, you could help your Dad out a little."

"My grandmother gives me a car to drive, and a hundred bucks a week for spending money. If I don't carry a three five in college this fall, the car goes away. As far as help, where's he been all my life? Family? I have a sister that I didn't even know existed, what's up with that?"

"Honey, chill, would you?" Derrick tried. "It's cool. The money will be good in Daytona, then it's on to Lauderdale. A lot of big tippers in Florida, am I right?"

He was looking straight at me and I couldn't help myself. "When you're right you're right, Dude."

When it became clear there was no money to be had, Derrick and Honey lost interest in a hurry. I bought lunch, and we walked out and said our goodbyes to the pair. Maggie insisted on a picture of them with Jasmine. Family was family, she said.

Derrick nodded and took me aside. He pulled a card from the wallet he had claimed not to have and wrote something on the back of it.

"Here, Dude, if you can shake loose from the girls, swing down to the beach. The club we're working at is wide open, if you get my drift. A guy needs a little variety, am I right? The name I wrote on the back will get you special access to the backroom. Anything you want back there, and I do mean anything."

"Probably not my thing, Derrick, but I'll keep the card in case we have to get ahold of you."

"Okay, but if you land in the dog-house, come to the Doghouse. We'll be there for a couple weeks." It took me a second, then I looked at the card. That was the name of the strip club, the Doghouse. Sounded classy.

Honey, still pouting that there would be no motorhome, started the car and they drove away without a wave, hugs, or nice to see you.

If it upset Jasmine, she refused to show it. "Well, that was pretty awful," She admitted. "My dad is kind of a tool. Not sure I even want to meet my sister."

"Sorry, Jasmine." Maggie put an arm around her. "I hate to say it, but I wouldn't bet that there is a sister. The whole deal seems sketchy to me."

"Yeah, you would think they would have given me a phone number or something. I wasn't expecting much, but having a sister would be cool." She glanced at Maggie and me quickly. "But what am I saying, I already have a sister, right? And Slater, you're kind of like my brother, my much older brother."

I grinned and slid my arm around her from the other side. "Forty is the new thirty, Dude."

Susy Foster texted me the next day and said she wanted to meet with me, alone. I drove to the restaurant a few miles from my house. I was early, but she was already there. I didn't recognize her at first. She had cut her hair, dyed it a dark brown and was wearing a faded sweatshirt, cutoff jeans, and a pair of tennis shoes. I walked right by her, then looked around for the woman I knew.

"Slater, behind you," she called out, pulling off the large sunglasses she was wearing.

I peered at her cautiously. "Holy Cow, I didn't even know that was you." I slid into the chair opposite her.

"That's a good thing. In my business, being recognizable is a liability."

"Who's going to recognize you?" I glanced around.

"I've been raising hell, trying to hone in on the trafficking and make the bastards pay for what they did to Davey and Sam. I think they're getting tired of me poking my nose into things. It didn't take them long to reorganize. They have a lot of resources, and some well-connected people in their back pockets. Frank and Gary Jeffries were just minor players. Most of the money is coming from overseas."

"This agency of yours, you have help, right? You're not going after them alone? What about the FBI, I thought they were all over this?"

"The FBI has a lot on their plate and Homeland Security has been busy lately, in case you haven't noticed. Our department is at the bottom of the barrel, so I'm lucky to be getting a paycheck. Protecting immigrant kids isn't a high priority right now."

"But a lot of these kids that are being kidnapped are US citizens."

"My mandate is to investigate child trafficking, especially immigrants. I keep fighting to widen the net, because like you say, a lot of these girls are American citizens, and I know for a fact that the organization that Frank and Gary were connected to didn't just target girls fresh off the boat. But it's political. My job is to make sure there aren't large groups of immigrant kids being sold into slavery, not because it would be horrific, but because it would look bad on the six o'clock news."

"So, you have fewer resources and the problem is getting worse, not better."

"The people I hoped to get to and maybe even indict are still in business, paying off politicians to redirect funding so agencies like mine don't have the manpower to investigate properly. I knew it would be impossible to arrest the big player from the Middle East, but there are a couple of Congressmen involved, and money out of Washington and New York."

"You said it was big. What about Gary's testimony? He can name names, right?"

"He's not been very helpful so far. He's a tough negotiator. I've been close more than once to pulling our offer and throwing him to the wolves. Once the organization knew where he was, prison or not, he wouldn't last long."

"Maybe, but he has a remarkable gift for staying alive. He supposedly died in that plane crash four years ago, and we both know that didn't happen. I still haven't told Maggie anything about him, but I need to, and soon. Hoping that won't land me in jail again."

She grinned. "You have my permission. I'm guessing that's going to be a difficult conversation."

"There's no way she could realize her uncle is alive, much less that he's the Diablo. She tries not to show it, but she's struggling with everything that happened. She says good riddance, but Frank was her father, and that has to hurt. I think finding out Davey was her half-brother is what's really kicking her ass. At least they had the chance to be close, even if she thought all along that he was just the neighbor's kid."

"What the hell? Davey Templeton was their brother? This is news to me. No wonder he wanted to get back to Point Road to protect his family. Why in the hell didn't you tell me this before?"

"It's not like you've made yourself available. I texted you a couple of times and you never got back to me, so I thought maybe you were holding a grudge. What possible difference could it make? Frank snuck across the road one night, no big surprise there. He spent his whole life being a scumbag and a liar. The only part of the whole thing that surprises me is that Edith Templeton could have been that stupid. But then again, she had Davey because of it, so maybe it was kismet or something."

"God, I'm so sorry for Maggie. That had to be a hard thing to find out."

"Her sister, Angela, knew for a while. Unfortunately, it gets worse. Frank was even more disgusting than we thought. He'd been molesting Angela for years, and he only stopped because Davey threatened to shoot him when he found out."

"Jesus. If anything is kismet, it's him hanging himself. Good riddance, I say."

I nodded, hard not to agree with that. "Bottom line Susy, I still want what you want, to get the people that killed Davey and Sam. Funny thing about Gary. When they sent that assassin after Frank's girlfriend, Gary said he was going to stop him, but that Andy got the drop on him. He would have been taking a hell of a chance trying to stop a professional gunman like that, unless he's damn good with a gun, or knew the guy. Maybe he was having a crisis of conscience, or maybe he knew he wouldn't be in any real danger because he could call the hit off. Maybe they weren't sending Frank a message, maybe it was Gary that they thought needed the message."

"You're saying maybe he's higher up in the organization than I thought? Maybe he's so valuable that they can't kill him, or it was some kind of power play?"

"Just a theory."

"Alright, let's assume that's true. Is he just waiting for a chance to escape? He's in a safe house, guarded constantly, and I've been thinking he would be worried about them finding him, but maybe that's what he wants. He keeps stalling and making demands for his testimony. That's why I'm here. I'm calling in that favor."

"I probably owe you." She had kept my name out of it. Killing a hired assassin would be considered justified, but it would have taken some explaining.

"Gary wants to talk to the girls, Maggie and Angela."

"Wow. That's a tough one."

"You just said you want to tell Maggie, this is your chance."

"Maggie maybe, but not Angela. She's fighting a lot of demons without having a dead uncle show up out of nowhere. She's struggled with depression and losing Davey all but killed her. Her dad, too, as illogical as that sounds to us. I can't speak for Maggie, but I'm pretty sure she'll be dead set against telling Angela, and if she is, I am."

"Gary says he talks to them or he doesn't turn State's evidence."

"He'll have to settle for Maggie, and I can't swear she'll do it. Not that you would, but Gary doesn't know Davey was his brother's son, so don't pass that information along. I'm thinking Maggie needs to be the one to tell him that, if she wants to. What a damn mess."

"Talk to her as soon as you can, okay? If we can make it work, I'll take you to the safe house where we have Gary. I'm staying in Titusville for now. I moved my sister to a place where she'll be safe, and I'm using the house. It's a good location, half way between Miami and here."

"One of the reasons I tried to contact you was about Davey's money. His mom and dad ended up with it, but some of that must have been Sam's too. Edith and I talked and I explained how Davey had been helping the girls like your sister and

Rosalyn Cabello. She agreed it would be good to give that money to as many of those girls as we can find. I took Rosalyn a hundred thousand dollars a couple weeks ago, and I was able to find Dedra too. I can get a check to you for Sandy, and if you know where Maria Lopez is, that would be great. I know there are a lot more of those girls that could use it, if we can find them without putting them in danger."

        "That's good of the Templetons. Nobody would blame them or be the wiser if they just kept that money. I could send Sandy a cashier's check, if that's alright. I don't want there to be any way that someone could find out where she is, even a digital money transfer could be dangerous."

        "What about Davey's list? Are those girls still in danger?"

        "I don't think so, at least not for a while. I need your promise, Slater, if I level with you about everything, you won't go crazy and try to take things into your own hands again."

        "You're talking about the man responsible for Davey's death?"

        "Yeah, promise me that if I tell you who he is, there won't be any more lying about what you know. You knew Gary Jeffries was the Diablo Blanco long before I did, and keeping that information from me could have ended up getting more people killed."

        "Granted I should have told you, but he's Maggie's uncle, and I'd known him since I was twelve. At the time, I figured I needed to talk to him first, about Davey."

"You mean beat a confession out of him. I get that."

"Fine, I give you my word, but it's a two-way street, we need to help each other."

"Rashad Dinar. Sound familiar?"

"Vaguely, but I avoid the news, too depressing."

"Big time oil trader, rubs elbows with sheiks and dictators all over the Middle East. He's well-connected in this country too. He has an unbridled enthusiasm for young girls, and absolutely no boundaries. He shares his harem with his business associates, it's one of the perks of doing business with him. There are parts of the world where that is just expected, it's part of the hospitality package when you agree to sell your oil. He was the man that wanted to eliminate Sandy and Dedra and the others. I'm sure it was his compound where they were imprisoned, but Davey refused to give the location away because he was afraid Rashad might find out and kill all the girls that were still there. He said it wasn't a place our government would go, no matter what the crimes."

"It's all about the money, I heard that more than once."

"After he killed Davey, and we grabbed Gary Jeffries, he got nervous and left the country. But with the price of oil so low, his revenue stream is drying up, so trafficking girls has become more than a dirty hobby, now it's a business. I think he's trying to expand. He has people working for him in this country, organized crime, or maybe just more people like Frank and Gary Jeffries."

"They're back in business and getting more organized?"

"The sex trade never stops, and someone is moving kids around again. A lot of these girls come from Central America, escape the gang violence there, then end up on the streets here. But things are changing. It's not just a random pimp here and there, it's getting more organized. It's more like the drug trade, a real distribution network with a lot of these immigrant kids as product, and Rashad's organization is responsible for a huge part of that. I don't know where Gary Jeffries fits into it, if he was just a mule or one of the heads of the operation. From what you told me about Rosalyn, he dabbles in the rough stuff too."

"I always thought he was a little crude when I was a kid, but not a complete pervert."

"Welcome to the real world, Slater, it's filled with soulless assholes. The Coast Guard stopped a freighter last week, because they suspected it was hauling drugs up from Ecuador. They found twenty-three girls, eleven to sixteen years old with six "handlers" hidden in the back of a cargo hold. The older girls already knew they were going to an eastern European brothel. They were told they had to help the younger ones adjust to the idea. How do you adjust to that? How can that happen in the twenty-first century?"

It surprised me when she started to cry, then stood suddenly and rushed to the bathroom. I was sure Susy Foster had seen some of the worst society had to offer, but it still got to her. Hard as that was for her, it was probably a good thing for those kids.

But I had a name, Rashad Dinar. I would try to keep my promise to Susan, but I had made one to myself, and to Davey Templeton.

Friday night supper was getting to be a thing, that and Angela's cooking. Being the dutiful boyfriend, I didn't argue and the food was pretty good.

Angela was dressed like Beaver Cleaver's mother. She had on a white apron and a blue and white print dress that stretched below her knees and billowed out like a square dancer's when she turned and walked back and forth into the kitchen. Her blond hair was pulled back and up and tied with a light blue scarf and her lips were a darker shade of red than usual. June Cleaver never looked so good.

Jasmine came in with Safeway in tow, showing him off to Maggie and Maggie's Mom. He nodded to me and rolled his eyes at all the attention the women were giving him as if he didn't like it, then started going on about his basketball career at the local high school. He reminded me of some of the guys that had chased after Angela when we were younger, a little too slick and self-entitled. Still, he was a big improvement over Cletus Johnson.

There was a lot of chatter and laughing and some ribbing about my upcoming birthday, then we all started sitting down at the kitchen table. Maggie jumped up when the doorbell rang, and Angela glanced nervously in her direction as she set a bowl of vegetables on the table.

"That would be my guest. RJ took me out for supper the other night, so I figured I should return the favor." She glanced at me apprehensively. "I know he can be a bit much, but try to be nice, okay?"

I shrugged. "I don't think I'm the one you have to worry about."

Randy Jenkins was on his best behavior for most of the meal. Perhaps that was because he was busy stuffing his face and guzzling wine. After we had finished eating, he sighed contentedly and pulled a pack of cigarettes from his pocket.

Maggie had ignored him up to that point. "You can't smoke in here."

"Oh, sorry, of course not." He glanced at Angela as if he was hoping she would argue his case. She had gotten up and started collecting plates. "Rich folks like you, don't you have a housekeeper?" Wisely, Mrs. Jeffries excused herself and left the table for her room.

"Jasmine's grandmother has a butler and a maid," Safeway volunteered. "But she owns half of North Dakota."

"Who's your grandmother?" RJ asked, eyeing Jasmine.

"Maryanne Thatcher, she has more money than God." Safeway spoke up again for Jasmine. I could see he was headed for trouble. If Jasmine could handle Cletus Johnson, she would eat this kid for lunch.

RJ leered at Jasmine. "Your mom is Divine Thatcher, the porn star? I've seen a couple of her movies. Yowzah!"

The blue-haired wild child smiled sweetly at him. "God, you really are a dickhead."

Maggie didn't attempt to hide her laughter. I bit my cheek.

"Kids these days." Randy smiled, then got himself in deeper. "What's the story with this one, Sweetie?" Angela had just walked back in the room, and as a group we were surprised by the term of affection.

"Who're you calling Sweetie?" Maggie asked.

"Slip of the tongue, Too Little. I have a deep affection for your sister."

Angela reached out and picked up our plates. "Deep affection? We had supper one night and I had to leave the tip so you wouldn't stiff the waiter."

"The service was terrible! You know I've always had a fondness for you Angie. We can talk about it later, after dessert. Come sit and have a glass of wine. You did all the work, these two can clean up." He waved in the general direction of Maggie and Jasmine. Maggie inhaled deeply, but I nudged her and gave her a wink.

"How about you and I do the dishes, RJ? Maybe Junior here can dry."

"Name's Jessie." Safeway glared at me. "I'll dry, if you wash."

"I'm not doing any damn dishes," RJ stated. "I'm a guest, guests don't wash dishes." He looked up at Angela. "Come have a glass of wine. I thought Charlie left you well fixed. Why don't you have a maid?"

"Our housekeeper is a family friend RJ, and she has a life of her own. I enjoy cooking and taking care of things. It keeps me busy."

"You shouldn't have to, is all I'm saying. Rumor is Charlie took very good care of you."

"You seem pretty interested in what Charlie left behind," Maggie pointed out.

"I just think she should be living the life she deserves. What do you think, Angie? Want to go to Miami for the weekend, maybe paint the town?"

Angela looked at him sadly. "I told you before RJ, I stopped drinking. Do you ever listen to anyone, or are you so busy talking about yourself that you don't have the time?"

177

"Angie! No need to be rude." He stiffened. "You were plenty eager to take me up on dinner, now all of a sudden I'm not good enough?" RJ slid his chair back.

"You're right about that, you're not good enough," Maggie remarked. "And it was Too Small, not Too Little."

"Maybe if she didn't have you harping at her all the time, she would appreciate the fact that I was willing to take her out," RJ blustered. "It's not like guys are beating the door down."

Angela teared up, then pointed at the door. "That may be true RJ, but you don't get to talk to my sister like that. She's someone that really cares about me. Jasmine said it, you're a dickhead. Goodnight."

The guy was thick, but he finally got the message. He stood up quickly, but looked like he might have more to say. I'd heard enough. I stood and pulled his chair out of the way. "The kid and I can handle the dishes, Randy. You best hit the road."

By the time I slammed the door behind him, Angela had disappeared and Maggie and Jasmine were carrying dishes into the kitchen. When I glared at Safeway, he jumped up to help. Maggie smiled at me and leaned next to my ear.

"Go talk to Angie, would you?"

"Why me?"

"You're a man. Give her a hug and tell her she looks pretty. She needs that right now."

I knocked softly on the door, then let myself in. Angela sat on her bed, wiping at her eyes, and looked surprised when she saw that it was me.

"How the mighty have fallen, right, Slater? Even Randy Jenkins doesn't want me."

"You know that's not true, he just wants you for the wrong reasons," I assured her. "Maybe dating isn't the best idea right now. You've been through an awful lot in the last few months."

"It was just nice to have somebody take an interest, even that self-obsessed jerk. I can't say that I've ever had a normal relationship. Charlie and I were very close, but it wasn't romantic in the normal sense."

"Look at you. Any man in his right mind would want you."

"I remember when you did." She smiled wistfully up at me.

I gave her a small kiss on the cheek. "And a part of me always will, Angie, it's just that I'm so damn scared of your sister."

She laughed and gave me a hug. "Me, too. Maybe a birthday kiss at the party, she'll have to give us a pass on that."

Evolution. It was a wonderful thing.

My birthday was on Sunday, the big four-oh. It's a day when a lot of people get caught up in self-reflection and over analyze what they've done and what they haven't. I wasn't that guy. I never was one to believe in Fate, or that there was some predetermined path that you were bound to stumble into whether you wanted to or not. Life was made up of choices, some good, some not so good; some worked out, and some didn't.

I did ascribe to the Butterfly Effect, the idea that tiny moments in a person's life could change their future, and by extension the lives of the people around them. Turning left instead of right on any given day could precipitate changes that we would never be aware of or could possibly quantify as we continued haplessly about our lives. I wondered, with over fourteen thousand days behind me, how many of those tiny choices I had made, and how they had affected where I was today.

I wasn't inclined to second guess myself too much. There were a couple of things I might have tweaked given the chance, but for the most part I was happy with where life had taken me. A huge part of that was the fact that Maggie Jeffries was a part of my life. I had to tell her about her uncle, and everything I knew about her dad. It scared me, mostly because I knew it would hurt her, and to some degree because I had kept it from her as long as I had. But she said it herself, at a certain point in time it would be like I was lying to her, and that would be a wrong turn. There were things in my life I couldn't control, but I planned to do everything I could to make Maggie Jeffries happy.

Somewhere out in the world, a Butterfly shook his wings and laughed at my plans.

There was never going to be a good time. After we took the plane up the next day to get Maggie ready for her flight test, I suggested we stop at my house to talk.

"Are you still hoping for an early birthday present, Slater?" She was on my side of the truck again and making it difficult to concentrate on my driving. I pulled away from her and must have looked serious. She knitted a brow. "What is it?"

"We need to talk, just talk. There are things I need to tell you about your dad and everything, difficult things. Maybe a cold beer would make it easier."

"It can wait if you want. I know I said you need to tell me, but it won't change anything between us. I know whatever you did, you always have my best interests at heart. You couldn't have known my dad would kill himself, I don't blame you for that."

"I'm afraid there's more to it."

"Now you're scaring me a little, but okay. A cold beer sounds good."

A myriad of emotions crossed her face in the three-minute drive to my house. It had occurred to me that she might react poorly and I didn't want her jumping out of the truck in traffic. We reached my house and went in, grabbed our beers and sat on the couch.

"I was going to wait for a good time, but I met with Susy Foster yesterday, and she asked me to talk to you about this as soon as possible."

"Last night would have been okay, but what does Susan have to do with this?"

"Alright, you know Susan works for Homeland Security. She tries to stop people from taking advantage of these immigrant girls, girls like Rosalyn Cabello."

"Sure, we talked about that. She was helping Davey, right?"

"Not in the rescue operations, her job is more enforcement."

"Busting people like the Diablo, and probably my father?"

"I told you that your father knew who the Diablo was, and that he was inadvertently involved with Davey's death."

"Yeah." She grew wary.

"The men your father worked with were trafficking girls, and he was part of it, that's how he got stuck in the middle. It's not like he wasn't involved, because he was. But there was a good reason your dad knew who the Diablo was."

"He worked with him?" Maggie asked cautiously.

"Yeah, but the reason he worked with him, that's complicated." I was struggling.

"Dammit, Slater, spit it out. We've established my dad was a scumbag, what else is there?"

"The Diablo Blanco, Maggie. He's your uncle. Gary Jeffries didn't die in that plane crash in the Everglades four years ago. He faked the whole thing and ran off to California. It was Gary that kidnapped Sandy Foster and sent her to the Middle East, and it was Gary that manipulated Davey, and slapped him around down in Miami."

Her eyes were wide and instantly shining with tears. "He made my brother watch, when he did those ungodly things to Rosalyn Cabello? His own nephew! Dear God, I wish he had died in that crash. Does he know? Did he have any idea that Davey was my dad's son?"

"The night I shot the man that was sent to kill Maria, I almost told him. But unless Davey told him, I don't think he could know. Davey was just someone convenient and vulnerable, someone he knew he could use and control."

"How long?"

I knew what she was asking. "I saw him the day Sam was killed, in a car outside of Rosalyn's house. That was the first time I realized he was alive. The pieces fit and I knew he must be the Diablo. I couldn't tell you, it was too much. It was too much for me, knowing everything I did, especially after I learned Davey was your brother."

She stared at me, pale and cold as the whole chain of events tumbled around in her mind. "I thought we agreed to always be honest, Slater," she said coldly.

"I am, now I am. I just couldn't get it out before, I knew how much it would hurt you."

"Why are you telling me this now, today?"

"He knows the man who had Davey killed, but he won't agree to testify unless he can talk to you first. He wanted to talk to you and Angela, but I told him there's no way Angela could do that."

"Of course you'd protect her." It was an accusation, one she took back immediately. "I'm sorry, you know I wouldn't have wanted to tell her either. She's had all the trauma she can handle for one lifetime." She put her beer down, settled against me and closed her eyes.

"How about I just sit here for a while and don't think. Just put your arms around me and I'll forget all about my fucked-up dad and uncle, and how I have a dead brother. Okay?"

"I can do that." There was no forgetting. I held onto her as she cried softly for a very long time.

Finally, she sat up, wiped her face and looked at me. "When? I want to get this over with."

"Okay, I'll call Susan. Does tomorrow morning work for you?"

Chapter Thirteen

No matter how we try to protect the people we love, there is always the chance that we'll fail. Doesn't matter if you call it Fate, bad luck, or just a poor decision; all but the luckiest of us have to face ugliness at some point in our lives and inevitably watch someone we care about face ugliness and pain, knowing there is little we can do to help them through it.

Looking at Maggie the next morning I would have done anything to spare her from what lay in front of her. In hindsight, I knew I could have done that. I could have found some way to take Gary Jeffries out of his brother's guest house the night I found him tied to a chair, spirited him away to a quiet place and gave him what he deserved, a spot in the Everglades with all those alligators. That would have been justice. And that would have stopped this moment from happening.

"What are you thinking about?" the redhead asked.

"How badly I screwed up when I didn't shoot your worthless uncle," I admitted.

She smiled sadly. "That isn't who you are. Maybe it's a good thing. Maybe he'll testify against the people that killed Davey."

"Then I get to shoot all of them?"

That made her chuckle. "If it were that simple, I'd help you."

"The way you shoot?"

"I asked for that. Looks like this is it."

Susan Foster had led us on a circuitous route through the back streets of Jacksonville to a small, brick house on a corner lot. A tall chain link fence separated it from the Interstate in the back, and the north side butted up to a small commercial looking building with no windows. That left two sides exposed to the street with good visibility. There were shrubs, but they were only waist high. I wondered about those, recalling the time I had used similar shrubbery to sneak up to the Jeffries Estate in Lauderdale.

Frank Jeffries and his girlfriend had had a dog, a half-grown pet that the hired assassin had killed. This yard had two dogs, both hundred pound plus German Shepherds that were undoubtedly well trained and a lot better at protecting their owner than that puppy had been. A full-grown man with a weapon could deal with one dog, but two could be a hell of a problem. We walked up to the wire gate and waited. The dogs sat calmly on the front step watching us carefully.

Susan Foster nodded at the pair of canines. "They know me, but if I opened this gate, they would shred me like a bag of kibble. Officer Grant will be out in a minute. He will have to check you for weapons. I trust you, but no one goes in armed, even me."

"Nice to see you again, Susy." Maggie offered. "Slater has told me stories of your exploits,

186

but I never really got a chance to talk to you much, other than on the phone."

"I feel like we're old friends, all things considered. Maybe someday there'll be a chance for coffee and we can really get to know each other."

"Right now would be a great time, but I don't suppose I can get out of this."

Susy gave her a shrug and a smile. "Sorry to put you through this, but we need his testimony. He says he needs to make amends."

"Nothing he says or does will accomplish that."

"Still, he wants to try. He can be a deceptively engaging man."

Officer Grant opened the door and called the dogs in. The bigger one stood its ground for a moment and gave out a half-hearted bark, alerting his handler. A half minute passed and he walked back out and waved us in. He frisked us quickly, even Susan.

The entry door didn't have any glass and it was steel, like the construction doors we used during our remodels. It hadn't been obvious from outside, but each window was filled with heavy steel bars, and there was a substantial crossbar securing the back door, which I could see behind Gary Jeffries. He sat quietly at the kitchen table. One arm was extended slightly, and I could see a short chain between a set of handcuffs and the crossbar securing the door. The room was spartan:

a table, metal chairs, refrigerator, and microwave. There was a sink, but no dishes. The garbage was nearly filled with paper plates and plastic glasses. Not Leavenworth, but not the Ritz either.

We walked into the room and stood ten feet away from Maggie's uncle. Susy spoke hesitantly. "You all know each other. Gary has requested time alone with you, Maggie. You need to sit on the opposite side of the table and have no physical contact. We will be in the office in the back should you need help or have questions. Gary has assured me he will be a perfect gentleman, and that it will just take a few minutes."

"I won't be alone with him." She stared coldly at her father's brother. "I'm not afraid, just so you know, but Slater needs to be here. If he wants to talk, he talks to us both."

Gary nodded. He looked smaller than when I'd last seen him, thinner. Perhaps TV dinners and constant worry had proven a good diet. I imagined that wondering when an assassin's bullet would find you would ruin your appetite. Rashad Dinar had to know by now that Gary might turn witness, and he would not be happy about that.

"Alright, you have ten minutes."

There were two chairs on our side of the table, and we pulled them back a couple of feet, then sat down. Maggie studied Gary for a good fifteen seconds, then spit out a few words.

"Did you know what my father was?"

"If you mean, did I know he was a weak, sorry excuse for a human being, yes. It takes one to know one, I guess."

"There aren't words for how much I hate him, or you. What possible reason would you have for wanting to talk to me?"

"Your Dad took the brunt of our father's anger after our older brother died and my mother committed suicide. He was a vicious, mean person. Sins of the father, I guess. It took something out of Frank, or maybe he didn't have it to start with. He was brutal, like our dad."

"And you're an angel?" Maggie asked incredulously.

Gary smiled and glanced at me, then nodded his head in acknowledgement. "I can't say that I am. But your dad was remorseless. Right up until the end, when he wasn't. I don't know if it was the guilt of thinking Maria was dead that made him do it, or if he just couldn't stand what he'd become. I admit I have done terrible things. I told myself the people I was doing them to didn't matter, and if I didn't use them, someone else would."

"How could you possibly do such vile things to Rosalyn? And Davey."

"I don't know. I am not that different from my brother, I guess. I took what I wanted, just because I could. It's an incredible feeling knowing someone is helpless, that you hold their life in your hands; that you could end it if it suited you."

Maggie lunged to her feet suddenly and stepped away from me. I don't know how, but she had hidden her gun somewhere, and now she pointed it at Gary's face.

She spoke quietly. "How does it feel? I could end your life if it suited me. Funny, I don't feel that rush, I just feel sick. Tell me why I shouldn't shoot you right between the eyes." She hadn't raised her voice, and Susan trusted us enough to not watch. I glanced back, to be sure she or the officer hadn't come out of the office, but I didn't try to take the gun. I was reasonably sure Maggie couldn't shoot an unarmed man any more than I could.

Gary didn't move, didn't show the least bit of emotion. After a tense few seconds, Maggie pocketed the gun and sat down. She was shaking, and her eyes filled.

"God, I wish I could kill you."

"Believe it or not, I am sorry for the pain I caused you and your sister. I would have liked to have had Angela here as well."

"Sorry, but she's a little messed up at the moment, dear Uncle. Seems like losing the father that had been raping her since she was twelve is something she can't quite wrap her head around!"

He hadn't known. It was on his face. "My God, I'm so sorry. I would have put an end to that if I'd known."

"Really? Caging a fourteen-year old child, raping her and shooting her full of drugs is in your wheelhouse, but you draw the line at incest? Good

190

to know. You're my hero! If you're so Goddamn noble, Uncle Gary, why did you have to drag your own nephew into it?"

Gary cocked his head, ashen. "Nephew, what do you mean?

"Daddy dearest slipped across the road back in the day, I'm surprised he didn't brag to you about it. Davey was my half-brother, and your nephew, you sack of shit." She was getting pretty loud and Susan stuck her head out of the office. I waved her away. "Did you set him up to get killed, or was that my father?"

"I didn't know, Maggie, I swear it. Frank didn't either." I knew that was a lie, but I was willing to let it go for Maggie's sake. Gary put his forehead down on the table, and when he lifted it, there were tears in his eyes. "I almost wish you had pulled the trigger a minute ago, but then you'd be paying for my sins, and Frank's. I didn't know about any of this. Davey, Angela, my God! What a nightmare we put those two through. Honestly, if I'd known Frank was doing that to your sister, I would have shot him myself."

"I can't look at you. You disgust me." Maggie gave into tears for a minute.

"Why are we here, Gary?" I asked.

"I hoped to explain to the girls, how things got so out of control. How we got involved with the group from the Middle East."

"You mean Dinar? He's the head of the snake, right?"

191

"Susan told you? She shouldn't have done that. Just knowing that name could get you killed, and my niece along with you. There are a lot of moving parts, but Dinar controls most of the supply chain from overseas, and no one dares do much without his say-so."

Maggie leaned forward, venomous. "Supply chain? These girls, these children, they are supplies to you?"

"I'm sorry Maggie, really I am, for everything I've done. Your father and I made excuses for each other. We figured most of these girls would end up on the streets anyway, so we thought it was okay to make some money off them. It was always about the money, like Davey used to say."

"You don't deserve to even say his name. You took my brother from me before I even knew who he really was. I'll never forgive you for that."

"I can't undo the past, but I have plans for the future. It's possible Susan is right, and Dinar will have me killed, but I think he plans to keep me around for a while."

"Not that it matters, since you are legally dead, but we liquidated the building in Lauderdale for a good chunk of money."

"Good! After everything, your mother and you girls deserve it." He tried smiling at her, but Maggie didn't respond in kind.

"You have plans?" I asked. "I thought the plan was to testify, then disappear."

"I could bring down a few people, but getting Dinar in a courtroom would be tough. He's tight with some men in Washington, and he controls the sale of huge quantities of oil. He would be protected from extradition and he would never stand trial. I want a more permanent solution."

"Kill him?"

"I know you two don't think a lot of me, but Frank was my brother, and Dinar has to pay for his death. And now there's Davey too, he deserves some kind of justice."

"You agree to testify, and he's going to kill you the minute he finds you." I pointed out.

"If I testify. If I don't, I might be able to talk my way back into the organization, get close to him and end it."

"Bird in hand. Susan Foster would never agree to let you try that, even as bad as she wants him."

"I don't expect she will."

It occurred to Maggie what he was implying, and she leaned over the table, getting close to his face. "You hurt anyone, if even one of those dogs gets so much as a scratch, much less Susan Foster, Slater and I will track you down and I swear on Davey's grave I will pull the trigger myself."

"I'm going to make him pay for Davey and Frank's death Maggie, anyway I can. But I'm done hurting innocent people, I promise you that."

"I don't believe your promises, and I'm going to tell Susy about what you have planned." Maggie didn't seem angry anymore, just tired, and resigned. "I wish I could say it was good to see you, but I really can't. Are we done?"

"All I hoped for was a chance to lay eyes on you and Angela. It's been a lot of years. I am sorry about Davey. I liked him, despite the way I treated him." He struggled to get the words out. "It's like a sickness. There's always this rage that doesn't go away. I can push it aside for long periods of time, but it's always there under the surface, waiting. My brother couldn't control it, and it ate him alive. Maybe we got that from our father's genes, or maybe we learned it. Don't let it ruin your life, Maggie." He extended a hand, and I was stunned when she took it, then turned without another word and fled out the door.

"I'll pass on the handshake," I muttered, backing away.

"I already told Foster my plan, but feel free if you don't believe me. And thank you, Eric, for saving Maria and those kids that night. It was a wake-up call for me, it really was."

The bastard had done it, I almost felt sorry for him. I backed from the room and walked outside into the cool morning air, feeling nauseous and unclean. Maggie and Susan were leaning against my old pickup. Maggie didn't look any better than I felt.

"I told Susy what he said. He's not allowed outside, no phone or any way to communicate with anyone, rotating guards. If they find him, they're more likely to kill him than invite him back into the gang, don't you think?"

"If they're smart," Susan said. "No offense, Maggie, but I wouldn't trust your uncle as far as I could throw him. He told me the same story he told you, that he wants to kill Dinar. He's not getting away from us, and if he did, they would shoot him on sight."

"He got what he wanted, talking to Maggie, so maybe he'll testify like he agreed to do," I said.

"We're going to sit on him for a while, until we can bring charges against the higher ups in the organization. I wish that could include Dinar, but I doubt it."

"I think we shook him up some. He had no idea Davey was his nephew."

"Maybe that will be enough motive to testify, his brother and nephew, both dead. You would think he would want to put the people away that are responsible for that."

Maggie snorted. "All he has to do is look in the mirror to see who's responsible. Come on, Slater. I have to get home and help with the birthday preparations."

"Whose birthday?" Susan asked.

Maggie gave me her first real smile of the day. "Slater is old! Forty. You're invited to the party if you want to come. It's Sunday afternoon at my house. You can meet my sister Angela. She has Davey's eyes."

"Thanks, but I have to go to Miami."

"Stay safe, okay?" I put in. "You wouldn't be the first undercover cop to end up on the wrong end of a gun."

"I can take care of myself. I can't shoot quite as good as you can, but I'm not bad. I am definitely going to start wearing my vest, just in case."

"Do you think he knew?" Maggie asked. We were in my truck, heading back to Point Road.

"Knew what? About Angela, or Davey?"

"That I wouldn't pull the trigger."

"Honestly, I'm not sure if he cared. And for the record, if you pull a stunt like that again I'm taking your gun away. It's Slater and Partners, remember? You shoot somebody and I'm liable, I have the license."

"Yes sir, boss." She grinned at me, and I did my best to look serious.

"I don't think he knew about your dad and Angela, or the fact that Davey was his nephew. He looked surprised by that. Are you going to tell Angela that he's alive? It seems like she has a right to know, but she may not be able to handle it."

"I'm going to hold off for a while. Maybe he'll testify. That would make him seem less horrible. Do you think there's a family curse, like Gary said? Am I going to lose it at some point? I have to wonder if that rage that my uncle talked about is going to come for me or Angela at some point."

"Angela has to deal with being bipolar, plus everything your father did to her. You're stronger than she is, you always have been. I don't think you have that kind of anger in you."

"Funny, that Gary would value family as much as he professes to, but not have the slightest remorse for what he did to Rosalyn or so many of those other girls."

"Not so different from Levi Davis. He has a different set of rules for people that don't look like him. Rosalyn Cabello wasn't from a good southern family, so she didn't matter to Gary."

"Well, Karma's a bitch, because now he doesn't matter to me." I didn't say anything. I wasn't sure if it was true or if I wanted it to be.

I'm not a guy that likes parties, especially when I'm the guest of honor. Fortunately, the party that Maggie and the girls were organizing wasn't going to be very big. I'd been away for a lot of years and most of the guys I hung out with from school were long gone. Davey Templeton had been my best friend, and he was dead, a fact I tried to push from my mind as I contemplated the second half of my life. The reality that he had been robbed of the second half of his, had been weighing on me after seeing Gary Jeffries again. If it took another forty years, I intended to make the people who had killed Davey pay for it.

I looked over the cars as I pulled up. Luis, my foreman was there, and Edith Templeton, Davey's mother, had made it. Tommy Ackerman and his wife were there, and Maryanne Thatcher, Jasmine's grandmother. I didn't see Jasmine's car or the Bagboy's flashy new Mustang. Him, I could do without. I was pretty sure Maggie's mom had left for Spain. She wasn't a demonstrative woman, and attending my birthday party probably wasn't high on her list of priorities. Adding Maggie and Angela to the guest list would mean ten or twelve people, tops. I could handle that.

Maggie kept alluding to a special birthday present. That sounded good, but I wasn't sure we were talking about the same thing. I was hoping for more than a new shirt for my birthday, and all the ear biting had aroused more than my curiosity.

She greeted me at the door, her long chestnut locks falling softly around her face as she slid against me and gave me a long kiss. "Happy Birthday, Slater," she said and winked secretively. "Let's make it a special one, okay?"

"I'm all for that, Red." I wasn't sure if there was innuendo. I have misinterpreted a woman's intentions before.

Angela rushed up and gave me a none too subtle kiss. She laughed when I pulled away. "It's your birthday, Slater, Maggie gave me a pass today. I get to smooch you as much as I want."

Maggie bumped her shoulder playfully. "I did not say that! I've got my eye on you two." There had been a time when she might not have been kidding, but we were past that.

Edith Templeton scurried up and wrapped her arms around me next. She buried her head against my chest and gave me a warm hug. "Happy Birthday, Eric. I wish Davey could be here to see you with Maggie! He laughed about how she used to follow you around when she was a little girl. He said way back then that she had a horrible crush on you."

"I wish he was here, too, Edith, but he is in spirit. I'll bet he's proud of you for taking care of those girls the way you have."

"Rosalyn has become a phone friend, and she's forgiven Davey for his part in what happened to her. She's helping other girls get off the streets. I hope I can meet her someday." Edith said.

"She realizes now that it was the Diablo Blanco, and that Davey wasn't to blame. We'll get the people responsible, sooner or later." Gary's name was on the tip of my tongue, and it almost slipped out. Nothing good could come of that.

"You be careful, Eric. I lost a son to those vile people, and you're the next best thing. Now that you proved Davey was murdered, maybe the police will do their job."

"The squeaky wheel gets the grease, Edith. I'm going to keep pushing until we get results. We know who was responsible, we just have to be able to prove it and get a conviction."

"You'd make a good lawyer, Slater." Tommy Ackerman wheeled up to us. "I see guilty people walk out of court every day because there isn't enough evidence. Happy Birthday. Uncle Wally would have been here, but he's up in Charleston for a few days."

"Seeing his muse? Lilly has a very understanding husband."

"They're both very good to him. He needs to spend time with her while he can, his health is getting worse, and his memory. He did tell me to say hello to you and Maggie."

"Probably our most successful case to date. I have my partner to thank for that."

"Slater!" Maryanne Thatcher wished me a happy birthday then looked at her phone. "I wonder what's keeping Jasmine?"

"Is she bringing the Bagboy? What's his name, Jessie?" I remembered.

"Not your favorite person?"

"He's okay. Just not good enough for Jasmine," I grumbled.

"From what she said, they aren't getting along the best, so he might not last. I kind of agree with you though, he's a little too smooth or something."

"Slick. Too good looking and self-entitled."

"Dare I remind you of her last boyfriend? At least Jessie's her own age and somewhat normal.

She needs normal for a while. The thing with her mom, and meeting her dad is bothering her."

"Her dad is a real piece of work, and his girlfriend is bad news. She goes out of her way to cause trouble. It sounded like Divine might have mislead Jasmine about them and the sister in California."

"Divine wanted leverage to entice Jasmine to move to New York, and that was just to work me for more money. I don't know what Derrick's angle is, but I think his showing up was a surprise to Divine. She told me to be careful, because he might try to fleece me. Ironic coming from her, after the check I just wrote."

We all stood around talking, mindless chatter about the weather and sports while we waited for the youngest member of the birthday party to make her appearance.

"What is keeping that girl?" Maryanne wondered aloud. "Maggie, have you talked to Jasmine? What is she up to?"

"I just got a text, she said there's a big surprise coming."

"Other than the one we had planned?"

"It would have to be, Slater's present is all taken care of."

"Alright, I guess we'll just have to wait and see."

"I'm starting to get worried." Maggie confided to me after another half hour. "Jasmine was really excited about the party. She said she was going to go talk to Jessie, because they'd had a fight, then come right over. That was two hours ago. Her last text didn't mention him, just that there was going to be a big surprise."

"Did you try calling her?"

"Yeah, it went right to voicemail. Twice."

"Do we know Jessie's number? Try him."

"I wonder if Maryanne knows." I was talking with Luis and Tommy Ackerman, but I kept an eye on Maggie. She returned shortly. "She doesn't know his number, but she gave me an address. I can't find him or his parents on Facebook. Who isn't on Facebook?"

"Suddenly I like him better. Maybe they patched things up and are, you know, being teenagers."

"She wouldn't miss your birthday party for anything, Slater. I'm getting worried. I'm going to run over to his parents' house, it's just a couple miles. I might be able to track their number down, but it will just take a second to go over there."

"I can go along."

"It's your party, Slater, I'll be back in ten minutes, then we eat, with or without her."

She hurried out the door and her sister walked over to me.

"What's Maggie doing? I thought everything was arranged for your birthday present. I think you're really going to like it." Angela leaned against me quickly with a hug.

"Jasmine is really late, and Maggie's worried."

"Yeah, I thought she would be here an hour ago. Drama with the boyfriend I would guess."

"Do you know his parents?"

"Dean and Kathy Pearson. He's a banker, and she sells real estate. I don't know them well, but I might have her card in the office. Want me to look?"

"Maggie ran over to their house, so by the time you find the card, she'll be back. She's kind of in a panic about Jasmine for some reason."

"She's worried about her, the deal with her father, and the fact that Cletus Johnson is out on bail."

"Cletus is out on bail?" The man had shot a hole in my airplane and my girlfriend's leg. How could he not be in jail?

"I guess. Maryanne, what's the deal with Jasmine's old biker friend?"

Maryanne had been talking to Edith Templeton. "Didn't I tell you, Slater? I was notified that he made bail. It sounds like he might get a plea deal and not serve any more time. Overcrowded prisons in Georgia, I guess. But I'm told he can't leave Fulton County until his hearing and that he's wearing an ankle monitor. I filed a restraining order, so if he shows up, it's right back to prison. I told Maggie all this a few days ago."

"She's had a lot going on, it probably slipped her mind."

203

"Or she didn't want to worry you," Angela said. "She's used to looking out for me, now it's your turn."

"No wonder she's worried. Cletus was obsessed with Jasmine. If he's out of jail, he might be crazy enough to come down and try to see her."

"Not likely." Tommy Ackerman joined the conversation. "An ankle monitor is pretty foolproof. If he leaves the immediate area his parole officer would know and Maryanne or I would be notified right away."

"Good to know. Jasmine probably just had some drama with her boyfriend and she'll show up any minute."

Ten minutes later we heard the squeal of tires in the driveway and Maggie burst into the house, visibly upset.

"Kathy Pearson said Jasmine was there earlier, but that she and Jessie had broken up. He supposedly headed to work and she left over an hour ago. I came back on the Old Farm Road and I happened to glance into the parking area of the rest stop. It's some kind of historical spot, there's a plaque, but that doesn't matter. Jasmine's car is sitting there with the windows down and Slater's card is sitting on the dash. What the hell happened to her?"

"Maybe a change of heart?" Maryanne said. "Maybe she patched things up with Jessie and he picked her up? Let's not panic."

"Call the Safeway, see if he's working." I suggested. "If he lied about going to work, maybe the two of them went somewhere to work things out."

"Slater, the car's a mile and a half from here. She wouldn't miss your party. If they were going to sort things out, they would have done it here or waited until after. She's been talking about your birthday for two weeks, no way she would miss this."

"I'll call the Safeway. Did you get Jessie's cell number?"

"I tried it and left him a message. Something's happened, I can feel it."

"Maggie, take it easy," I said. She looked frantic. "Call Mrs. Pearson and see if they are tracking Jessie's phone. Rich, seventeen-year old kid with a car like that, they probably are."

Maryanne didn't seem alarmed. "She wasn't the least bit distraught about the breakup, but she was worried about how Jessie would take it. They're probably just sitting somewhere having a long heart to heart. God knows her mother put me through worse than this when she was a teenager."

"She would have locked her car. I'm telling you, she would not miss this party if there was any choice!" Maggie insisted.

Angela came back into the room. "I called the Safeway. Jessie didn't show up to work."

"There, see? They're probably parked somewhere, patching things up."

205

Maryanne's phone chimed. She pulled it out and smiled. "It's Jasmine." In a moment her smile faded and she fell into the nearest chair. "My God! Read this." She handed me the phone.

Surprise! We have your precious granddaughter. If you want her alive, don't call the police. We'll be in touch. PS This phone will be going for a swim, so don't bother tracking it.

Chapter Fourteen

What do we do? Slater?" Maryanne's calm had disappeared. Her eyes filled with tears and she was shaking. "I've had people try to shake me down before, but not like this."

"I still think there's a chance this is a prank." I reasoned. "Maybe they went to a keg party and someone got ahold of her phone. Maybe it's just a horrible joke. We need to track down Jessie and see what he knows."

"Slater." Maggie rasped out. "Jasmine absolutely loves you. I told you five times, she would not miss this party for anything. Certainly not for a few beers. I think this is real. I'll try both their phones again, then I'll call Kathy Pearson and see if she can tell us where Jessie might be."

Everyone looked back and forth at each other, stricken. Tommy Ackerman wheeled his chair forward. "If this is real, if she's been kidnapped, I have to presume they'll want money. The question will be, do we call the cops, or do we try to negotiate on our own."

"No cops." Maryanne said. "I know as my lawyer you're obligated to tell me that's the wrong thing to do, but don't bother. Having the police involved would mean the press too. All that attention would just motivate whoever it is to kill her."

"It might be someone she knows, or it might just be someone who knows you have a lot of money. It would make a difference in how we negotiate if we can figure that out. First thing we do is track down this Jessie clown, see if he knows anything."

"I have an address." Maggie walked back into the room. "Friend of Jessie's that has a lot of parties. Kathy said if he ditched work, he probably went there."

"Alright, I'll go over there. Luis, can you ride along?" He nodded.

I expected Maggie to speak up and she did. "I'm coming too."

"I have another set of keys for Jasmine's car," Maryanne said. "We'll go over and pick it up and look it over." She drew a shaky breath. "For blood or anything."

"Just bring it back and try not to disturb things inside too much. There might be fingerprints and if you decide to call the police, they're going to want to go over it. Call us if you hear anything more, but this shouldn't take long."

Jessie's friend lived a few miles further out of the city. Most people considered it country living, which was fortunate for the neighbors, because the yard resembled a scene from any one of a number of teen movies. There were a couple dozen cars, loud music, and plenty of drunken kids. No one looked happy to see us. We spotted Jessie's car out on the road and parked at the end of the line, then walked up to the house.

A small group of girls stood near the driveway and eyed us cautiously. The tallest of the group stepped in our direction. "Is there a problem? Is the music too loud? I can tell my brother to turn it down. The last thing we want is to make the neighbors mad, but we talked to the Turners and the Petersons and they said they're okay with it."

"We're not here about the noise." I explained. "We need to talk to Jessie Pearson, and it's really important. Could you ask him to come outside? I really don't want to have to go in and find him."

"Yeah, that would be trespassing. I don't think he's here."

"Listen little girl." Maggie pushed by me and put her face inches from the girl's. "His car is out there, so you go drag his privileged ass out here or we're going to have about a dozen fucking cops here in the next five minutes. This is serious shit, so if you don't want my foot in your ass, I'd start running for the house and find that little prick."

"Jesus, Lady, chill. I'll go get him." As a pack, they turned and fled toward the front door of the house.

I had learned to trust Maggie's instincts, but it was clear she was closing in on irrational. I slid an arm under hers and leaned close.

"Remember, we want to keep this from turning into a media circus. If the press gets wind of this, it's going to make finding her impossible. Jessie probably isn't involved, so we have to be careful what we say to him."

"I know that," she said sharply, then softened. "Sorry, you're right. I'm just so damn worried I'm not thinking straight. He's scared of you, so you have the best chance of getting something out of him. Feel free to slap him around if you think it will help."

It was a poor time for levity, but I chuckled. I also knew she wasn't kidding.

Jessie stumbled down the front step of the porch led by the tall blonde that I guessed might be a year his junior. She stopped a dozen steps from us and gave him a bit of a shove in our direction. A few of the young partiers looked curiously in our direction, then returned to their debauchery.

Jessie eyed us cautiously. It looked like he had already had a few too many. "Whas-up?" He asked bleary eyed. "Jasmine already broke up with me, isn't that enough? I maybe called her a name or two, which I guess I shouldn't have, but shit, she didn't have to call out the Family Guard. I really like her, so sue me. Are you gonna' kick my ass, Mr. Slater?"

"No Jessie, not that. She hasn't come home yet, so we're just worried about her. We thought maybe she was with you."

"Me?" He mumbled and weaved around with a perplexed look on his face. "We had a fight and broke up, and she wouldn't talk because she had to get to your party. Because your birthday was a big deal and I didn't matter to her. Happy birthday, Mr. Slater."

"Do you remember what time that was, Jessie?" Maggie asked calmly.

"I was 'sposed to work at five, but I came here instead. Whoops." He chuckled. "A guy gets a day off when he gets his heart stomped on, right? Stupid job anyway. So, maybe four-thirty." He frowned, thinking. "She was really in a hurry to get to your party. Is she okay? I really like her, Mr. Slater, but I blew it."

"Sorry kid, but at your age relationships don't usually last."

"I was pissed about that biker guy that she used to date, 'cause he called her and she told me the whole deal. I didn't handle that well. Dude was old. Weirded me out, you know?"

"He called her? When?"

"Couple days ago, I guess. She said they had a long talk and straightened some shit out, but that they were done, because he was a loser. But she said she actually cared for him when they were hanging out. Kind of like me. It weirded me out because he was so old, and then she told me to go to hell, just like the old guy. Guess I'm a loser too, huh, Mr. Slater?"

211

"You're just seventeen, Jessie," I said. "But pull your head out of your ass and quit the drinking before you wrap that pretty car of yours around a tree, okay? Go drink a couple glasses of water and take a nap. If I hear you were drinking and driving, I will come back and kick your ass, is that clear?"

"Yeah, okay." He took a step back, then eyed me mournfully again. "But tell Jasmine I really like her okay? If she was to take me back, well, just tell her I said I really like her, okay?"

"We have to go Jessie. Remember, don't even think about getting in your car tonight."

"Don't want you kickin' my ass, that's for sure." He turned and stumbled back in the direction of the house and the girl we had talked to earlier. She latched onto his arm and pulled him toward the house, then gave us a brief wave. I got the feeling she intended to help him mend his broken heart.

"Cletus called her? And he's out of jail?" Maggie asked as we drove back toward her house.

"Maryanne said she told you he was out. He's in Atlanta, under house arrest with an ankle monitor on. If he skipped town, Tommy or Maryanne would be notified the same day."

"Why would she even answer his call? The guy is nuts, and he's obsessed with her."

"Maybe he has a new phone number. Or maybe she feels sorry for him." I reasoned.

"He shot at us, nearly killed me. Why would she feel sorry for him?"

"The Little One, she has a very good heart." Luis spoke up for the first time. "I think it must have skipped a generation, but she has a heart like her grandmother. Divine, she is very pretty, but her heart is like a stone. If the Mrs. hadn't already given her money, I'm just saying, I would put nothing past her."

"Maybe not her, Luis, but she doesn't keep very good company. There are quite a few people in Jasmine's life that I don't trust. We need to sit down with Maryanne and go over our options. Hopefully they make contact again soon."

Maggie slid her hand into mine and looked at me wide-eyed. "I've never been so scared in my life, Slater."

"I know. Me either."

It was getting dark when we pulled up to the Jeffries' house, but there was no missing the shiny new job trailer sitting in the turn-around with the big bow on it. Maggie gave me a weak smile.

"I forgot the dealer was going to deliver that. Happy Birthday. Angela, Maryanne, Jasmine and I all went together on it. Now she isn't here to see you get it!" Luis got out of my old pickup and the tears came in a torrent. I held onto her until she stopped shaking and sat up. "Sorry, I have to keep it together for Maryanne. We'll figure out who has her and get her back, right, Slater?"

"Absolutely, partner. Don't you think that trailer is a bit much?"

"I told you, the building in Fort Lauderdale was worth twice what we thought, and it's just money. Angela and Maryanne can both afford it, and Jasmine kind of borrowed against her inheritance, I guess. We all love you, Slater, get used to it."

"Still a little much, but thank you." I gave her a quick kiss. "Before long I'll be able to thank Jasmine too."

"Right now would be good, but we'll find her." Maggie lifted her chin and clmbed out of the pickup.

"The food is cold, but we all should eat." Angela pointed toward the table. "I know everybody is worried, but you need to keep your strength up."

We all sat down and picked at the food and I thanked Maryanne and Angela for their part in my new trailer; then we ate cake and sat around staring at each other, waiting for the phone to ring.

Tommy brought up something that had been on my mind. "Maybe I'm stating the obvious, but secrecy has to be absolute. No one but the people in this room can know about this until it's resolved."

"I don't know what to do about Divine." Maryanne admitted. "She isn't known for being prudent. If she told one of her worthless friends it would be in the tabloids the same day."

"She made you Jasmine's guardian," Maggie pointed out. "If that means protecting her from her own mother, so be it."

"Unfortunately, I have to agree. Alright, for the time being it doesn't go beyond this room, and I trust you all completely. All we can do is wait to hear their demands. I presume that will mean money and an exchange of some kind."

I tried to be reassuring. "We'll hear soon, I'd bet on it."

It was nearly midnight before the text came in. Surprisingly it was from Jasmine's phone again. There was a picture of Jasmine lying on a hardwood floor with her hands and feet tied, a piece of duct tape across her mouth, and an angry, defiant look on her face.

Included is a picture of your granddaughter before we moved her to a secure location, so don't bother trying to track this phone. She is perfectly fine and will remain so if you agree to our demands and DON'T CALL THE POLICE. You will be contacted in a couple days regarding a donation to our favorite charity. If you call the police, I swear, I will kill her.

"Days? What kind of kidnapper would want to wait days to get their money?" Maryanne asked, after sharing the text.

"I can make some guesses," I said.

"You're my investigator, Slater, you and Maggie. By all means, start guessing."

"I'd say whoever this is, they're amateurs. They gave away a lot in that short text. First of all, it's they, so more than one person. Then he said he would kill her. "I swear I will kill her." It's almost like he needed to convince himself. And maybe his partner isn't willing to do it. Not to be sexist, but that implies his partner might be a woman."

"That is sexist," Maggie said. "It could be a woman, or it could be someone who knows her, someone like Cletus Johnson. He called her, maybe he's still obsessed, or maybe he thinks getting some of Maryanne's money would be a good way to get even."

"Cletus is wearing an ankle monitor, and he isn't supposed to have any contact with Jasmine," Tommy said. "My understanding is he found a job and is able to move around Atlanta when he's working, but he can't leave Fulton County. Not to say he couldn't have a partner. For some people, jail is a training ground. Maybe we can turn this around on them, and figure out who it is before they make their demands."

"I can't believe she didn't tell me that he called. But then I couldn't believe she was hanging out with him to start with. My granddaughter is full of surprises," Maryanne said.

"Which is a good thing." Maggie chuckled. "She'll give those kidnappers as much trouble as she can. I wouldn't be surprised if they volunteer to give her back for free."

"Okay, you two need to try to figure out who this is. Maybe, if we're lucky, you can find her without some dangerous exchange going on. In the movies, that's when someone gets shot, and I don't want it to be Jasmine."

"Maybe tomorrow we'll go to Atlanta and track down Cletus. It's a start, and I have a few other ideas. It's like you say, the dangerous part will be when it comes down to getting her back. If a kidnapper kills their victim, there's no payday, and then they're just murderers. But it is odd that they're not in a bigger hurry to have it done with."

Maggie shrugged. "Maybe they're such complete idiots that they're still trying to figure out what to do next. Maybe they saw her on the road, recognized her, and grabbed her spur of the moment, without a plan."

"Whatever is going on, they have every reason to keep her alive." I tried to put appositive spin on it. "I say we all get as good a night's sleep as we can. If you don't want the police involved, I would suggest you see about having some cash on hand. Sooner or later that will be what it comes down to."

Maggie walked me out and said goodnight.

"Is it going to be alright, Slater? Tell me that it is, please!" She was near tears again.

"It has to be, Maggie. We both know that Jasmine is about as strong and tough as anyone can be. I almost feel sorry for those kidnappers."

"I was going to spend the night at your place tonight, but I better not. Angela is holding it together pretty good, but she'll go off the deep end as soon as everyone goes home. She loves Jasmine almost as much as you and I do."

"Getting Jasmine back is the important thing right now, we're good."

"Come over early and we can start figuring out how to find her." She kissed me quickly and said goodnight. I doubted I would get any sleep, and I knew she wouldn't.

Chapter Fifteen

It's hard to imagine anything worse than having your child disappear. Having them killed tragically would be horrific, because kids are supposed to outlive their parents. I had delivered that news to parents as part of my job while I was in the Navy, and it always tore me apart watching their grief. But at least they knew. There wasn't the constant hoping for unexpected good news, all the while thinking the worst; knowing at any minute a body could be identified that had been the center of your world for the last five, ten, or fifteen years.

Even seeing it first hand on many occasions, that kind of pain had always been abstract to me, unimaginable. Not now. Jasmine wasn't my flesh and blood, but in the few months we had known her I had come to adore her as if she were my own. It's hard to define what makes us love the people we do. Familiarity plays a part, but in Jasmine's case it was so much more: the crazy blue hair, the comical mix of sweetness and sarcasm in just the right dosages, and the realization that Maggie and I had played a major part in turning her life around, all combined to make me think of her as family.

Now there was an ache somewhere behind my breastbone that refused to go away and a gnawing in my head that followed me into sleep and continually told me that there was something very wrong with my universe. Edith Templeton told me one time that the pain of losing Davey never left her, that it was the first thing she thought of in the morning, and the last thing at night. I understood that better now.

I was reasonably sure Jasmine wasn't dead, so there was still hope. But I wanted to find the person that had taken her, and end him. While I was at it, I would have liked to find every bastard like Frank and Gary Jeffries that had ever taken a child from their parents and end them as well. Those parents' pain wasn't abstract to me anymore. Davey Templeton's death had been reason enough to go after Rashad Dinar. Now that I knew that pain, I wanted Dinar more than ever. I wanted him dead. If the time and opportunity came, I might not be able to do it, but for now, it was a place to put my anger.

"Slater!" Maggie pulled me back to reality. "Are you alright? You were gone. Thinking about Jasmine?"

"Yeah, and what I want to do to the people that have her. And I'm not talking about jail."

"I know, but we'll find her. We need to stay positive. I'll be the good cop this morning. We have to concentrate on trying to figure out who has her, it's our best chance. I spent half the night thinking of all the horrible possibilities and it didn't help in the least. She is really strong and smart. She'll do what she has to, to survive and escape if it's possible. We have to stay sharp and do our part."

"Okay coach, point taken. I still say the first person we look at is Cletus Johnson. Just because he's under house arrest, doesn't mean he doesn't know somebody he could line up to kidnap a rich heiress. Jasmine spent weeks with him, and he probably picked her brain about her grandmother's money, which would be plenty of motivation."

"He didn't strike me as a mastermind, but he was so crazy, he might have had her taken somehow. Maybe he thinks he can talk his way back into her good graces."

"That would be crazy, but obviously the guy isn't playing with all the cards. Who would be dumb enough to help him with a plan like that? They're asking for money, so even if Cletus only wants her heart, somebody wants her money."

"Maybe he had to include ransom to get help, since he can't leave town. People have done crazier things for seventeen-year-old girls."

"Maybe, but they were usually seventeen-year-old boys, not middle-aged bikers."

"Been on the internet lately?" Maggie asked dryly.

"Too depressing, but I get what you mean. I just think Cletus would have more sense than that now that he's off the meth or whatever the hell he was using. If he got a job as an electrician, he must have gotten a recommendation. I'm calling Sidecar and see if Cletus has talked to him."

"Sidecar? Oh, you mean Brandon, the guy that owns the electrical business where Cletus used to work? What was his last name?"

"Kramer, I think. Yeah, Kramer Electric in Fargo, North Dakota. I really doubt he knows anything, but it will only take a few minutes. At the least he'll know where Cletus was applying. If we go up there, I don't want to have to contact his parole officer and risk tipping him off. It would be better if we could do some surveillance before we talk to him."

"You call him, I'll call Maryanne and see if she's heard anything."

"Eric Slater! Wow, it's great to hear from you. Are you and Maggie married yet?" Brandon's wife Gracie answered the phone. We had led them to think we were engaged as part of our backstory when we rescued Jasmine from her crazy boyfriend.

"Not yet, Gracie. Any chance I could talk to Brandon, it's about Cletus Johnson."

"I told you that guy was batshit crazy. We heard there was trouble after we left that morning and he started shooting at your airplane. Next thing we hear, he's in the slammer."

"Yeah, it wasn't good." She wanted to chat, I didn't. "I really need to talk to Brandon."

"Slater?" She must have handed him the phone. "I hear the pea flipped and Cletus went off the deep end. I told you he was in love with that little girl, the crazy bastard."

"I need a little information about him if you don't mind. He's out of jail and that's making us all a little nervous. I wouldn't want him coming after Maggie and me, much less Jasmine."

"Do you still talk to Jasmine?"

"Yeah, she and Maggie ended up being good friends. They talk pretty often." There was no reason to tell him any more than I had to. "We understand Cletus is on work release and is wearing an ankle monitor, so it's unlikely he could show up, but Maggie is worried he might hold a grudge for our part in their breakup. I was thinking I might drive up there and have a talk with him. I figured if he has a job, it's probably being an electrician, and he'd need a reference from you. If I can't find him at home, I might try to catch him when he's leaving work."

"I have his phone number, that might be a better option. He told me he's in a drug program and going to meetings most nights. He claims he sees where he went wrong with Jasmine. That doesn't mean he might not react badly if you show up. But he did say he likes you, and that you have a good right hand."

"Odd reason to like someone. I hit him as hard as I could and he just shook his head and came back for more." Nonetheless, I was feeling quietly proud.

"Guys like him respect somebody that's willing to stand up to them. Probably why he liked that little Ballbuster so much."

"Jasmine. She has a name." Lack of sleep was making me irritable. "It was funny the first couple times, but she's a great girl."

"I know, spunky as hell, that's all I meant. Sorry, but I make up nicknames for everybody."

I grinned into the phone. "I do that myself, Sidecar."

"Good one! I might have to have a tee shirt made. I don't remember the name of the outfit he went to work for, but I'll check my emails and text it to you. Nice talking to you, and good luck with Cletus. If he really has got his shit together, I might even have a job for him. We're busy as hell."

"Thanks for your help and stay warm."

Within a few seconds the text came through. Lights Out Electrical.

"I just have a gut feeling that we're barking up the wrong tree here," Maggie said as she climbed into the passenger seat of my pickup. "I can't imagine Cletus orchestrating a kidnapping from Atlanta. If I was going to take a guess, I'd say it's her father's girlfriend. Maybe it's just wishful thinking on my part, because I know they wouldn't kill her, but Honey seemed pretty bitter that Derrick's daughter is in line for millions and she still has to shake her money-maker to make ends meet.

Derrick would do anything she told him as long as it didn't involve work."

"The guy Divine was with didn't strike me as the most honest person either. What was his name again?"

"John something. No, maybe John was his last name."

"John Cox, that was it. John Cox and Derrick Longfellow. Couple of real winners. Not their real names, I hope. How the hell did Jasmine ever turn out so good? Divine seems fairly normal, but she sure can't pick her men."

"Present company excluded, finding a good one is a battle."

"Thanks for that. We're going to have to bring Susan Foster in on this sooner or later. She can access information we can't, and push comes to shove she can call the FBI in."

"So far there isn't much that she could do. The stretch of road where Jasmine's car was parked doesn't get a lot of traffic, and there sure weren't any cameras nearby. We can't ask for tips from the public, obviously. I wonder when they'll call back."

"I doubt they will. By now they tossed Jasmine's phone in a canal somewhere, and they wouldn't dare use a burner. They'll figure there's a chance the FBI will get involved, so they won't risk it. I'd guess they'll use the mail. I think that's why they don't seem to be in a hurry."

"But they track down bombers and idiots that send threatening mail to politicians, why not something like this?"

"That takes a whole lot of man power, and most times those are packages. You can drop a letter in a mailbox anywhere. Unless they're dumb enough to walk into a big Post Office with a camera, and go to the same place every time, it would be about impossible to track them down. At least in the time we have."

"If it is someone like Honey and Derrick, they would never hurt her, do you think?"

"Even as goofy as those two are, I can't imagine them thinking they could get away with it. Anyone who knows her would have to realize she is going to identify them." I reasoned. "Maybe they think they could convince her to take a cut and claim she didn't know them. Jasmine would never do that, but people expect you to behave like they would. Even complete idiots believe they're smarter than everyone else, especially someone like Derrick Long and Honey. Still, I'm with you, I hope it's someone that knows her."

"You mean, because a stranger would be more likely to kill her?"

"I'm afraid I do. Why would a kidnapper leave the only eye witness alive? Sorry to say it, but they'd probably spend the same amount of time in jail either way."

"You're not making me feel any better, Slater."

"I'm no expert on kidnapping. That's why we need Susan."

"Soon as we get back, we should sit down with Maryanne and explain that. Maryanne thinks she can just hand them a pile of cash and they'll give Jasmine back. It won't be that easy will it?"

"I doubt it."

"Do you have a plan as far as Cletus goes, or is this just busy work to keep my mind off what they might be doing to Jasmine."

Hers and mine both, but I didn't say that. "We have to start somewhere, and until the kidnappers contact us, Cletus is as good a place to start as any. It would be good to eliminate him as a suspect. We don't have the luxury of watching him for long. Tommy talked to his parole officer on the pretext of being sure that Cletus was adhering to the terms of the restraining order. Supposedly he has a room not too far from work and he goes to an NA meeting every night. Model offender, follows all the rules and stays out of trouble. He has a hearing next month, and if that goes well, he's planning to go back to North Dakota. At least that's the story he's telling. Tommy has been planning all along to go to his hearing and make sure that any contact with Jasmine would be an infraction of his probation."

"But he's already done that. Why was he calling her?"

"We can ask him that tonight. Can you get on your laptop and find out where there's an NA meeting near that electrical shop? He doesn't have a car and his bike was impounded, so he either gets a ride, or walks to his meetings. He must be somewhat serious, because he wouldn't have to go every night."

"You ready for round two? Tough guy, like Jasmine said." Maggie laughed lightly.

"Not likely he'll start something when he's on probation. My guess is he's going to be as worried about Jasmine as we are."

It was late in the afternoon before we managed to find the neighborhood of Atlanta where Lights Out Electrical had their shop. It looked to be a thriving business on the north edge of the more metropolitan area of the city. There were a lot of electrical vans coming and going. I did a quick drive-by, then drove the six blocks to the little church where Maggie said the nearest NA meeting was taking place.

The Cletus Johnson I knew didn't strike me as someone who would go to such a meeting. Not to say he didn't need it. The morning of our fight he was about three lines into some sort of powder that had made him mean and tough. Very tough. Cletus was one of those guys that despite being built like a watermelon, was strong as three normal people and quick as any flyweight. Coupled with the fact that he carried about three hundred pounds on his considerable frame, I felt lucky to escape our last altercation with all my body parts and face intact. I was really hoping he wasn't looking for a rematch.

We parked in the back of a large lot, the best part of a full block from the front door of the Church and sat telling Jasmine stories to each other as we waited to see if Cletus would show up. At a few minutes before six one of the vans designated with a big bolt of lightning on its side pulled up and dropped Cletus Johnson off. He waved to the driver, then turned and walked into the church. I had never been to an NA meeting, but I figured it was going to last an hour, maybe more.

"I say we check out his place. Tommy gave me an address. It's a run-down motel a few blocks from here and they rent by the week. For a guy on probation waiting for trial, he seems to be doing alright."

"Probably not the Plaza." Maggie offered.

Not the Plaza, or anything close. At one point in time the road in front of the motel had probably been a busy street and the businesses in the area thriving; not so at this point in time. The old motel was a single-story red structure in need of a paint job and a tow truck to drag a few of the broken-down vehicles out of the lot. I didn't want to be too quick to judge since I was driving a rust bucket myself, but three of the old cars had flats, and one was missing a windshield. Despite that fact, I could see lights on in several of the units and a sign blinked repeatedly in one of the windows near the street identifying it as the office.

"We might as well go in and see which unit is his. Not like he's going to be hiding Jasmine under his bed, but I am curious about that phone call."

"Still worth the drive. I want to show that asshole my scar," Maggie muttered.

We walked into the dilapidated office and rang the bell sitting on the counter. There was a television blaring in the living quarters which was separated only by a ragged blanket that sufficed for a curtain. Someone turned the noise down, and soon a bent, scraggly looking man with a cigarette hanging from his mouth pushed through the opening and greeted us.

"Just two rooms left, busy night. You're lucky you came when you did." He paused and shifted his gaze slowly up and down Maggie's five ten frame. "You might be wanting the honeymoon suite, it's extra special nice."

Maggie stepped in front of me, leaned against the counter and gave the old pervert an eyeful, then did a reasonably good Daisy Duke impression.

"We don't want us a room, we're here to see my brother. He got hisself in a spot of trouble, and I got to talk to him. Cletus Johnson? My Daddy, he's pissed, and he sent me down here to give Cletus a proper tongue lashing for getting his dumb ass in so much trouble."

The term "tongue lashing" seemed to rouse the old codger's imagination. He continued to stare

230

at my Maggie's chest, dropped his cigarette into the ashtray, and grinned a fractured smile.

"Well aren't you a good sister. Most families don't give a squat for one another anymore. Me and Cletus, we're like this." He raised a pair of brown fingers. "Did you want to wait in his room? He always comes walking in here about seven thirty, says he goes to a meeting at the church every night. Whatever his trouble was, he seems to have things figured out now. Who would have thought he would have such a pretty young sister?"

"Aw, thanks. You're an old sweetie. We been driving half the day, and it would be nice to park my big behind somewhere soft." I was getting nauseous.

"You just follow me, and I'll open his place for you. Ain't much, but it's affordable." He bent over behind the counter and came up with a set of keys. "Sure as the dickens your behind ain't that big, but the room comes with two nice soft chairs." He led us to the back of the parking lot and turned the key in one of the darkened rooms, all while trying to keep one eye on Maggie. "You tell Cletus I was extra nice to you, alrighty Darlin'?"

"You are the sweetest, and thank you again." Maggie touched his shoulder and smiled. The old man chuckled, took one more look, then shuffled off to his television and forgotten cigarettes.

I gave her a shrug. "I can wait in the truck, if you and the old guy want to be alone."

"I got us in, didn't I?"

"The sign in the road says safe and secure rooms, but not so much, if you have the goods."

"The goods?" She snickered. "Leave my girls out of it. Let's look around quick and then wait in the truck. We don't want him catching us in his room."

"No doubt. It's not going to take us long, there's no place to hide anything in here."

A couple of worn chairs faced an old television and there was a small dresser and a single bed. The idea of the three-hundred-pound Cletus sleeping on a single bed boggled my mind, but it was probably more comfortable than a cot in the county jail. There was a tiny refrigerator with a built-in sink and two burners for cooking on the side. Very efficient, and sparse. Maggie checked the kitchen and I looked under the bed and pulled the drawers of the tiny dresser open. There was a small table, a lamp beside the bed, and a Gideon Bible in the drawer. I flipped it open and found a few pages of notes.

"Nothing here except some notes about staying clean." I thought about it for a moment, then shared my other discovery. "There is a letter to Jasmine, but I don't think I should read it."

Maggie pulled it out of my hand. "Kind of why we're here Slater. If he's still obsessed with her, we have to know that." She sat on the bed and scanned the letter, then looked up at me sadly. "He says that he does still love her, but that he understands they can never be together. It goes on and on about how much he cares about her, and how he just wants to make amends because it's part of his recovery. At the end he says he hopes he can see her again someday, just to show her that he can be a normal person. Slightly obsessed maybe, but now I feel bad for him."

"You'll be feeling bad for us if he catches us in here. Let's get out of here and wait for him in the truck."

"I was afraid this was a waste of time."

"We have to eliminate suspects, so it still was worth the trip. You never know, it's not like he'd leave a ransom note just laying around. But considering how he's living, orchestrating a kidnapping does seem unlikely. I still want to talk to him. Funny, the Bagboy knew he called Jasmine, but nobody else."

We sat in my pickup for another forty-five minutes until Cletus Johnson walked in from the street. It looked like he had lost a few pounds and he had replaced the bib overalls with regular jeans and a sweatshirt that was three sizes too small.

"Let me see about the reception," I said to Maggie, then opened my door.

Maggie snorted, and flung her door open as well. Surprised, Cletus took a step back, then rushed forward. Expecting the worst, I spread my feet and waited.

"Eric Slater! Am I glad to see you." Cletus reached out, grabbed my hand, and started pumping it enthusiastically, grinning like I was an old friend just back from the war. He sobered instantly when Maggie walked around the truck. "I'm glad to see you too, Maggie. I am so horribly sorry for what happened to you when I shot at your airplane that day. I just thank Jesus that you weren't hurt any worse than you were. I was out of my mind from the drugs, and losing Jasmine. But there is no excuse. Can you ever forgive me?"

"I'm good as new, just a scratch, really."

"I am supposed to make amends, but I can never make that up to you. All I can do is say I'm sorry, really, really sorry."

"Maggie spent some time in the hospital and was laid up for a couple weeks, so it was more than a scratch," I put in. He didn't have to look at the scar, but she didn't have to let him off the hook completely!

"Oh God, I am sorry. I will do anything you want to try to make that up to you. As soon as I get back to North Dakota and go back to work for Brandon, I'll start sending you money, to pay you back for the doctor bills."

"It's alright Cletus." Maggie rested a hand on his arm. "You can pay me back by helping us and being honest with us about what's going on with you and Jasmine."

"We know you called her, which is a violation of the restraining order," I added.

"I didn't harass her, honest. I just wanted some closure, you know?"

"So you haven't had any contact since, no phone calls or messages that someone might have delivered for you?"

"I know it's hard to understand, with me being twice her age, but I really cared about that girl. I had to apologize to her, too, as part of the program." He looked back and forth between us. "Don't you guys live in Jacksonville? Did you come all the way up here just to get me in trouble for calling her? I'm not going to call her again, honest. I thought about sending her a letter, to kind of explain some things I forgot to say, if that's alright. As soon as I can, I'm going home to Fargo. I'll probably never see her again."

"We're not here to get you in trouble, Cletus. I have to tell you something and I don't want you to over react, but you might know something that will help us."

"Is Jasmine okay? Is something wrong with Jaz?" There was desperation in his voice, real concern, and I didn't think he was that good an actor.

"Jasmine's disappeared, Cletus. She may have been kidnapped." Maggie spoke up. "We thought there was an outside chance you had something to do with it."

"We're just covering all the bases," I assured him. "We thought you might be holding a grudge. Nothing personal."

He started pacing frantically and ringing his hands. "Shit. Oh shit."

235

"What is it, Cletus? Don't flip out on us. I only told you on the off-chance Jasmine might have said something when you talked to her on the phone. It seemed like she was worked up lately, and I thought she might have said something to you."

"That's just it." Cletus leaned against my truck and put his head down. "When I was first in County, I met a guy named Diego Salazar. Smooth talker, and a funny guy. I kind of wanted to impress him, being new to jail and everything. I told him all about how crazy I was about Jasmine, and about how her grandmother was Maryanne Thatcher and how she owns half of North Dakota."

"You think he'd be capable of a kidnapping?"

"You thought I might be," He said shrewdly. "He got out a few days before I did, and he showed up to help me find a place to live. I thought he was just being a nice guy because he knew how I felt about Jasmine, but he suggested I call her. I used his phone without thinking. I was afraid she might not pick up if she knew it was me. Bottom line, he has her number on his phone now. He was in jail for writing bad checks, but he's been in the can more than once. The way he talked, I don't think he's ever done an honest day's work in his life, it's always about scamming someone out of money."

"Big jump to kidnapping."

"But big money when Maryanne Thatcher is involved. I'll kill him if he hurts Jaz."

236

"You need to keep doing what you're doing, Cletus," Maggie said. "We didn't tell you this so you would jump probation and do something crazy. Let us handle this Salazar guy. Any idea where we might find him?"

"He said he was headed back to Daytona. He hangs around down on the beach at the White Sands. That's a bar and strip club where a lot of bikers go. He said he goes there to pick up girls. He thinks he's a real player. I've been there before." He glanced at Maggie. "Lots of drugs and girls for sale."

"We'll keep you posted okay?" I put out my hand.

"You're not really a lawyer, are you, Mr. Slater?"

"Not that smart, Cletus. Promise me, no funny business. We'll call you when we know something."

"I promise. Here's my phone number, you let me know what's going on. I maybe can't be with her, but I really love that little girl."

As we started driving out of the lot, the manager opened his door and started talking to Cletus. It was probably a good thing we were leaving Atlanta.

Chapter Sixteen

We didn't get back to Jacksonville until three in the morning and the lights were still on in the Jeffries house. Angela sat at the kitchen table, drinking a cup of coffee and reading a book. There was an uncased handgun sitting on the table.

"Why are you still awake? And what's with the gun?" Her sister asked. "Angela, you weren't thinking..."

Angela glanced at the weapon and smiled. "Pills would be my choice, you know that. No, I keep hearing noises and I couldn't sleep, with Jasmine being gone. Maryanne promised she would call the second she heard anything, so I'm waiting."

"Is the gun a good idea?" I picked it up and opened the breech, it was loaded.

"I told you, I heard noises. And for what it's worth, I can shoot a hell of a lot better than your girlfriend."

That wasn't saying much, but I kept that thought to myself. "Wind is picking up, that's probably what you heard."

"Atlanta was kind of a bust, but we do have the name of someone Cletus talked to about Jasmine," Maggie said, helping herself to some coffee.

"There, did you hear that?" The blonde looked at us. "That was something. Why aren't the security lights working?"

I started to speak, but then I heard a metallic sound, followed by a loud bang. Not the wind. I yanked my gun out, walked quickly to the switch and turned the lights off.

"Sit tight, okay? I'm going to circle the house, so stay inside. I don't want to accidentally shoot you." There was just enough light for me to see the two women nod their heads. Angela picked up the revolver from the table and she and Maggie backed against the nearest wall.

I eased out the entry door. The front yard was illuminated by a street light, but none of the motion sensors seemed to be working. I plastered myself to the wall, feeling naked and vulnerable in the open, and slid quickly along to the corner where I had some cover from the bushes planted there. The wind had freshened, so it was possible that was all it was, but I didn't take any chances. I waited for a thirty count, peering through the darkness for anything out of place, then worked my way around the house.

I made it to the back of the house where the pool and the slider for the deck were. At that point I was reasonably certain it was just the wind, but as long as I was there, I checked to be sure the door for the pool entry was locked. I reached for the door and the motion sensors picked that moment to start working, turning the floodlights in the backyard on and bathing me in bright light. I caught just a flash behind me and spun quickly, bringing my gun up.

I had spent years in the Navy training with guns, running drills with stationary targets and live simulators. I had been in several live fire situations when knowing when to shoot and not to shoot had saved a life or two. The first rule involving a gun is that before you pull the trigger, you make damn sure you know what you're shooting at. Instinct and alarm nearly made me forget that rule, but I pulled up short of firing and saved a life.

The noisy intruder that I had nearly dispatched with my 9 mm had four legs, floppy ears, and a tail, which he proceeded to thump happily on the concrete. I drew a breath and laughed quietly at my nerves, then held out a hand. The dog was a large, emaciated looking yellow Lab that looked at me mournfully, then moaned and yawned nervously. He had no collar but he followed me back to the front door when I called him. I was reasonably sure he was friendly, and he sat as instructed when I opened the front door. I reached around the corner and turned the lights on. "Found the intruder," I said and called the dog softly.

"Oh my God! What a beautiful puppy." Within a few seconds, and against my advice, Angela and Maggie had both fallen onto the floor with the scrofulous canine and were fussing over it and sharing dog kisses that had to be anything but sanitary.

"We never could have a dog because Daddy was allergic." Angela grinned as the exuberant hound continued to wash her face. "Can we keep him?"

"It's your house, Angela," I pointed out. "I would bet if you feed him, he'll be your best friend for life. No collar, and it doesn't look like he's eaten for a week. But you probably should run an ad. He does seem well trained, and he certainly isn't mean."

"What should we call him?" Maggie asked, lost to the affections of the starving hound.

"It's after three and I'm dog tired, no pun intended." I admitted. "Is it okay if I sleep here?"

When I climbed into Frank Jeffries old bed just off the living room, I could still hear them laughing and playing with their new dog like they were a pair of schoolgirls. Times had changed, and that was nice.

My phone buzzed at a little after eight. A short night, but the sun was well into the sky when I walked out to drink my coffee and call Susan Foster back.

"Gary Jeffries wants to see you. Just you this time. He said it's urgent. It's always urgent with him lately, but he's my star witness, so I have to keep him happy."

"Toss him in a real jail for a while, he'll be begging to testify."

"If he lived long enough. Dinar's organization finds out where he is and I won't have a witness. Can you meet me at the safe house, say ten-thirty?"

"Sure, but I'll have to tell Maggie. No idea what it's about?"

"None. He said he'd only talk to you."

"Ten thirty it is then."

The house was quiet, but I wanted to go home to shower and I had to talk to Maggie first. I tipped-toed up the stairs, intending to knock on Maggie's door. Angela pulled her door open just as I reached the top of the stairs, dressed in a housecoat and followed closely by the yellow Lab.

"You won the coin toss?" I asked.

"Maggie's feeling generous, I guess. Duchess gets to sleep with me."

"I hope you don't mean in your bed. The dog slept in your bed, didn't it?"

"Well, he was lonely and scared. Hard telling how long he's been homeless."

"Why did you name a male dog, Duchess?"

"He's fixed, so it kind of works, and we like it. Go bother Maggie and quit picking on Duchess and me."

"That dog is already spoiled rotten. I'll bet the owner won't want it back." She didn't bother responding and the pair disappeared down the stairs. I knocked softly on Maggie's door and opened it a few inches. "You awake, Maggie?"

"Yeah, come in, Slater. I can't get up yet." She slid the covers back and patted the bed next to her. I climbed in and she snuggled up against me. "Any word from Maryanne yet? Once I get moving, I'll go over there and see how she's doing."

"Nothing yet, but I have to think we'll hear today. Angela seems pretty attached to that dog already. Nice that you're not fighting over it."

"She needs something to hold onto, a therapy pet. I've got you, so she can have the Lab."

"I hope you think you won that exchange. I don't drool, a lot." She grinned and leaned into me and kissed me for a long minute. I really didn't want to leave that bed, but I knew I had to. "Your uncle wants to see me this morning, and just me for some reason. I have to be there at ten-thirty, so I better get going."

"Bummer. I feel safe with you here. I wonder how Jasmine is doing this morning."

"We'll find her Maggie, no matter what it takes."

"Okay, if you say so. Go talk to my asshole uncle and I'll go see Maryanne. Are you going to tell Susan about our situation?"

"What do you think? I feel like that should be Maryanne's call, but she doesn't know Susan Foster. I trust her completely and she could be a lot of help."

"And Maryanne trusts us. Still, maybe give her a call and see how she feels about it. We don't want her thinking we're not being honest with her. Maybe I'll hang around over there for moral support. Come over after the meeting if you can."

"Yeah." I rolled off the bed. "I'll call her right after I get home and shower. See you later, okay?" A quick kiss and I headed for the door.

"Hey, Slater?" I turned back toward her. "You know I love you right? I didn't say that to Jasmine enough, and it would suck if I never get to."

"She knows." I assured her. "And I do, too."

"No word, nothing at all. It's a day and a half. Is she dead?" The eldest Thatcher woman said, her voice raspy and shaking.

"No, of course not, Maryanne." I wasn't as sure as I sounded. "It's clear it's money they want, and there would be no money if they kill her. When does your mail come? I'm guessing you'll hear today."

"Noon here at the farm, anything that's addressed personally. But all the business stuff goes to my office in town. Since Tommy already knows the situation, I'm having a courier deliver everything to his office first. I'm sure it will raise some hackles with my staff, but they're going to just have to just wonder for the time being. We have to keep this absolutely quiet, but everybody who knows realizes that."

"I'll call Edith and remind her. She tells her housekeeper Claire everything, but she can't this time. You know Luis would never risk Jasmine's safety. But there is one more person that I think we need to bring in." I gave her a brief explanation of who Susan Foster was and of our history. "She has access to things we don't, forensics, police records, even the FBI if we need them."

"I have to trust your judgement, Eric. I've never had to deal with anything like this before. Jasmine and her mother both ran off and gave me a lot of trouble, but it was trouble of their own making. Nobody ever texted me and threatened to kill them."

"Try to relax. Maggie said she's going to come over and keep you company. I'll stop after I talk to Susan."

I suspected Gary Jeffries was bipolar. His brother Frank had surely been, and Angela had been diagnosed years earlier. If that was the case, he was in a manic phase.

As before he was handcuffed to a short chain and the chain was affixed to the bar that secured the back door. The previous visit he had been calm, eerily serene for a man who had just lost a brother and knew that a sniper's bullet might find him at any time. This time he was like a caged leopard, pacing back and forth as much as the chain would allow, stretching occasionally to look out the window.

"Hoping for a rescue, or a bullet?" I asked. "I think the only way you're getting out of here is in a body bag, so be careful what you wish for."

"No idea, you have no idea." He paced again. His face was flushed and he kept pulling at his shirt sleeve. He stopped and stared at me. "You have no idea what they're capable of."

"I know they tried to kill Frank's girl and a five-year old kid, so I'm guessing they're capable of just about anything."

"Willing. They were willing to do that. Capable I said."

"Explain the distinction to me. Murder is murder."

"They were a little too sure of themselves last time, and you weren't something they planned on. They won't overlook you again." He pulled at his handcuffs and wiped his sweaty brow with the back of his hand. "It will be hard to protect you and the girls."

"The girls, Angela and Maggie? Are they going to go after them so you don't testify? I thought Dinar had left the country."

"He likes it here. He's in Algiers this week, then Dubai, but he'll be back. I can't be sure the girls are safe, not from here."

"There is a solution. Put him in jail Gary. Testify, then the girls will be safe."

"Idiot, what did I just say." He yanked at his chain and leaned toward me, grimacing. "I said you don't know what he's capable of. Turn on the TV, turn on the news. They traffic kids out of Miami every day and blame it on the coyotes. But the coyotes that bring those girls in are all dead. They buy the cops and the courts, and when they can't do that, they buy the politicians. He's capable of doing anything he wants, including killing me, you, and everybody we love." He collapsed into a chair, apparently spent.

I stared over at him. "I don't believe that you love anyone."

"I have to get out of here," He muttered. "I have to leave."

"You sure as hell can't leave. You're under arrest, and even if you could get away, Dinar will kill you the minute he finds you."

"My brother and I, we weren't always this way." He could have been talking to himself, or God, it was like I wasn't in the room. He seemed diminished suddenly, his shoulders collapsed and he slumped back into the chair and drew a shaky breath. For just a moment I thought I saw real emotion when he finally looked up at me. "Our father was a bastard. We were punching bags, and when we weren't, it was my mom. That's why she killed herself, not because of Clarence getting killed in 'Nam. After she died, it got a lot worse, the abuse. He had special ways to punish us, disgusting things no father should ever do to his sons."

I didn't want to think about what that meant. "I don't know that anyone is born bad, Gary. Some people do wretched shit just because they figure out they can get away with it, and I guess there are a few psychopaths that don't feel anything, and then there are people like you; people who were dealt a really bad hand and don't have what it takes to find a way out. They become what they hate the most. I would feel sorry for you, but you knew what you were doing was wrong, no matter what your father did to you. Still, you keep getting chances to do the right thing. Now's the time to start."

"I keep telling you, there is no right thing!" He slammed his fist on the table and the cop in the backroom stepped out to look in on us. Gary continued in a normal voice. "I have to go back. I can keep him off you and the girls as long as you stay out of his way. You need to stay out of his way from now on, Slater."

"He'll kill you, sure as hell."

"I have leverage over some really important people, people he needs. And he likes me, as much as someone without a heart can like anyone. I'll see nobody gets hurt when I go, even those damn dogs that Maggie's so worried about."

"How? I'll have to tell Susan what you said."

"Deals off then." He looked at me coldly. "If she winds up dead, it's on you."

"You can make that happen?"

"I can prevent it, if you keep your mouth shut. Rashad couldn't care less who dies. All those women and children mean less to him than those two guard dogs mean to Maggie. They're all just property."

"Why am I here today? This heart to heart is great, but I have other things to do."

"He knows about you, Slater, and he sure as hell knows about my nieces. He knows about you helping Rosalyn and Dedra, and he knows you work for Maryanne Thatcher. Like I said, he is capable of anything, and right now he is willing. He says the word and a lot more people will disappear."

"More?" Could he possibly know about Jasmine? Was her kidnapping a part of all this?

"Like all the girls he keeps scattered around the world, gone, never to be seen again. I'm telling you, stay away from this business and keep my nieces safe. Let me deal with Dinar. It may take a while, but I'll get him."

"All bets are off if anyone dies here."

"I said I'll see to it. Tell my nieces that I love them."

"You're dead, remember?"

"Angela still doesn't know that I faked the plane crash?"

"Better she thinks you're already dead than she finds out you were involved in what happened to Davey. I don't think Maggie is feeling too generous right now either, and she might share that fact."

"I know it doesn't seem like it, but I do care about them both. That's why I have to deal with Dinar, so they'll be safe. My brother took the easy way out, but odds are I'll be dead soon enough, too. I can see why he did it, I'm starting to relish the thought of not living with this."

"I'm having a tough time feeling sorry for you, Gary, because I keep remembering you put Rosalyn Cabello in a cage when she was fourteen years old and sent Sandy Foster to a brothel in the Middle East when she wasn't much older. But I can see where living with that would be hard."

"You have no idea, Slater, you couldn't imagine some of the terrible things I've done." He buried his head in his hands for a moment, then looked up again. "You just keep my nieces safe, and stay away from Dinar."

"Buy you a coffee?" Susan Foster was waiting outside for me, leaning against her car.

"Better not, I have to meet Maggie."

"What did Gary want?"

"He's worried about Angela and Maggie. He says anything is possible with Dinar. He wants me to stay clear of this whole business, says that Dinar knows who I am and that I helped Rosalyn and Dedra. I'm not sure if he knows about the trust we set up with Davey's money, but Dinar knows I'm the guy that killed the assassin he sent after Frank's girlfriend. You would think he would send someone after me just for that."

"Dead assassins don't cost him any money. He'll probably stay clear of you if you don't make any more trouble for him."

"I have bigger problems right now, and I need your help."

"Starting to lose track of who owes who, but we're kind of in this together. What's up?"

I explained everything to her, including the fact that Maryanne didn't want the police or FBI involved.

"I can't advise you to keep law enforcement out of it, Slater, but I get why you're doing it this way. I have to say, dealing with kidnappers doesn't usually go well. I'd say the main thing is to not give them anything until you know the girl is alive, then dole out any money carefully. Could be a simple exchange, or things could go to hell."

"Other than the fact they have her and want money, we don't have any details yet."

"Any chance she could be in on it? Sounds like she's a little rough around the edges."

I chuckled. "She is, but in a good way. Absolutely no chance, and for Christ's sake don't even suggest that to Maggie. She likes you, but that would be asking for it. Jasmine's like the kid sister she always wanted."

"You too, it sounds like."

"Yeah, me too. I'll call you when I know more. I have a couple of people to run down who know about Maryanne's money and might be desperate enough to try for ransom. More than a couple, but I'll call if I need help. Hopefully we'll hear something today."

I drove down the long driveway of the Thatcher Estate and pulled up next to the big house. Maggie sat on the top rung of the white fence that held the horses, so I walked over to her. Dolly, the cantankerous mare that craved the taste of my flesh, was standing quietly while Maggie stroked her forehead. I risked climbing up onto the fence and was surprised when the horse nuzzled my leg without taking a bite.

"She knows something is wrong," Maggie said, near tears again. "She can sense that something is going on with Jasmine."

"I don't know about that, but she can tell you're upset. I've never been this close without almost losing a digit." We sat there for a while stroking the horse without talking. Not a therapy dog, but it didn't hurt. After another ten minutes Maryanne Thatcher came walking down from the big house.

"Tommy just called and there's a letter he said looked suspicious. He's sending it over, and he said to call him when we know what's going on."

We stood there waiting for the next page in Jasmine's life to arrive, talking nervously about the horse and the fact that the fence was due for a paint job until a beat-up old Buick came roaring down the manicured lane and slid to a stop near us. Jarrod, Tommy Ackerman's dopey intern jumped out of the car and walked quickly over to us. He walked straight up to Maryanne Thatcher. For a moment I thought he might salute, or bow, or do something equally as stupid. He had a small packet of letters that were all tied together and he reached out with both hands and handed them to her like he was delivering a kidney.

"Mr. Ackerman said these were super important and that I should get them here as fast as humanly possible. I drove like nuts, thought I'd get pulled over for sure."

"Thank-you Jarrod, I appreciate your getting them here quickly. Drive carefully on the way back." She turned and started for the house with Maggie right behind her. Jarrod watched, crestfallen.

"What's the matter kid?" I asked. I wanted him to be gone.

"I thought maybe Jasmine would be around. I think maybe I finally worked up the nerve to ask her out."

"She's not here, kid. I'd hold off for a while if I was you. Her and that Jesse kid aren't going to last. I'll give you a heads up when she's single again, okay?"

"But you said to talk to her, that it wouldn't hurt to ask."

"And now I'm telling you to wait. Go back to work Jarrod, We're busy."

We want five million to start. Five more when you get the girl back. She's a feisty little thing, but my partner is working on that.

Yesterday's paper, just to prove she's alive. Check the want-ads."

There was a computer printout of Jasmine holding a newspaper up with one hand, but not the front page as I would have expected. She had handcuffs on, but her other hand was raised and she was extending a middle finger, presumably at the cameraman. She appeared to be shouting and had a large ugly bruise on one side of her face and a swollen eye.

"On a positive note, she hasn't given up," I tried. "Are we sure that's yesterday's paper?"

"It's the financial section. Jasmine knows that's all I read." Maryanne was staring at the printout of her granddaughter and her black eye. "What do they mean, check the want-ads?"

"Do you have the newspaper? They probably bought a small ad and want to communicate that way."

After a few minutes of searching we found the portion of the newspaper that was still set aside for want ads and personals. After a quick search we found the site on the internet as well, and all started looking at the same time. It took a while to find because it was posted under roommate wanted, presumably as a ploy to disguise its true intent.

Maryanne, your old roommate wants to return! Please advise here if terms are suitable. Sincerely, Missing you.

"I'll call the paper and see if we can get a name, but odds are they mailed the ad in and paid cash."

"I can call and get a reply in tomorrow's paper, set up the first payment."

I gave my opinion cautiously. "Maryanne, doing it in two payments doesn't make sense. Five million is a lot of money, and once they get that, they might just decide to run for it and eliminate the witness. Sorry, but that's the reality."

"I won't do anything to jeopardize Jasmine's safety, but I see what you're saying."

"Why is she holding the financial section in the photo and not the front page?"

"Most people read the financial section, Slater," Maggie said.

"I don't. Maybe that's something rich people do. My stock portfolio is non-existent. The fact that they know you do, says something about them, if only that they have an idea of what your habits might be. Jasmine's too smart to tell them anything."

"What are you saying, Eric?" Maryanne asked.

"Not many people are privy to what you do in your office most mornings, right?"

"Edgar of course, but he's up in Connecticut. His sister is ill, and he would never do anything like this."

"Not who I was thinking of."

"Divine? Slater, my daughter is heartless, but that would be a stretch. Plus, I just gave her a substantial amount of money to go away."

"I was thinking of her latest boyfriend. Can we verify his whereabouts?"

"I believe he and Divine flew back to the west coast. He's booked for a few movies, such as they are."

"Okay, but double check with Divine if you can without tipping her off. If he's out there, it would be unlikely he could manage a kidnapping."

"I can have a professional out there check him out and have them make sure he's where she says he is."

"Her real dad is a sleaze-ball," Maggie put in. "And his girlfriend was hinting really hard about needing money. She seemed bitter about her lot in life."

"I hate to say it, but they did seem pretty desperate." I agreed. "They have to be considered suspects. No hint of when the kidnappers want the first part of the money, but I'm guessing it won't be long."

"I'll arrange to have it ready. It says she's feisty, but they're working on it. That doesn't sound good, and that's an ugly bruise."

"Knowing Jasmine, she would put up a fight." I put a hand on Maryanne's shoulder. "I'd be more worried if she didn't. The picture looks like she's giving them hell."

She and Maggie both chuckled a little. "What now? I'll talk to Tommy about getting me the money, but there's nothing about denominations or anything. Five million in one hundred-dollar bills is over a hundred pounds, and it'll fill up a couple of gym bags."

"How could you possibly know that?" I wondered aloud.

"Arrogance, Slater. There was a time when I wondered what it would be like to have a million dollars, so one day I had the bank bring it to me, just to look at. It seems vain and stupid now. I'd give them every dime I have if they'd just give me Jasmine back. I need to get a reply in the paper. What should I say?"

"Maybe try to stall a little. If they want to play this game in the newspaper, we can come up with something. Maybe something like: *Missing-you, No to down-payment terms, want you back right away. Maryanne.* That'll let them know you don't want to drag it out. If they insist on two payments, we cross that bridge when we come to it."

"The waiting and not knowing are the worst."

"I have to think the next ad will give us more directions. It'll probably come tomorrow or the day after, and I'm sure it'll post online first. We could try to track the source of this letter, but not without a lot more resources than we have and bringing the police into it. I think Maggie and I should go to Daytona. Cletus mentioned a guy named Salazar that he knew in jail, and the fact that he knows more about Jasmine than he should. We have to consider him a possibility. I really doubt Derrick would kidnap her and expect to get away with it, unless they think they can skip the country. He's a loser, but he wouldn't hurt his own daughter. Odd that she doesn't seem to be afraid of the kidnappers, whoever they are."

"When has Jasmine ever been afraid?" Maggie laughed. It was for Maryanne's benefit and I laughed along with her.

"Alright, we'll go to Daytona tonight and see what we can find out. If everyone's where they're supposed to be, we have to presume it's someone else, someone we haven't considered yet."

"Five million dollars is a lot of motive, but like you said, how do they expect to be able to get two payments without getting caught?" Maggie asked.

"Good question. We'll just have to see what their next communication says."

Chapter Seventeen

Maggie was holding up pretty well, and I knew keeping busy would help ease the worry that was creeping through both of us. I didn't have any experience with kidnapping. I was going on what seemed like a logical process of elimination. The kind of money Maryanne had was bound to attract unwanted attention. But it was a big leap between the occasional would be scam artist and a kidnapper. Maryanne was undoubtedly good at fending off schemes to fleece her of her fortunes, but I could see she was struggling with panic in our current situation.

Hard as it was for me, I tried to make it seem matter of fact, just eliminate each suspect until the guilty party was identified, then go get Jasmine. It was fine to tell Maryanne that, but Maggie wasn't fooled.

"Slater, what motivation do they have to keep her alive? It doesn't matter if she knows them or not, she's seen them, and she can identify them."

"That's why I don't think we should give them any money until we make the trade. But bottom line, that's Maryanne's decision."

"Why would they even want to do it that way?"

"We know there are at least two of them, so maybe they don't trust each other. If the guy that picks up the first payment runs for it, the person watching Jasmine still has her and the possibility of getting the second half. Probably a good plan from that person's perspective."

"Person, maybe not two men? You still thing Derrick and Honey are a possibility?"

"Unlikely, but that's why we're going to Daytona. If Honey's up on stage shaking it, we know she's making her money the old-fashioned way."

"You're being sexist again," She pointed out.

"Neanderthal, remember?"

It's a quick drive from the south end of Jacksonville to Daytona Beach, especially if you're riding with Maggie Jeffries.

"How the hell do you not get speeding tickets?"

"I just say I had no idea I was speeding and apologize a lot, seems like they appreciate that."

"They appreciate the way you look. The sexist thing works to your advantage when you want it to."

"Maybe, and that's probably wrong, but it's payback. Women put up with a lot of crap you guys don't have to deal with."

"I notice you don't."

"I did when I was little, and it wasn't just my father. There's always some sleaze-ball that doesn't care how young you are. Back then it wasn't popular to call the bastards out, but you have no idea what girls are subjected to, and I mean almost all of them. You wouldn't believe the stories I've heard from other women, things that happened when they were nine or ten.

"Look at Lilly Franklin. She was so afraid of her Dad and her ex-boyfriend she had to sneak out of town and let people think she might be dead rather than face them. And she was eighteen years old. Men can do anything to a woman and never be held accountable. That's the real reason I started Taekwondo."

"Not all guys are predators, Maggie. Where is this coming from, did something happen to you that you haven't told me about?"

"No, but I was always afraid that my dad might try again, maybe even rape me. It ruined so many things, always being afraid. Every day, Slater, a little girl or boy is being touched by some deviant, just because they're bigger, stronger, or older. Just because they can, isn't that your favorite saying? Right or wrong, that's where Me Too came from, women fighting back."

"That's a can of worms, but nobody should ever touch a child. There's a place for those people and it's full of hungry alligators."

"And yet there are people willing to sell them, girls ten or twelve years old. How can that be?"

" From what I hear about this Dinar asshole, he's willing to sell girls or boys, any age."

"Who exactly is this monster? Is he the big shot that Davey was worried about impressing; the mystery person that Angela and he talked about that last time he was home?"

It wasn't a conversation I wanted to have with her, but as usual, I had said too much. "Probably. Rashad Dinar. We know he's the man that had Davey killed, and the man with the brothel out in the desert that Davey pulled Susan's little sister out of. It was Dinar that gave your father the ultimatum, you and Angela, or Maria and her child. Your dad couldn't live with having to make that choice, and I'm pretty sure that's why he killed himself."

"Is it possible that Dinar is involved with Jasmine's kidnapping?"

"It seems pretty amateurish for his organization. There was always the chance that Maryanne would call in the FBI, and that would have been more attention than he would want. If he took her, it isn't likely she would still be alive."

"Why is the world so full of these sick bastards, Slater?"

"We're not all that way."

"But you get what I'm talking about. It's ingrained in our culture; guys dominate and women submit. It's hard for a woman to know that the guy they're with isn't going to suddenly turn on her and change from someone to love, to someone to fear. Most of us have seen it happen before. It's a leap of faith for any woman to trust."

262

"Are we talking about some women now, or you? Is this about your father, or is it about me?"

"Remember Tommy talked about us selling Dad's Lauderdale property? Well, Angela is better, and I can't live with her and Mom forever. I made an offer on a house, just a mile and a half further down Point Road to the east. I want you to look it over and see what you think." She glanced at me quickly and I misinterpreted.

"I should bring Luis over and he can have a look. He knows a lot more than I do about construction. Are there structural issues, or any sign the roof is leaking?"

"No, there's nothing wrong with the house, it's perfect. Cripes, Slater, don't be so dense. I'm kind of asking you to come live with me. When you're ready. If you want to."

"So, you're willing to take that leap of faith with me?" My face hurt. I was grinning that hard.

"Don't get a big head, but I do think you're one of the good ones. Having Jasmine jerked from our lives makes me realize that life is short, and you're definitely on my bucket list."

"You're not worried that it's too fast? Do I dare point out that we haven't actually slept together yet?"

"Slater, I've been in love with you since I was ten years old and had to pedal my bicycle half way across town just so I could ride by your house a couple times and fantasize about the day you would make love to me. I'm pretty sure we'll do fine in the bedroom."

I had to gloat. "I knew it! I knew you had a little girly crush on me."

"I'm all grown up now Slater. Once we get Jasmine back, I'll show you what I mean."

The Doghouse. Where did they come up with these names?

Strip clubs by their very nature aren't what most people think of as being classy. During my time in the Navy I had been in a few, often as not for a birthday or bachelor party for one of my shipmates. I won't pretend that anyone put a gun to my head, I went willingly. Some of those had been upper end places with strict rules, pretty girls that didn't necessarily take all their clothes off, and sometimes there were a small number of women customers that appeared to enjoy the music and atmosphere. The Doghouse wasn't like those places, not at all.

It was early evening when we walked into the poorly lit, squalid looking building that stood three blocks from the beach on a side street. I cringed at the thought of leaving Maggie's car parked on the street, but there was no other option. We walked a hundred yards to the front door and sidestepped two homeless men that were sleeping just off the sidewalk. I hope they were just sleeping, they never moved. Two women leaned against the building smoking and spared us a glance, then walked into the street when a car pulled up and rolled down its window. I had thought they might be dancers, but it was clear they were escorts, getting an early start.

Maggie glanced at them sadly. "Ever go to a prostitute when you were in the Navy, Slater?"

"If I said yes, would you make me get tested?" I bumped her shoulder. "No, I can honestly say I never did. I did date a girl in Hawaii that worked some odd hours and had a surprising amount of cash on hand. I never asked her what she did for a living."

"Sometimes I think it should be legal. Then there would be no pimps beating girls up and getting them hooked on drugs, no minors forced into it by people like my dad and uncle, no crooked cops taking advantage of them. How old do you think those women are?"

"Not old, but they look at least twenty-one. Old enough to be legal, if what they're doing was legal."

"They couldn't do it if they didn't have customers."

"You're preaching to the choir, Maggie, I agree with everything you're saying." I pulled the door to the Club open and held it for her. "But the world has an annoying habit of being what it is, not what we would like it to be."

"Just saying, it's hard to look at."

"For tonight, let's just see if we can find Dumb and Skanky and make sure they're not involved with Jasmine's kidnapping."

She laughed quickly, then gave me a disapproving look. "That was mean. Accurate, but mean. There aren't that many dancers, I would think we could find them right away."

We got a table near the back and ordered beers. There were a few dozen men sitting around and half a dozen girls that were all at one table near the front. They were scantily dressed and were cheering on the dancers, probably waiting their turn on stage. As is always the case, there was a small contingent of young men with a seemingly endless supply of dollar bills and testosterone collected in a circle close to the stage, being as inappropriate as they dared while two disapproving bouncers looked on.

"I see now why I don't come to these places," Maggie complained. "Maybe if they just watched and weren't trying to stick their hands where they shouldn't, it wouldn't be so bad. This is really depressing."

One of the girls at the front spotted Maggie and wound her way back through the chairs to our table. She was pretty, had long legs, and wore a little too much makeup. She smiled happily and raised her beer.

"Hi guys. Are you a dancer, Gorgeous?"

Maggie shook her head. "No, I couldn't do that I'm afraid. One of those drunks reached in my pants like that and I'd break his fingers."

The leggy blonde laughed. "They don't mean any harm, they're just drunk and horny and they get carried away."

"I was looking for a friend of mine actually, a girl named Honey?"

"Honey? Every other stripper in here goes by that name, you need to be more specific."

"Here, I have a picture." Maggie pulled out her phone and brought up the picture of Jasmine, with Derrick and Honey. "She's the one on the right, the older one."

"I would hope so, the little one better not be stripping. Yeah, I know that gal. She moved on. Her and her old man were making all kinds of demands, like they were headliners or something. They wanted appearance money on top of the regular tips, just because they had been in some third-rate porno that no one had ever heard of. Our manager told them to hit the bricks."

"When was that?"

"Just a few days ago. They weren't here long. I heard they went down to the White Sands. It's a nicer place than this, but they kind of expect the girls to hustle on the side. They don't all do it, but if you're looking for a sure thing, that's the place to go."

"Why does that sound familiar?" Maggie looked at me.

"Diego Salazar hangs out there, Cletus Johnson's buddy."

"You know Cletus?" The stripper laughed. "Big, heavy, biker guy? Small world, am I right?"

The White Sands did look like a nicer place. It was across the highway from the beach, maybe a mile from the spot where Angie, Davey and I had partied as teenagers on a night that seemed like a dozen lifetimes ago.

So much of that night made sense to me now, now that I understood the pain they had shared and how they managed to help each other through it. Angela Jeffries had been lost to the torments of an evil, twisted father, and it had only been because of Davey that she had survived; she and another dozen or so girls that he had managed to rescue from a different, yet similar torture. Now it was my turn, mine and Maggie's, to find and save another girl from some unknown torment. If only that damn Butterfly would leave us alone.

"Slater." Maggie brought me back to the present. "Do you have some cash? There's a door charge and I left my purse in the car."

"Yeah, sorry." I handed the large attendant a pair of twenties. "Any new girls?"

"Lots of girls, Buddy, but most of them don't hold a candle to what you got here."

"Thank-you sir." Maggie turned her nose up. "He still insists on coming to places like this and drags me along. I don't think he appreciates me."

268

He grinned at her and talked past me. "Hang in here until about three, Sugar, I'll appreciate the hell out of you."

"We're looking for a friend, a dancer named Honey." Maggie played along. "She's short, mousy blondish hair, runs with a guy named Derrick?"

"Yeah, I know who you mean. They friends of yours?"

"Acquaintances, more or less."

"They're in there, always bragging about their time in the film industry. Annoying if you ask me. We're close to capacity so it might take a while to find them, but good luck."

The music was too loud and the room was too full. There were a number of girls spread out across the long stage, some clothed, some not. There were possibly a hundred guys, college kids that had escaped the snow and ice of the frozen north, lined up four-deep in front of the stage. Behind them, scattered loosely around the huge room were dozens of tables where more people sat, some peering in the direction of the stage, some with their own personal dancers. Some of the dancers, in the darker, quieter corners of the room, were doing more than just dancing for their tips.

Maggie looked at the mob of drunken college kids and winced. "This really sucks. Let's find Derrick and Honey and get out of here."

"We have to see if Diego's around too. It's so loud in here it's going to be hard to strike up a conversation with anyone. Why don't you sit here, order us a beer, and ask about Honey. I'll go up to the bar and see if one of the bartenders knows anything about Salazar. Will you be alright here, all by your lonesome?"

"No worries. Any two-bit celebrity grabs me by the pussy, there's going to be bloodshed."

The bathroom was next to the bar on the far end of the club, so I went in there first. When I was done, I stepped to the sink, washed my hands and was toweling them dry when a man stepped out of the stall and walked up to the adjacent sink. He was nearly my height, but slim and weathered, with oily black hair. The jagged scar on his cheek looked fresh.

He nodded at my reflection in the mirror. "Looking for a girl for the evening? I can fix you up."

"Kind of why I came," I said, fishing. "Buddy I know from up north said I could find just about anything I want in here if I talk to the right guy. Kind of looking for him."

"Yeah? Who's that?"

"Salazar, Diego Salazar." I caught a reaction. "Friend of a friend, but my buddy said to look for Salazar and he could fix me up."

"Seen him outside earlier. He's small time, and he's usually buying, not selling. Just out of the joint and he's laying low. I got three or four girls I could put you on. One's very special, if you're into it."

"Special, how's that?"

270

"Young stuff, and a really sweet girl. New in town and I been keeping her off the street, saving her for special customers. Cost you plenty, but I guarantee it'll be worth it."

"How young are we talking?"

"Real young, fresh out of Honduras. They must start early down there 'cause she's a wild one already. She claims she's sixteen, but I'm guessing younger. You a cop?"

"If I was, you'd be in handcuffs by now. The girlfriend, she and I both like 'em young, but that's a stretch. We're on vacation, and I don't want to spend it in jail."

"Dude, I'm impressed! Your girl goes for that? Then spend a few bucks, and give the old lady something special to remember Daytona by. I'll be outside later if you change your mind, but the price goes up at closing time. I'm Ramone, just ask the girls if you can't find me." He grabbed my hand and shook it, then turned and left.

I washed my hands again.

"Any luck?" Maggie asked when I returned with our second set of beers.

"Met a charming pimp in the bathroom that tried to line me up with a date, she's all of sixteen years old. He did say he knew Salazar and that he might be around."

"Soon as we leave, I'm calling the cops." Maggie took a drink and looked around the bar. "The waitress said she saw Honey and Derrick, and she's going to send them over."

"Want to just go? If they're here, they're not our kidnappers."

"How do we know they don't have an accomplice? As long as we came all this way, we might as well talk to them."

"I guess. If they're planning on a big ransom, I don't know why they would hang out here. I can't imagine why anybody would hang out here."

"What's the story with this young girl?" Maggie asked casually.

"I know that look. We can't save them all, Maggie. Remember, we're trying to find Jasmine."

"I know, I'm just asking." She smiled innocently. I wasn't buying it.

"Eric Slater!" Derrick called my name loudly, then came walking up to our table. "Shirley said there was a couple of tourists looking for me and I hoped it was you two. Where's my kid? They don't pay any attention to how old people are around here, she could have gotten in."

He was just too much of a dumb-ass to be deceitful. There was just no way he could be our kidnapper.

Maggie must have agreed. "We were down here looking for someone on a case, and we thought we'd stop by."

"Oh yeah, the Private Eye deal. Who you looking for?"

"Diego Salazar, he supposedly hangs out here."

"Oh yeah, I know him. Big talker. He's a funny guy, and he thinks he's a lady's man. He was trying to get with Honey. He's usually in here, but I haven't seen him tonight."

"What does he look like?" I asked.

"Normal guy, except for the hat." Derrick shrugged. "Cuban, I think. Kind of good-looking, and he always wears one of those hats, like he's Bogart in Casablanca."

"A Fedora?"

"Yeah, only it's bright white, weird. Honey is dancing in a few minutes, you should come up front and watch."

Maggie bumped my foot under the table. "We have to get going," I explained. "It's getting late for an old guy like me, but we wanted to be sure and say Hi, since we were in town."

"Are you sure? Honey will feel bad that you missed her act."

"That makes one of us, but give her our best." Maggie's sarcasm was wasted.

Derrick frowned unhappily. "Sorry you can't stick around and see the show."

"Yeah, I've seen enough," she said. He gave her a curious look, then tipped up his beer and walked away. Maggie sat back and sighed, then gave me an accusing look.

"What? I can't help that I was born a guy."

"As a group you're a disgusting lot, but for some reason I like you."

273

"That's a good thing since I'll probably be living at your house pretty soon. I presume the invite is still good." I took the eyeroll as a yes.

We left our beers and walked back to the entrance. The bouncer at the door gave Maggie a big smile again. "Leaving already, Beautiful?"

"Yeah, a little bit of Honey goes a long way." Maggie joked. "We were looking for another guy too, but he isn't in there. Diego Salazar?"

The bouncer frowned. "You two cops?"

"Private, not the real kind," I volunteered. "We're trying to track down an underage girl for a client, and we hear Diego might know where she is."

"Sounds like Diego. He thinks he's quite the stud, and he doesn't card his girlfriends. His parole officer had a talk with my manager, and he's not allowed in the club. Some nights he sneaks in, but not on my watch."

"So he hasn't been around?" Maggie asked.

"I didn't say that, Sugar. Some of the girls go out the side door to smoke in between dances. Salazar is always out there trying to hook up. Bunch of new girls started last night, so I'd bet he's over there trying to make a new friend. Walk around to the south side of the building. There's a light over the back door so the girls feel safe. You can't miss him, he wears this ridiculous white Fedora."

"Thanks," Maggie glanced at his nametag. "Jimmy. You're very sweet."

"Appreciative too, just saying." He looked at me and winked. "Take good care of her, Sherlock, or I'll come calling."

We walked around the corner and saw the light Jimmy had mentioned. Sure enough, there was a small cloud of smoke, three strippers, and a white Fedora, all clearly illuminated by the overhead. I took Maggie's hand and we wandered down the street as if we were walking to our car. When we were even with the little group, we cut across the grass and walked up to them. They stopped chatting and looked in our direction.

"Diego Salazar?" I smiled, hoping to make it simple. The strippers all dropped their cigarettes and crowded through the door back into the club.

"Yeah? Who's asking?" He glanced at Maggie and gave her a smile.

"Name's Slater. I'm wondering if you know anything about a girl named Jasmine Thatcher?"

"Shit!" He exclaimed and turned tail. It wasn't much of a race. Maggie and I ran most mornings and I was in pretty good shape from working construction. He had been smoking with the girls and his legs were considerably shorter than mine. I caught him within a hundred feet and rode his back down to the street. His white hat flew off when I slammed him to the ground and rolled him over so I could talk to him. He whimpered a little and put his arms up. "Not the face! Not the face!"

"You are not that pretty Diego, and I just want to talk."

"All I did was call her once. Okay, twice. I called her twice, but I didn't know she was only seventeen, honest."

"Don't lie to us." Maggie knelt down, holding his hat. "Crap, there's more hair gel in this hat than most people use in a year. Slater's right, you just aren't that pretty."

"You're going to be a lot less pretty, if you don't tell me why you called Jasmine."

"Okay, okay. Just no hitting, alright?" I stayed on top of him, just in case. "I was in the can with Cletus Johnson. He said she went for older guys and she had a lot of dough. I'm older, and I got a lot more to offer than Cletus."

"That's debatable," Maggie said.

"I just thought I'd give it a shot, so I called her. First time she was nice enough, but she said she was seeing someone already. I've heard that line before, so I tried again. The second time she gave me an earful, so I backed off and never called her again. Nasty temper, that little Chica."

"And that's it? You never went to see her?" I cocked my fist, and he covered his face again, wailing about his good looks. Maggie shrugged and tossed his hat down next to his head. I got up slowly and bumped him with my foot. "You stick to women your own age Diego, or I'll be back and I won't be so nice, got that?"

"Yeah, I got that, Mr. Slater."

"I'd have been alright with you punching him." Maggie muttered as we started back around the building.

We walked around the front, since our car was down the street to the north. Jimmy stood at the front door and gave Maggie a little wave and a smile. There were a couple cars in the street, with women standing beside them, negotiating. Maggie just shook her head and kept walking.

After we walked down the street away from the lights, a man stepped from the shadows suddenly. It was the pimp I had encountered in the bathroom. He grinned at me, appraised Maggie, then motioned toward the bushes.

"Think any more about that threesome, senor? She is very young, and very sweet. A special night for you and your woman."

The light was dim, but I could just discern the shadowy figure of a small girl backed up to a row of shrubbery. She had her head down, and her long black hair was hanging in her face. The night was cooling, but all she was wearing was a sleeveless shirt and a pair of cutoffs. I stepped back a little. The cops were starting to sound like a good option.

"She is pretty." Maggie surprised me, walking closer. "How much?"

His smile broadened. "For you, Darlin', an even grand. Another five hundred includes a room for the night, and anything you would like for her to do. Her English is not so good, so you might have to show her what you like. That can be a good time too, am I right?"

I was ready to shoot him just for using that expression, and I was pretty sure Maggie would have been okay with it. She grinned at him and nodded. "Can I go and check her out? That's a lot of money, I want to know what we're getting."

"Sure, look her over good, feel her up if you want. She is shy at first, but very willing."

Maggie walked over to the young girl and reached her hand out. She leaned away from Maggie's touch and pushed herself deeper into the bushes, never lifting her head.

"Chica!" The pimp yelled sharply and pointed at her, then started shouting instructions in Spanish. The girl lifted her head and moved forward slightly. Maggie slid an arm around her back and pulled her closer.

The pimp smiled at me and held out his hand. "It looks like we have a deal, Senor. Your woman, she likes the little one. I told you this girl was very sweet, didn't I?"

"She doesn't look sixteen to me, Ramone. Fifteen will get you twenty." Maggie and the tiny girl were talking quietly, and I wanted to keep the pimp busy.

"She says sixteen, but she has no papers so I cannot be sure. If she is lying, what can I do? I am a businessman, and she is going to be very good for business. Am I right?"

"Stop saying that!" I really wanted to hit him. "No Goddamn way that girl is sixteen, you slimy asshole. She looks like she's twelve."

"Senor! She is small, but she knows what is what, I can tell you that for sure."

"What is what doesn't matter from jail, dumb ass." I was losing it.

Ramone wasn't happy either. "You know, I don't like this name calling, it makes me upset. Maybe we will have to call this deal off, before I have to call my friends. Or perhaps I will have to hurt you myself." He pulled his hands out of the pockets of his jacket. He held a cellphone in one hand and a knife in the other, which he flipped open with a practiced, casual flip of his wrist. "Perhaps you should go back to Wisconsin or Ohio, or whatever shithole place you call home, before you get hurt."

Maggie had stepped closer. The girl was crying and holding onto Maggie's hand, hiding behind her as she watched. I pointed my gun at the pimp's face. "Perhaps you should walk the hell away, before you get hurt. That little girl is done being your meal ticket."

"You have just made a huge mistake, Senor." He turned and spoke to the girl in Spanish. She didn't answer, but Maggie gave him an earful, also in Spanish. The knife disappeared and he stepped back. I kept the gun pointed at him. It surprised me when he lifted his cellphone and took my picture, then Maggie's.

"What the hell are you doing?" I asked.

He smiled and punched at his phone. "This is the twenty-first century, Senor. I am sending your picture to the man who is going to kill you for stealing my property. This Chica is worth a great deal of money and you cannot just take her from me."

"Watch us." Maggie walked behind me with the girl in tow. The pimp was yelling obscenities at all of us as I backed away. We ran the half a block to Maggie's car and she threw me the keys. She climbed in the back seat with the girl and I hit the gas. It was hard to say how far away the pimp's friends were, or how many of them he had. I just wanted to get us all back to Jacksonville as fast as possible.

Chapter Eighteen

You did what? You kidnapped a thirteen-year old girl?" Susan Foster was shouting and I had to move the phone away from my ear.

"It wasn't kidnapping, it was a rescue. Her parents were murdered by a gang in Honduras a year ago because they wouldn't give her up to the local gangs. She managed to run away and almost starved, then got picked up by the local police, who sold her to a coyote that brought her to this country; all to get trafficked by some scumbag pimp in Daytona. She's like a poster child for the people you're trying to protect, Susan, an immigrant child with absolutely no rights or protection."

"Exactly. She has no standing, no legal right to be here."

"What do we do, ship her back to Honduras so the whole thing can start all over? She wouldn't live through it, she'd kill herself if someone didn't do it for her. She's thirteen, Susan. Trust me, Maggie and Angela aren't going to give her up without a fight. And, for what it's worth, the pimp that had her took our pictures with his phone. So sooner or later something might happen there."

"That doesn't sound good. It's what I've been talking about. Dinar's organization is expanding all over the state and the east coast. Pretty soon, there won't be any small-time street corner pimps. They have to join up or they wind up dead. They serve the master, but they get his protection."

"Dinar already knows our names, and a couple people at that club do too. It isn't likely he'll be happy to hear we took one of his young girls off the streets. But for now, all I'm worried about is not having ICE knock on our door."

"Lawyer up, today. The sooner she claims refugee status, the better your chances. The fact that her parents have been killed will get you a hearing, and the courts are backed up for two years. But I can't stress that enough, call your lawyer right now. I don't know what to say about Dinar. He may come and try to take her, or he might just let it go. You're not some low life street thug that he can just execute out of hand, and he's well aware that we still have Gary. But I'd be damn sure the security is working at Maggie's house."

I called Tommy Ackerman and explained our case to him. "The good news is, we've crossed a couple of suspects off the list of kidnappers. The bad news, I guess the bad news is obvious."

"I'll get working on it. That's an area my intern is interested in, so I'll get him looking into case law. I know a couple of immigration lawyers, but they're all busy as they can be right now. For all the hype, there are ways to do this that are legal. Adopting an immigrant child isn't that difficult, but that's a hell of a commitment. One of the girls could be her foster parent, but that's temporary and doesn't guarantee that the girl will get a green card. First thing we get her a hearing and establish that she has an asylum case. Then we have time to figure the rest of it out."

Gabriela Martinez was less than five feet tall, thirteen and a half years old, and already in love with Duchess the dog. That's why it was doubly painful when the Lab's owner showed up the next morning. Angela had done the responsible thing and put a notice on Facebook and Twitter right away, and shortly after breakfast there was a knock on the door.

We had talked security after my conversation with Susan, and I went to the door and looked through the peephole, as I had instructed Angela to do. A full security camera system was on the horizon, but it hadn't been installed yet. A slender dark-haired guy in his early fifties, dressed in a plaid shirt and blue jeans waited patiently while I checked him out. He had a leash in his hand. I eased the door open.

"Morning!" he said cheerfully. "I talked to a woman named Angela, and she said you found Buck?" Maggie and Angela walked up to the door and Andrew Mitchel introduced himself. "He ran off after a rabbit the other night just as it was getting dark, and I couldn't get him to come back. Stubborn sometimes, like me, I guess. I sure have missed him."

"We already love him so much, Andrew is it?" Angela held a hand out and he took it, ignoring Maggie's for an amount of time that became embarrassing. She finally gave up and took my arm as we both watched the sparks ignite.

"Yeah, Andrew, I don't like Andy. Angela or is it Angie?" He was looking into those magnetic blue eyes. I knew the feeling.

"I would love it if you called me Angie." She was looking back, so that was interesting.

"So Buck, my dog? I really should take him home."

"Can I get you some coffee first? We have a young girl staying with us, and she needed a few minutes to say goodbye. She is quite taken with your dog."

"He loves everyone, that's for sure. But I could go for a cup of coffee."

Andrew was a self-employed web designer that lived near the little airport where I kept my airplane. He talked about the marshes that stretched east of the runway and how he and Buck took walks there every night.

Angela worked her magic. "With Slater and my sister gone as much as they are, they're private investigators you know, and gone all the time; I really loved having Buck here. My Dad never let us have a dog, but he passed away last year. My mom went to Europe for a couple months, so it gets really lonely. Because I'm all by myself."

"I know what you mean, my wife has been gone for three years now."

A despondent widower no doubt. It was getting ludicrous, like stumbling into a Disney movie. Maggie laughed a little too loudly and brought the pair back to reality. "I should check on Gabriela and bring you your dog," Angela said.

Gabriela shuffled down the steps behind the Lab in a pair of oversized pajamas that made her look even younger than she was. Her face was covered in tears and she fell on the floor beside the dog and threw her arms around its neck, wailing and blubbering in unintelligible Spanish. Even the dog, happy as he was to see his real owner, didn't have the heart to break that grip. Andrew sure as hell didn't.

"Maybe you could just keep him for a while for me? I have to go out of town next week anyway, and it's obvious he's getting plenty of attention around here."

"Oh Andrew, that's so wonderful of you." Angie's smile lit up the room. "If you would consider it, I would buy Duchess from you, anything you want."

"Duchess?" He muttered, then looked back into Angela's eyes. "Maybe I could come see him once in a while? I won't take any money, but maybe you could make me dinner some night, as kind of a payment? Or, maybe I could take you out to dinner?"

It was like Maggie and I weren't in the room. Andrew stumbled through another few minutes of conversation, said goodbye to his dog, and left with a big smile on his face. After Maggie explained everything to Gabriela, she cried even harder and wrapped her arms around Angela's neck. Pure Disney.

After everyone calmed down about the dog, Maggie and I got in my pickup and drove to the Thatcher Estate. Maryanne seemed to be doing pretty well, so I dropped Maggie off to keep her company and drove back to Tommy Ackerman's law firm. If a letter came, it would be late morning and I wanted to get my hands on it as quickly as possible.

Jarrod had his head buried in the computer, but he greeted me cheerfully. "It's a cool thing, you helping that girl from Honduras, Mr. Slater."

"You can help her just as much as we did if you can get her immigration figured out."

"Stuff like this is why I want to be a lawyer, so I can help people."

Maybe I'd misjudged the kid, he didn't seem so bad. "Tommy alone in his office?"

"He is, go right in."

Tommy was at his desk, studying his computer screen. "Courier is bringing the mail over shortly. We'll see if there's a letter."

"It would be a fast turnaround for the US mail, but maybe they sent something out before our ad in the personals came out. I expect they're going to try to set up a meeting. I just hope she's doing alright. I'm scared Tommy. Not that I know, but kidnappings don't usually end well."

"The ones we hear about, anyway. Who knows how many get paid out and never make the news? I think your advice to Maryanne is good, if that helps. Two payments is asking for trouble."

There was nothing in the mail and after being in the way for another twenty minutes, I drove back to Maryanne's. They had checked the ads online, and there was no response. We drove back to the Jeffries house and had supper with Angela, Gabriela, and the dog. After supper the girls sat down with Gabriela for language lessons, Angela to learn Spanish and Gabriela to learn English. The girl had adapted quickly to the safety of her new environment, and I hoped to keep it safe.

"Okay if I sleep in your Dad's room tonight? Until we get the rest of the security updates done, I think I should hang around."

"Of course, Slater, we have a lot of beds." Angela answered for them both. Maggie had a book out and was busy showing the young girl something. She didn't acknowledge my existence.

I went home and did bookwork for my remodeling business. Luis was doing a great job with the actual construction, but it was still up to me to write checks and bid on houses. My new job trailer sat in the front yard, untouched. There would be time for that after we got Jasmine back. If we got her back.

The lights were still on when I got back to Angela and Maggie's house just before eleven. Angela sat at the kitchen table alone, studying a book about Spanish. I poured myself some cold coffee and put it in the microwave, then grabbed a stale doughnut and sat on a stool.

"Everybody else in bed?" She nodded and I decided it was a good time to tease her a little. "That Andrew guy, he seems nice."

She smiled and peeked over her book at me. "He seems like a really good guy to me, good looking too. Is he Slater approved?"

"I know I said you probably shouldn't date, but that's not my choice. Maybe he's the right guy, and it's the right time. So much happened, but if you feel ready, I say go for it. Guys think differently than women, and what do I know? I just want you to be alright." I was always afraid conversations with Angela would turn awkward, given our history, but it didn't.

She put her book down and looked at me. "My dad was a sick man. When you're a child you trust everyone: your teachers, the cops, the babysitter, but especially your parents. When he did those things to me, I lost all that trust. Maybe it drove me to the booze and pills, or maybe I would have found those on my own. But he's gone now. I can't forget what he did to me, but I'm not going to let it define the rest of my life, that would be giving too much power to whatever sickness it was that made him behave that way. I'm finally sober and I'm going to stay sober. I miss Charlie and Davey more than I can tell you, but thanks to you and Maggie, all of a sudden, I have a chance to do something good for someone other than myself. A purpose, and it's really empowering."

"Gabriela?"

"Her, and maybe other girls like her. I'm in a unique position to help. Other than my privilege, girls like Gabriela are not so different from me at that age, abused and lost. Of course, I was so self-centered and entitled, I can't imagine why anyone put up with me. You did, you and Davey. You were both more than I deserved."

"You're becoming someone Davey would really be proud of." My voice broke a little from the unexpected emotion of the moment. This was the Angela I had always hoped was hiding behind those blue eyes.

"Thanks Slater, you are too."

I dumped my coffee out, untouched. "Don't know why I would want coffee at eleven o'clock at night. I need to get some sleep."

"Good luck with that, I'm heading up to bed." She gave me a quick peck on the cheek and started up the steps, then stopped and looked down at me with an odd smile on her lips. "Slater, I'm glad that after everything that's happened, it's you and Maggie that are together."

"Me too." I husked out. I turned off the light and went into Frank's old room. I wasn't alone.

Maggie slid an eye open and looked up at me, smiling. "I gave Gabriela my room. I hope you don't mind sharing."

"You don't snore do you?" I knew she did, but I was pretty sure it wouldn't bother me.

"Glad you two finally got that out of your system." Angela laughed as she dropped a pair of plates loaded with eggs and bacon in front of us the next morning. "Rosa will be here pretty soon. She's going to be scandalized."

"She'll get used to the idea." Maggie laughed. "Not like she didn't know this was coming. Does she know about the new house guest?"

"Yes, and I told her eventually I want to take in more girls like Gabriela, so she'll still have a fulltime job, even after you two move out. Have you closed on the new house?"

"Signed the papers, but I can't take possession for a month or so. Morning sleepy head. Manana Dormilon." Gabriela stumbled down the steps with Duchess close behind her.

"Hello. Slater and Maggie." It wasn't perfect English, but she got it out. We had breakfast like a real family, and Gabriela even snuck Duchess a table scrap, like a normal teenager.

Somewhere during the meal, I called Maggie, Sweetheart; because of all the sex, and

290

because I'm a guy and we're always confused about the rules.

"Slater, don't get weird on me. It's still just me. I didn't turn into a Princess overnight. I appreciate the effort, but don't change how you act just because we did the hokey-pokey."

"Hokey-pokey?" Gabriela frowned.

"See, scandalized." Angela laughed.

Maggie and I took the dog for a walk, then went for a run. It had been a few days and we both could feel it. When we got back to the front door, Maggie sat down on the stoop and started crying.

"Jasmine?" I asked.

"I'm sorry. I feel guilty, being this happy while she's out there. We're good, Angela's the best I've ever seen her, and we have a dog and a child. I just wish Jasmine was here to share in all this."

I sat beside her and put an arm around her. "Me too. But you're allowed to feel good about what's good, even when there's bad stuff going on. We'll get another letter or ad today, and then we'll know what to do. Okay?"

When we walked back inside, Angela had turned on the small television above the counter in the kitchen. The news was detailing another shooting, possibly another homicide. I barely glanced at the screen; it happens so often you forget to be shocked. But this time was different. I recognized the building with the police tapes surrounding it.

It was Gary Jeffries' safe-house.

Chapter Nineteen

I had never met any of Susan Foster's coworkers and I wasn't sure she had any in Florida. On the one occasion when she had needed help, she had enlisted local law enforcement and I knew she worked with the FBI sometimes. We took Maggie's car and drove to the scene. The reporters were all gone and most of the gawkers. Two uniformed cops stood outside and I could see activity inside the building. It looked like the back door had been yanked from its frame, which seemed to indicate that they had probably taken Gary, not just killed him.

We walked up to the police tape and I waved at one of the officers.

He nodded dismissively. "Move along please, we aren't releasing any information."

I pulled out my PI card, feeling a bit like a Cub Scout trying to join the Army. "I knew the individual that was being held here, and I have information about what happened."

"That person was my uncle." Maggie joined in. The cop went into the house for a few moments, then waved us in. There was a blanket on the floor covering what could have been a body. I saw the edge of a paw.

The detective looked at us skeptically. "Alright, what do you know about this."

"The man being held here under protective custody was my uncle," Maggie offered. "And Susan Foster is a friend."

He nodded at me. "And your name?"

I waved my PI license again. "Eric Slater, this is Maggie Jeffries."

"Just making sure. Susan was hurt, but it isn't serious. She pulled up halfway through the deal and exchanged fire with them. The officer assigned to her is critical, but hanging on. They yanked the back door open somehow and came in shooting, killed the dogs and wounded our guy. He was conscious long enough to tell us that it looked like a jailbreak, not a kidnapping. The guy they pulled out of here, he was yelling orders, and they were listening."

"But Susan was shot?"

"Twice, leg wounds. Could kill you, but it would be bad luck if it did. She said if you showed up, to get you to the hospital. Her cellphone got lost in the shuffle and she couldn't come up with your number offhand. Of course, she was on a gurney, and they were pumping drugs into her, so that's understandable."

"Which one, we'll head over there."

"St. Mary's. There's a uniform outside the room, but I'll tell him you're coming."

"Why a guard?"

"This has mob written all over it, well organized and armed. She doesn't make a lot of friends doing what she does, not in those circles. Brave-ass woman is what she is."

Susan Foster was awake, barely. She smiled when we came in the room. "How're my favorite gingers?"

"I haven't heard that in forever," Maggie said with a laugh. "How are you? My uncle isn't worth all this, you should have just tossed him in jail, I would have been fine with that."

"I got hit, twice, I think they said. Can't feel anything right now, some kind of good drugs they have me on." She seemed to doze for a moment, then startled awake and slid up in the bed. A plump nurse came out of nowhere and scolded her.

"You can't move, Miss Foster. If you can't stay still, your visitors will have to go. If you open those wounds and lose more blood, you'll need a transfusion."

"Okay Sarah, I'll be good." She watched the nurse leave, then scooted up again. "Who knew getting shot in the ass could hurt so bad?" She giggled at us, then winced. "Once in the knee, must have turned me around and then I got it in the butt. No vest on my backside." The drugs must have made everything seem funny, she laughed at her own joke. "Did they tell you about the dogs? I don't know if the breakout was Gary's idea, but they sure weren't trying to kill him. I heard him yelling, warning them not to shoot me. I don't think it was because he likes me, but because he promised you." She looked up at Maggie.

"I told him how I feel."

"Still, he cares about you and your sister. He feels bad about Davey too, now that he knows he was a blood relative. I think that's why he broke out. That's why I needed to talk to you."

"Why did he break out?" I asked, trying to keep her awake.

"Dinar, he's coming back to the States from the Middle East soon. Gary thinks he will come after you, you and Maggie, for interfering with his business. He told me he had to go back and run things, take over the Florida operation, so that if Dinar comes for you, he can kill him. I said I wouldn't let him do that, that the best way was for him to testify, but here we are. I'm in the hospital and he's out there."

"The people that helped him escape and followed his instructions, do you think they're loyal to him or will they protect Dinar?"

"Can't say. Shot me in the ass." She was dozing again. "Just be ready, 'case they come for you." She fell asleep and we didn't bother trying to wake her. Sarah came back and scowled at us.

"We were just leaving," I explained.

"Bastards kill Duchess and they're done," Maggie fumed.

"To say nothing of Angela and Gabriela," I reminded her.

"Dogs just do what they're trained to do, they should be off limits."

"We need to get those cameras up and be ready in case they try something. I can't believe he would risk the exposure just to get Gabriela back."

"New territory, maybe he wants to make an example of us. Sorry I got us into this, I'm the one that grabbed Gabriela."

"What else were we going to do, leave her there? Normal, civilized people don't force thirteen-year old girls into prostitution. There was never a choice."

"We better go over to Maryanne's and see if she's heard anything."

"Five and five. My partner is enjoying her company, but I'm sick of this.

Sell some of those oil wells bitch, and get that money!"

"That doesn't sound good." Maryanne looked over her big desk at us. "Is he saying she's being molested?"

"Maybe, but molested is alive, Maryanne. And it doesn't have to mean that. It might be they just disagree on what to do. The oil well comment is odd, unless Rashad Dinar is involved." Once again, I had said too much.

"Dinar? I know that name. I deal with a Rashad Dinar, an oil trader from Dubai." We both nodded. "How is he involved?"

"He may not be. But he dabbles in young girls on the side. He had Davey Templeton killed because he was helping some of the girls get away from that life."

"Rashad? I've met him several times, and that's hard to believe. He's young, good looking and rich, a real charmer. Why would he need to be involved with something like that?"

"Money problems maybe, or just because he's disgusting," Maggie suggested. "Would there be any financial advantage for someone like him if you did sell some of your oil wells?"

"Not that I can think of, just the opposite. Are you certain we're talking about the same man? I could call him up right now and ask him if he's heard anything about this, we're that close."

"Maryanne, please!" Maggie leaned across the desk. "We just came from the hospital. Dinar's men nearly killed Susan Foster breaking my uncle out of a safe house because he could testify against the bastard. He's not who you think he is. He may be charming, but he's the person that killed my brother."

"Your uncle? I thought he was killed in a plane crash years ago. And your brother? Now I'm completely lost, what the hell are you talking about?"

"Davey Templeton was my half-brother." Maggie sank back into her chair. "Slater, tell her everything, would you?"

I gave her the condensed version but pointed out that we were concerned Dinar might be plotting against us for taking Gabriela. "Susan Foster has been after him for years, and she has stacks and stacks of evidence. He's protected from extradition by some of our own people in Washington, oil and money, sex, and more money. They keep the FBI off his back and he pays them off and does favors for them. Correction, his underage slave girls do favors for them. Susan is convinced he's expanding his organization, and most of it's human trafficking, immigrant kids."

"That's awful. To think I've done business with him for years. That stops today. I will make some calls, but not to that bastard. Hard to shut someone with his contacts down completely, but I can give him a good kick in the pocketbook. You're absolutely sure about all this?"

"Absolutely, we know he's the guy behind it all."

"If I raise hell and it starts costing him money, sooner or later he'll figure out where it started and tie it back to you, Slater. Is it worth the risk?"

"He might come after you too, Maryanne. But he killed Davey. Anything we can do to him is worth the risk as far as I'm concerned. Maggie?"

"Absolutely. I'll talk to Angela and Gabriela about it, but somebody has to stop him, we owe Davey that."

"Okay then, let's deal with one scumbag at a time." Maryanne set her jaw. "What about this ransom note? Five and five?"

"Let's say we give them five million. They're not going to show us Jasmine, because they can't give their location away. Now they have Jasmine and a small fortune. What is stopping them from cutting their losses right then. They take the money they have and get rid of the only witness. Sorry to be blunt, but that's the reality."

"That was always going to be a possibility, I know that, Slater. What if you watch them somehow, follow them or track them? I suppose they would be expecting a tracking device."

"Depending on how and when they want to transfer the money, there might be a chance to follow them back to Jasmine."

"Two payments means two chances, if they don't deliver her. There's always the risk that they'll kill her, we all know that."

"Okay. Agree to their terms, but tell them you want very specific instructions. From their perspective, the first run is to see if you'll do what they want and not bring the cops. Since there are at least two of them, one guy will probably hang back with Jasmine. It's insurance for them, because they can always threaten to kill her if we try something. It all depends on how they want us to deliver the money, that will be our chance. Obviously, you can't just put it in the mail, or leave it outside the door, there has to be some sort of an exchange."

"Maybe just keeping her alive is all we get for the first half."

"How about a video? A thumb drive of her, timestamped, so we know she's alive and reasonably well? We get that and they get the first half. Anything we get might give us an idea of who they are and where."

"That's good. How should I word the ad?"

"Missing you. Worried about your health. Need a video of that smiling face, then I can deliver the first five at the location of your choice. Be specific."

"They should be able to figure that out," Maggie said.

"Maybe Jasmine can give us a clue, but I imagine they'll be careful about that."

"Think they might have us just leave it somewhere? They do that in the movies."

"Five million dollars? They wouldn't leave it for long, and they would expect a setup. We'll just have to wait and see what they come up with."

That Butterfly, or the uncertainty it represented was tearing me up. Somehow, Jasmine had been ensnared by it. It might have been as innocuous as stopping on the side of the road to use her cellphone and never getting the chance. Maybe she had forgotten something in the house on her way to the party, and that slight delay had put her in the wrong place at the wrong time.

People run red lights all the time and sometimes the consequences are tragic. One second, or a portion of that sometimes means the difference between a sudden death or a close call with some horn blowing and hand signals exchanged. Was it all random, turning left instead of right somewhere along the line, or did the Butterfly know what it was doing? And was that Butterfly just a pawn in a bigger game? Was it guided by some ultimate purpose?

It was difficult watching my mother die. At times like that, and now this, I think everyone wonders about the big questions, and their own beliefs about a higher power. It's tough for me to think that our end is predetermined, that there is one day and minute that an omnipotent being has picked for our demise. That seems too simplistic, and robs us of our free will. At forty, I still hadn't settled those questions in my own mind, but I had said a couple quiet prayers for Jasmine, just in case I was wrong about that damn Butterfly.

When the next letter arrived three days later it contained a thumbnail, and we all gathered around Tommy Ackerman's laptop to watch the clip. Jasmine was sitting in an overstuffed chair with a rope tied around her neck that disappeared behind her. She had on a sweatshirt and shorts that neither Maryanne nor Maggie recognized.

"They must have bought her clothes," Maggie muttered close to my ear.

Jasmine looked better than I would have expected, her voice was strong and defiant.

"Hi guys! Still alive and as good as I can be. I miss you all. This is the sixth time I've recorded this stupid thing because Beavis and Butthead here want it just right. Twice I lost my temper, and twice I blurted out their real names. The last time I tried to sneak a hint in, but they aren't quite as stupid as they look." She glanced up at whoever was doing the recording. "Not a hint, dumbass, you are stupid-looking." She appeared to be listening for a second, then looked back at the camera. "I'm supposed to tell you that my life depends on you doing exactly as they say, blah, blah, blah. Same thing kidnappers always say...but I wouldn't mind coming home. I am going to owe you big time, Grandma, but I promise to get good grades. I'm thinking about being a cop so I can shoot assholes like these two morons. Hey..."

The clip ended before she was finished, and despite the fact that we were no closer to finding her, it was a relief to see that she hadn't given up hope. It brought a smile to Maryanne's face.

"Leave it to Jasmine to give them as much grief as she could get away with."

"She told us there are two of them," I pointed out. "And she implied that she might know them. She knows their names now at least, I'm not sure if that's a good thing or not."

303

"And, that they're stupid looking." Maggie chuckled. "Her bruise is mostly healed, and she didn't look too bad."

"Let's see what their demands are." Tommy unfolded the ransom note.

Maryanne, video included. Alive and well if you follow these instructions! Check GPS in tomorrow's ad. From that address drive gravel road three miles south, stop and wait. I will blink my headlights three times. Put the money on the road and leave the way you came. 5 million in unmarked hundreds. If there are no surprises, after next five, you get the girl. Midnight, on the dot.

"Gives us some time to prepare at least," I said. It had been a nerve wracking few days for all of us and we had gathered at Tommy's office to strategize. I didn't know if I should blame the postal service or the kidnappers for taking their sweet time in replying.

"I was hoping we might get a glimpse of an arm or a hand," Maggie put in. "Jasmine was trying to say as much as she could. She knows more than just their names."

"Kidnapping is a capital crime, so being recognized is not a mistake they can afford to make," Tommy pointed out. "These days, presuming no one is killed, they wouldn't get a death sentence, but they would end up in jail for a very long time. At least we have some idea of how it's going to go down."

"Midnight on a gravel road somewhere, any thoughts?" Maryanne looked at me.

"Luis could make the delivery, and I could try to follow them with the Piper after they pick up the money. No moon, so if we disable the lights it would be hard for anyone on the ground to see us if we stay high enough. The FAA frowns on that sort of thing, but I'm not going to worry about that. If Maggie goes up with me, she can watch for other planes and keep us out of their way if need be. If we're not near a commercial flyway we won't raise any red flags."

"From the air, you might be able to follow them right back to Jasmine," Tommy said hopefully.

"It will depend on where it is and what direction they're going. If they come back into town, we would need someone on the ground. Luis might be able to identify the vehicle if he gets close enough. If not, we just watch them from above and hope we get lucky."

"Will Luis be okay doing this?" Maggie asked.

"I'll talk to him, but I'm sure he'll do anything necessary to help," Maryanne said. "Could it be dangerous for him?"

"They've talked about killing Jasmine, so I'd say yes. People have died for a lot less than five million dollars. I'll talk to him about the risks. The second that ad gets posted tomorrow we have to start making our plans."

"Should we meet here, or at my place?" Maryanne asked. "The cash is in my safe, so maybe there would be best."

"The ads have hit just before noon, so Maggie and I will be there then. I'll make sure the plane is ready. I'm going to stop and see Susan Foster and run this by her. She might have some insight."

"Is she out of the hospital?" Tommy asked, then glanced at Maggie.

"I explained how we know her, Slater," the redhead told me. "And the shooting was in all the papers."

"She's out of the hospital, but staying here in town until she heals up. No worries, Tommy, if we can't trust our lawyer, who can we trust." Nobody laughed.

"This is downright embarrassing," Susan complained. She was dressed in some loose-fitting pajamas and perched on a stack of pillows at the kitchen table of the cop we had talked to the day of the shooting. "Captain Green and his wife were nice enough to take me in or I would have had to hire a nurse and been staying in a motel. No way I was ready to be alone in Titusville."

"Why didn't you call?" Maggie exclaimed. "We have a ton of room. My mom went to Europe for two months and her bed is empty."

"Thanks, but I'm here now, so I'll stay put. A few more days and I'll be able to get around. I haven't been able to get any kind of lead on your uncle, but that's not surprising. How is the girl doing that you brought back from Daytona?"

"Kids that age are unbelievably resilient. She already seems like your normal, happy teenage girl. Loves to shop and thinks she should have a cellphone."

"I would wait on the cellphone. Sometimes those girls have been so indoctrinated and terrorized, no matter how good their situation is, they're convinced they have to call their pimp. Gabriela may believe if she doesn't call him, he will come and kill you all. It's part of the brainwashing they're subjected to, especially the younger ones. She wouldn't do it to hurt you, she would think she was protecting you. I've seen it before. In time her ability to trust that she's safe will come back."

"No cellphone, got it. I would have never thought about that," Maggie said.

"I've seen dozens of girls like her," Susan said sadly. "There's a pattern."

"We're trying to save another one at the moment." I pulled up a chair and slid one over to Maggie. "The kidnappers made contact and it sounds like we're going to deliver half the money tomorrow night. Two payments, only way they would do it. I need your ideas."

"Two payments, and two kidnappers?"

"Right, and it doesn't seem like they're on the same page all the time. The correspondences were odd, whoever wrote them tended to overshare."

"If there are just two of them, you have to be prepared for the first one to make a run for it. Once he gets the money, why would he go back? He leaves his partner with nothing, just the cleanup. At that point, a lone operator might just decide to kill her and cut his losses. It's possible they're tight enough that that won't happen, but the guy watching Jasmine is taking a hell of a chance, or he's an idiot."

"Not what we wanted to hear," Maggie said. "How do we know what the guy is going to do? The idea is to watch him from Slater's plane and follow him if we can."

"May come down to your gut. If you think he's making a run for it, try to stop him. That's what I would do anyway."

"What if he calls his partner, and he kills Jasmine?" I put in.

"Then he dies in prison, while the other guy gets away? If you're able to stop him, killing Jasmine would be the stupidest thing they could do, unless he wants to try to shoot it out with you. I've seen you shoot, Slater, that wouldn't end well for him."

"Maryanne wants to do whatever it takes to get her granddaughter back safely. What if there is shooting and we kill the guy? Then how do we find Jasmine?"

"Most likely these two kidnappers are associated somehow, and you could track the other one down. Not a perfect plan, I admit. I can get you a piece of equipment that may help if you decide to do it my way. If you stop him, or pin him down, you probably don't want him calling his partner."

"A cell-scrambler? I know they exist, but how effective are they?"

"Police issue will shut down any cellphone within a couple hundred yards."

"And if his partner is sitting there waiting for a confirmation call?"

"Not a perfect plan, like I said. It'll be a judgment call when the time comes. I can line up the blocker and a set of night goggles. Pretty dark at midnight."

"You're a lifesaver." Maggie stood up and hugged her.

"Hope so, nice to win one once in a while."

I dropped Maggie off at home and went back to the airport. I took all the running lights out of their sockets but left the landing light operational. I spent a couple hours going over everything mechanical I could think of to check and washed off the spots where an errant Gull had left its mark. Being the poor mechanic I am, I didn't want to tinker with too much, so I closed it up and went to find Luis.

My crew consists of three men, plus Luis. They're all Hispanic, all legal, all better carpenters than their employer. What I lack in skill, I try to make up for with enthusiasm, but lately I hadn't found much time to even show up. My timing was right, and I helped unload a lumber truck before taking the foreman off to the side.

"Things are almost set for tomorrow, Luis. Are you sure you want to be involved?"

"Of course, Jasmine is like my own daughter."

"It may mean following them, or even ramming their vehicle if things go to hell. You can drive my pickup, if that gets smashed up it wouldn't hurt my feelings any. Do you have a gun?"

"A shotgun, to shoot the quail."

"Can you shoot a handgun?"

"Maybe." He grinned. "I've never tried."

"Bring the shotgun, you can scare them if nothing else."

"Close up, I can do more than scare them."

"Let's hope that isn't necessary. Sorry, but I have to go downtown and get some equipment. Maybe give the guys tomorrow off with pay. You and I both need to be wide awake come midnight."

"I will come to the Senora's tomorrow and we can make a plan, like you say. We will get her back, Senor Slater, I have a good feeling."

"I wish I was as sure, Luis."

Chapter Twenty

I felt better about things by the next morning. Watching Gabriela play with the big Lab while Maggie and I ate was cathartic. Young people are amazing. Despite all the tragedy and horrors she had seen, a good meal and a loving dog had Gabriela well on the way to recovery.

Hopefully, whatever Jasmine was going through could be put behind her as quickly. There was a sense of excitement mixed with dread, and my gut told me that one way or the other, tonight's delivery was going to shed light on who had Jasmine and what our odds were of finding her alive. Given the opportunity, I wanted to end it.

The more I thought about Susan's advice, the more I agreed with her. Giving the kidnappers five million dollars without getting Jasmine in return seemed like asking for trouble. It seemed confusing that Jasmine wasn't more scared of her captors. She was a strong girl and one that wasn't likely to be cowed, but if the bruise on her face was any indication, she had been knocked around some. No matter how independent, she had to realize there was a chance they would kill her. Yet the girl on the tape didn't seem frightened in the least. She had been combative, but the interaction she had with her kidnappers didn't seem like that of someone who considered them to be a threat. Their off-camera conversation, what was intelligible, had seemed more like banter than a heated exchange.

The idea that she could be involved had flickered through my head briefly. She had done some unexpected things in her seventeen years; but the wild child that I knew was more sweet, than saccharin, honest about what she felt, and committed to having a normal life with the people who truly loved her. People like myself and my partner. I had to go with my gut, and I trusted Jasmine. But she had been at the mercy of her captors long enough to have formed a bond of sorts, Stockholm syndrome, when the captive becomes so dependent on their captor that they lose their perspective.

From the first note, it had seemed like the two kidnappers might be at odds about Jasmine. The author of the letter had referred to his partner enjoying her company. That could mean the obvious, and if the writer's intent was to shake us up, he had succeeded; but it could also be taken in the literal sense. Maybe the second kidnapper actually liked Jasmine, or maybe she had wormed her way into his heart, as she had mine. And maybe I was grasping at straws, convincing myself that the second kidnapper wouldn't kill Jasmine, even if his partner told him to. I ran my thoughts past Maggie.

"I know Jasmine is brave and all that, but did you get the same impression from that video that I did?"

"That she was angry and bored, not scared? Yeah, but I didn't want to say anything to Maryanne. Maybe she managed to charm the second kidnapper, hoping for a chance to make a getaway. But the letters sounded serious, they still might kill her."

"I think we have to try to stop the guy that's picking up the money. He could go back and put a bullet in both his partner and Jasmine, then go on his merry way."

"What if he puts up a fight? You kill him, and we have no clue where Jasmine is. Maybe then the other guy flips out and kills Jasmine?"

"I just want it done with." I admitted.

"Me, too, but second guessing crazy kidnappers isn't a good idea."

"I'm going to run all the possibilities past Maryanne."

"I think she's being overly cautious, but she just got her granddaughter back from the drugs and a crazy biker, she doesn't want to lose her this way."

"Who is Jasmine." Gabriela asked in her fledgling English.

"Someone you are going to love," Angela said walking into the room. "Can you translate for me, Maggie?"

Gabriela smiled and spoke slowly again. "I know love."

That got to me.

After breakfast I went downtown and picked up the equipment Susan had lined up. The night goggles were top of the line, military issue that would magnify even dim starlight enough to see what we needed. The cell jammer was bigger than I expected, mostly because of the battery pack.

"We have a more powerful unit, but it has to have one ten power. That baby can shut down a square mile, but it takes an act of congress to use it." A uniformed officer spun the instrument around and gave me a quick lesson. "We don't use this very often either because there are all kinds of privacy issues and FCC regulations."

"Susan Foster must have a lot of pull for you to let me use this," I observed.

"Who? Never heard that name before." He gave me an exaggerated wink, had me sign a form, and I was on my way. I resisted the urge to turn the device on when I saw the person in front of me talking on his phone and weaving all over the road. It would have been fun, but I needed to save the battery.

"Explain to me how all this is going to go." Maryanne Thatcher sat in her plush living room nursing a bottle of water and looking at each of us in turn. "We have a limited number of bodies available but I really don't want to bring anyone else into this. Luis, thank you for agreeing to make the delivery."

"Anything I can do for Jasmine, Senora." He nodded.

"Camille offered to follow them with our car if that becomes necessary," Tommy said.

"That would be too dangerous, but thank you. I would like you here with me if that's alright, should any legal questions come up. I can't imagine what those would be since this whole thing is outside the law, but still. Slater, you and Maggie have a plan figured out?"

"Maggie and I will be overhead with the night scope, I'll fly and she'll keep watch. Luis will follow the instructions. He has a shotgun just in case he needs to defend himself. He'll make the drop, then go back to the end of this road, wherever that is. I'm guessing the GPS coordinates they give us must be near a highway or a bigger road, so he can hide his vehicle and wait there. Having him follow the kidnapper would be too risky, he might get seen and they might do something stupid."

"Like kill her," the older woman said grimly.

"Yeah. Maggie and I will try to follow them back to wherever they're keeping her, but if they get into traffic or go into the city, we won't be able to keep track of them. We talked about a tracking device, but there again, we don't want to have them find it and do something crazy."

"So, we're back to waiting? Give them the first half, and hope they deliver her the next time?"

"We could try to stop them, or him, because I'm sure one of them will stay back to watch Jasmine, but a shootout is going to be on the news. Then Jasmine's really in danger."

"So, we're stuck? We just do what they say?"

"The police would do this differently, Maryanne, but we don't have their resources and the chances are if they were involved, Jasmine might already be dead. We just have to play it by ear and if things change, we have to adapt. Maybe they'll do something we can take advantage of."

"If you have a chance to save my granddaughter, Slater, you do what you think is right."

"Kind of what I wanted to hear," I said. "Spur of the moment, we might catch a break."

"Any new information concerning the man we talked about?" I knew she meant Dinar.

"No, nothing from my end. Did you make the calls?"

"Nobody wanted to hear what I had to say. Money and oil, like you said. Making money is usually more important to people than doing the right thing. But my business is going elsewhere, and it's not a small account. I'll keep trying to apply pressure." Tommy looked between us, but held his tongue.

"Nothing to do now but wait for them to put the ad up." Maggie stated.

The ad must have been late, but thanks to the instantaneous delivery of the internet we had our instructions by early afternoon. They didn't offer a lot more information, just an address west of Jacksonville and another admonition to not involve the police. A quick look at a Google map confirmed our guess. The address was a church, ten miles north of Interstate 10, just off the main road heading up to the Georgia state line. It was situated on the end of a dirt road that wound its way west, in and out of a state forest and petered out somewhere in the middle. It was as desolate a spot as they were likely to find in north Florida, and one that would provide plenty of cover and places to hide from observation, both from the ground and from the air.

"Maggie and I will go up there in the Piper and look it over while it's still light."

"Would it be possible to trap them somehow?"

"We know there are two of them. The person that's left behind may be expecting a call. We could probably stop the one that picks up the money and jam his phone, but there again, the person who has Jasmine might be waiting to hear, and kill her if he doesn't. Common sense should tell them that if they don't have a live hostage, they aren't going to get any more money. But if they had any sense, they wouldn't be kidnappers."

"Should I drive out there?" Luis asked.

"They might be watching the road. We'll make one pass, plenty high up so we don't draw attention to ourselves. I just want some idea of what we're getting into. Hard to tell from Google, but that road doesn't look like much."

"Midnight is a long time from now." Maryanne said glumly. "Too soon, but not soon enough."

"Not much of a road." Maggie had the binoculars pointed down into the tall pines of the state forest a mile below us. "Do we dare get closer?"

"There's a possibility that whoever this is would recognize my plane, don't you think?"

"Can't imagine anyone doing such a thing for a few million dollars, or that it's someone we know. I'm starting to think it's someone out to hurt Maryanne. They told her to sell some oil wells and called her a bitch. It could even be a competitor."

"We're too close to chase down anymore leads. We just have to hope we can follow them back to where they have her."

"I'm with Maryanne, I want it to be over, but I'm scared of what's going to happen. The road looks like more of a trail, and there are a lot of swamps. Not many houses."

"When we get back, we'll have to look up the owner's names, see if any of them rings a bell with Maryanne."

"You're pretty good at this PI thing, Slater."

"Thanks, Partner. We're going to need to be good, and lucky, to get Jasmine back."

It was worth a try, but none of the few landowners along that road were familiar to any of us.

"How screwed are we if we get caught flying without running lights. I just got my license, and they'll take it away, won't they?" Maggie asked as we lifted off shortly after eleven.

"I'm certified for night flying, but you're right, we'd be screwed. Right now, all I care about is being able to see them, but them not seeing us."

"Kind of creepy, thinking that we can't be seen by other pilots."

"That's your job, to watch for other airplanes. Most people aren't dumb enough to fly over an area like that at night. If we had to put down, it would be the highway, and that would definitely get us in trouble." We flew west for several minutes, then I reached out and switched the cockpit lights off.

"I haven't been up at night in a single engine very often. Are you okay without any instrument lighting?"

"I can fly this old Piper by the seat of my pants, no problem." I assured her. "I can see the horizon and feel everything else. Plenty of room up here Maggie, safer than being on those roads down there with all those crazy drivers whizzing by."

"I know, I'm just not used to how pitch black it is in here."

"Darker it is in here, the better I can see outside."

"It's fine, I trust you not to kill us both."

"Check out the night goggles. They should be ready to go, just hit the button."

She looked down at the traffic far below us. "Wow, they compensate when you look at something bright. I'm curious just how much I'll be able to see when we get out where it's really dark."

"Won't be long. I'm going to take us in at about four thousand feet, half throttle with the flaps dropped some, slow and quiet. Luis will deliver the money right at midnight, and then we just circle and wait."

At five minutes before midnight Luis called me.

"He just went by the church." I told Maggie after I ended the call. "He said there's a parking area in the back, so he's going to park there and wait after he makes the drop, see if he can maybe get a picture of the car or the plate when they come back out. That looks like him."

Dark as it was, I could still make out the ribbon of lighter colored road against the dark woods surrounding it. Far to the south I could see the lights of the Interstate and a few cars trickling by on the trunk highway, disappearing to the north. I put the Piper in a slow turn and circled as we watched the headlights of my pickup make its

321

lonely way the three miles to the drop point. There was no sign of another car, at least not yet.

We hung there in the sky for another ten minutes before anything happened. A hundred yards from where Luis had parked, the lights of a vehicle flashed suddenly, one, two, three. Three quick flashes, then darkness.

"Wow, why didn't I see him?" Maggie said, shifting the scope.

"He must have been parked back in the woods. Hard to believe he could see the road with his lights off."

"It looks pretty bright through these glasses. He's just sitting there, waiting for Luis to leave."

"Any guess about the car?"

"Kind of big, and looks older. A Caddy I think, but I don't recognize it."

Luis must have dropped the duffel bags that held Jasmine's ransom. I could see the headlights moving back, then flash in a quick circle as he turned around and drove back in the direction of the church.

"Pretty cocky, thinking we wouldn't have somebody on the end of the road to follow him." Maggie commented. "I see movement, the road is actually a lot lighter than the trees. He drove right up to the bags so he must be able to see a little bit. I wonder if he suspects we're up here, and that's why he's keeping his lights off. I can't see, but I don't think he even got out of the car. Back to our first theory, maybe it is someone we know."

"Luis is in position, but he's not going to follow him unless he gets a call. He'll have to turn his lights on when he hits the main highway, then we can stay on him."

"If he goes to the highway. He's turning around and going the other way, still no lights."

"Dammit." I hit the throttle and turned the Piper sharply west.

"Where's he going? I thought this road ends in the middle of nowhere."

"Good place to disappear. He's ditching his partner and making a run for it. He's pulling a D.B. Cooper."

"D.B. Cooper?"

"Before we were born, but I understand the concept. He going to just disappear into the woods with all that money. Maybe the road goes all the way through or maybe he's going to ditch the car and walk, but I'm betting his partner isn't in the direction he's going. He's taking the five million and he's going to leave a very unhappy partner behind. Unhappy kidnappers have been known to kill their victims."

"What are we going to do?"

"Plan B. Stop him any way we can."

"What are you going to do, Slater?"

She already knew, I just confirmed my insanity. "There's a sharp turn a few miles ahead, I'm going to put the Piper down past it and block the road. It's got to be fast and you're going to have to use the scope to look for powerlines, because I'm not going to turn on the landing lights."

I still didn't see headlights and I was hoping he wouldn't turn them on. Dark as it was, he wouldn't be going very fast and we could get ahead of him. It would be a dicey landing at best, and we would still have to get him stopped.

"You okay with this Maggie? We have to stop this guy, but if we clip a tree it could be rough."

"I'll watch for limbs and powerlines, you get us on the ground."

"Soon as we're down, you turn on the cell blocker, then we get out as fast as we can. Call Luis and tell him to head this way, we'll trap this asshole."

I put the Piper in a dive to get as much speed as possible, taking a wild guess at where the sharp corner I remembered was in front of us. We came over the top of the road suddenly, a diagonal gray hashmark cut against the darkness of the pine trees, and I realized that I had overshot the corner by half a mile. I laid the Piper on its side, dropping into the small opening that a swamp afforded, and came down fast. Beside me, Maggie spit out an expletive and scrambled for the night scope and phone that had escaped her grasp.

I could just make out the trees on either side, ominous dark giants that rushed by us and loomed ever closer as we neared the ground. Their branches reached out for us, narrowing the opening as I struggled to keep us centered on the road. I'm not sure if we touched a limb or if there were telephone poles, but I felt a bump as the right wing caught something and the Piper careened sideways for a second. I corrected, but the left wing-tip dropped and I knew if it caught the ground or a fence post we were done for, so I put us down hard and fast. We slammed into the packed clay that sufficed for a road. The gear crumbled and the Piper slammed into the ground and dug a trench with the prop as we did an almost perfect nose stand, then dropped back onto the hard ground.

"Nice," Maggie said dryly, then spun around and fumbled for the two switches needed to activate the cell blocker.

"Out, quick." I yelled, but she was already sliding down the wing. I tumbled to the ground behind her and pulled her to the side when I heard the roar of the approaching car.

He came around the corner fast, despite the fact he still didn't have his headlights on. I'm sure his eyes were accustomed to the darkness and he could see the road, but he didn't see the Piper lodged in his way until it was too late. At the last second he tried to brake, veered sharply and caught the edge of the ditch, then piled into the left wing and fuselage of the Piper. If the landing hadn't totaled my airplane, the kidnapper's car did.

Maggie lunged from the other edge of the road before I could stop her. She had her gun out and moved quickly. I tried to get to the car first, fearing that the kidnapper would start shooting, but she jerked the driver's door open before I could reach her. The car was teetering between the road and the swampy ditch, and when the door popped open the man inside tumbled out into the barbed wire fence that paralleled the road.

The Piper picked that particular moment to burst into flames. Aviation gas burns quickly, and I was expecting an explosion. The man on the ground was flailing his arms and trying to get to his feet, so I grabbed a handful of collar and dragged him away from the growing blaze. Maggie reached into the back seat of the car and grabbed the bags with the ransom money, and we ran and stumbled away from the carnage, back onto the road. The kidnapper got to his hands and knees, then stood slowly and raised his arms cautiously. Maggie already had her gun pointed at his face, a face illuminated by the growing glow of the burning Piper. I had my gun out, standing behind him.

"You!" Maggie shouted over the crackle of the flames that were devouring my airplane. "You son of a bitch!" I stepped over beside her and looked at our captive.

Randy Jenkins, big talking con man, unremittent reprobate, and now a kidnapper.

"Hi guys, let's not do anything stupid here, okay?" He had a small cut on his face, but other than that he was unscathed, and remarkably defiant.

"Where's Jasmine?" I asked, keeping my gun leveled. Headlights flickered, and Luis came sliding around the corner in my pickup and stopped a few yards away.

"Where's Jasmine, you degenerate asshole, tell me!" Maggie screamed. The gas tank of the Piper blew, throwing debris in our direction and creating an even bigger fire. Instinctively RJ and I both ducked and shielded our face from the blaze. Maggie didn't. She stepped closer to RJ, waving her gun within inches of his face. "I said, where is she? If you hurt her, I will kill you, I swear to Christ. Tell me where she is!"

True to my belief that he wasn't the brightest bulb, RJ tried to negotiate. "You let me walk away right now or my partner kills the girl. I'm no murderer, but the kid is nuts, he just might put a bullet in her. If I don't call him to say I have the money, it's hard to say what he'll do."

"Where's your phone?" I asked. I couldn't be sure the phone would work, but the fire was licking at the cabin of the Piper and the cell-scrambler was likely to burn up within seconds.

"In the car." He glanced at the old Cadillac, but it had joined the inferno. "Let me take the Mexican's truck. I can stop him from hurting her." He licked his lips, just the whisker of a smile appearing. "Let's make a deal, I take the truck, the money, and disappear. I'll tell you where to find Jasmine."

"You'll tell us right now!" Maggie leaned toward him, shouting, with tears streaming down her face. Suddenly she stepped back a couple feet and raised her gun. She wasn't screaming or crying now, she was calm, and dangerous.

"RJ, it's over. We'll find her either way, and I don't believe your partner has the balls to shoot a seventeen-year-old girl. But so help me God, tell us where she is or you won't walk away from this." She aimed her gun at his head.

"Maggie, don't." This time I wasn't sure. A part of me was afraid she would kill him.

"Put the gun down, Darlin', I know a bluff when I see one." RJ smiled. He shouldn't have done that.

Maggie lowered the gun and pulled the trigger.

Randy let out a squeal of fear and pain. "You shot me, you dumb bitch, Jesus, you shot my Goddamn foot!" He collapsed, howling, with tears streaming down his face. "Oh God, it hurts, it hurts."

Maggie leaned down in front of him. "An address, you piece of shit, or I'll blow a hole in the other one."

"Call Susan," I said to Maggie as we turned onto the tar. I could see the flash of emergency lights just over the horizon, probably the fire

328

department, very possibly the police. "They see Luis, they might not be as objective as they should be." She produced her cellphone and dialed the number. I had to ask. "Would you have shot him again? Or even killed him?"

She snickered. "I didn't mean to shoot him the first time. I was trying to put one between his feet and scare him. Oops." I slowed the truck to the speed limit as she talked to Susan so we wouldn't get stopped. RJ had given us an address, but the possibility still remained that Jasmine was in danger if the cops went roaring in there. We had decided to go it alone. Randy had been suitably scared when Maggie pointed her gun at him the second time and had volunteered an address and the name of his partner. I was pretty sure we could handle it.

The address RJ gave us was about six miles closer to Jacksonville and on the other side of the two-lane highway. Undoubtedly, our second kidnapper was familiar with the area and had suggested the drop point, not realizing that the far end of the road would have allowed for his partner's escape with all the money. No honor among thieves.

We slowed down and caught a glimpse of a long driveway and the glimmer of lights. By now the doubt would be settling in, and the realization that RJ might not be coming back with the first half of the money. Given that he had been foolish or stupid enough to trust Randy Jenkins, it seemed reasonable that the man wouldn't hurt his meal ticket. I was pretty sure that had never been his intention.

We parked the pickup a quarter mile down the road in an abandoned driveway and ran back, ignoring the blaring horn of a bored motorist. When we could see the lights of the house, we cut through the woods and approached quietly. Like most old houses in the south there was a porch, hearkening back to the time before air conditioning when the best way to cool down in the evening was to get outside. The boards creaked ever so slightly as I stepped up and moved around the corner out of sight of the front door. Maggie stood behind a tree and flipped a stick at the front door, then a pine cone.

We were nearly certain this kidnapper was unarmed, but we wanted him outside before we confronted him. I heard stirring and the sound of someone climbing steps, then the front door opened. "RJ? Did you get the money?"

From behind the tree Maggie let out a grunt of sorts. Maybe it was supposed to sound like RJ, or maybe a bear. It didn't sound like either to me. Whatever the intent, it drew our target further out onto the porch. No doubt about who it was, same stoop to his awkward frame and the same unkempt hair.

Just to be sure there was no funny business, and because a part of me wanted to inflict some damage as payback for all the worry he had put us through, I hit him at a full run and gave him a pretty good shot to the back of the head. We fell into a pile on the deck of the porch and as Maggie rushed past me, I rolled him over and shook him a good one. He was just barely conscious, so I indulged myself and gave him a good slap across the face.

Jarrod Kinsley opened his eyes and stared up at me vacantly. When realization hit him, he started to cry. "I'm in a lot of trouble aren't I, Mr. Slater?"

I stood up and yanked him up behind me, then shoved him through the open doorway. I heard Maggie call out from the basement. "Down here, Slater. Bring Jarrod."

I held him by the collar and followed him down the steps. He was weaving slightly from the blow to the head and spouting a string of apologizes and excuses.

The basement wasn't much, an area for the water heater and furnace, an old couch and chair that I recognized from the video. There was a black and white television, and a couple steel supports to hold up the sagging floor. A toilet and wash sink were hidden in the corner. There was a chain bolted to one of the steel posts with six or eight feet of slack and the other end led to the handcuffs that Jasmine was wearing. She had dropped her hands and was leaning into Maggie, who was holding onto her and sobbing. Without comment,

Jarrod handed me a set of keys and I tossed them to Maggie.

As Maggie unlocked the handcuffs Jasmine looked over at me. She had been crying, but she gave me a small smile. "About time you showed up, Slater."

Once free, she went right after Jarrod, slapping and kicking at him until I eased in between them, only because I thought she might hurt her hands on his hard head. Spent, she returned to Maggie's embrace and buried her face in her shoulder. Jarrod stood with his head down, practically catatonic while the two women held each other and I made a call to Susan. There was a lot to explain, and we needed her help if we didn't expect to end up in the jail cell next to Jasmine's lanky captor.

"Why?" Maggie finally asked, with a look of pure hatred.

"I knew she would never have looked at a guy like me. I thought I could convince her if she just had time to get to know me. I thought maybe I could get her to love me, like I love her."

Maggie looked down at Jasmine but didn't ask the question I knew we both wanted to.

"He didn't rape me or anything, and he kept Randy away from me." Maggie touched the corner of Jasmine's eye which had nearly healed. "And he didn't do that. I fell down the stairs trying to make a run for it."

Jasmine glared at the gawky young man. "How could you be so stupid, Jarrod? Why wouldn't you just call me up and ask me out, like a normal human being?"

Jarrod dropped his chin onto his chest. "RJ said once you got to know me you would see how much I really care about you. He said we could take our half of the money and go away somewhere, together."

Jasmine softened a little. "That's not caring, Jarrod, that's really sick. You don't put someone you care about in handcuffs and let them wonder if they're ever going see their family again."

"Upstairs." I pointed and followed him up the steps.

We had another party, this time to celebrate Jasmine's return. Luis had managed to keep RJ alive, despite all the blubbering and the fact that he was missing two toes. He was the who had come up with the plan, and Jarrod had volunteered enough financial information to make it seem like a good idea. RJ was going to take that first five million and disappear into the swamps of north Florida where his three ex-wives and the victims of his latest scheme couldn't find him. Now it looked like some other poor miscreant would suffer the cruel and unusual punishment of having his company in the penitentiary for the next twenty years.

Jasmine surprised us all by testifying on Jarrod's behalf, both to the fact that he had protected her from RJ, and that she was pretty sure he was insane. She had volunteered the second part. The first portion of her testimony did seem to sway the judge, and a psychiatric evaluation didn't dispute the second half. Jarrod would be incarcerated for a while, but he got the lighter of the two sentences.

I went back to pounding nails but I kept my place next to Maggie in Frank Jeffries' old bedroom. Maggie's new house was ready for occupancy, but Maggie's mom had extended her stay in Europe, and neither one of us wanted to leave Angela and Gabriela alone in the big house. There was still the question of Gary Jeffries' whereabouts, and if Rashad Dinar planned to insert himself into our lives again. As spring gave way to summer, I fooled myself into thinking all that trouble was behind us. The Butterfly knew better.

Chapter Twenty-One

Nice truck, Slater." Jasmine Thatcher stood beside Gabriela and Maggie watching me fuss over my new pickup. The insurance money from the Piper had covered most of it, and a new airplane didn't seem like a priority at the moment.

"Your grandmother helped, finders' fee for getting her granddaughter back, again."

"Twice now," Jasmine admitted. "I always attract the wrong kind of guys."

"Cletus went back to North Dakota, so at least he won't be bothering you anymore."

"Other than the kidnapping thing, Jarrod isn't a bad guy, he's just confused."

"She's talking about going to see him in prison," Maggie volunteered with a sour look.

"He was just really lonely," Jasmine defended him.

"He chained you to a post and planned to make you his love slave," I reminded her. "When you start college, you'll have plenty of guys to choose from that are sane, you can move on and find someone really nice."

"If you don't scare them off. Jessie is still afraid to talk to me."

"Good, him I don't care for."

"We're going into town, Slater, want to come?" Maggie asked.

"I'm making a run to my house to pick up the job trailer, then I have to go help Luis and the guys for an hour or so."

"See you at supper then."

They drove off in Maggie's car and I started picking up the cleaning supplies I had scattered around the lawn, and rolled up the hose I had been using. It was midday and a breeze was coming off the water. Someone had cranked open the windows to let in the summer air, but I would have heard the scream anyway. It was a shrill, blood-curdling shriek that started loudly, then fell off into a broken wail, followed by a choking sob.

I was close to the front door and burst through, gun drawn and ready. Angela Jeffries was huddled in the corner of the dining room, her back to the wall, with Duchess clutched tightly in her lap. The Lab sensed her terror and snarled in my direction before recognizing me and whining apprehensively in the direction of the patio. Angela was shaking and almost incoherent.

"I swear, I haven't been taking anything, I swear. And I haven't had a drink in months, Slater, I swear it."

"What is it?" I asked. "What did you see?" I ran to the patio and stepped out and walked around the corner of the house. There was no sign of trouble, so I went back in. Angela was still sitting on the floor with her face in her hands, crying softly.

She looked up at me pitifully. "I swear, I haven't taken anything. Am I having a flashback, or am I losing my mind? Slater, I saw him, a ghost maybe? I am, I'm losing my mind. I have to take care of Gabriela, I can't be crazy!"

I put my arms around her and tried to reassure her. "You're not crazy. What did you see, or what was it you thought you saw?"

"Garrett. My uncle Gary. Older, different looking, but it was him. I swear to God. He was over there, near the patio, looking in at me. He was back by the bushes, but I could see him plain as day. Am I losing it, Slater?"

The timing wasn't great, but Maggie and I had been talking about telling her that her uncle was still alive, and this seemed like the moment. I led her over to the kitchen table.

"You aren't crazy Angela. There's something I have to tell you about Gary."

I explained everything about Gary's fake accident and the chain of events that led to Davey's death, whitewashing her father's involvement. I took the brunt of her anger, though I knew she was saving some for Maggie; but in the end she agreed that we had probably done the right thing. "I'm still mad at you two, but you were right. If I'd known that Gary was alive and that he was involved with what happened to Davey, I couldn't have handled all that. Does my mom know?"

"No, just Maggie, Susan Foster, and me."

"What does this mean, and why would he come here?"

"It's possible he just wanted to see you, to know that you're okay. But he's alive, and we weren't really sure of that, so I have to talk to Susan. It means we have to tighten our security again, we've gotten lax. The man responsible for all this is the same man that put Gabriela on the streets when she was thirteen and a lot of other girls like her. He's trafficking kids all over this country, and probably the world. The cops and the FBI have been cracking down on child prostitution operations all over lately: Minneapolis, Seattle, here in Florida. According to Susan Foster, Gary's boss is feeling the pinch since he's the one behind most of it."

"Is Gabriela in danger? I know you took her from some pimp."

"That pimp was protected by Dinar. He could decide to make an example of her, and Maggie and me, since they have our pictures. The last time I talked to your uncle, he said he could protect you and Maggie. That's why he escaped from detention."

"Fine time to start protecting us. He can go to hell." She stood and walked to the steps leading up to her bedroom.

"Most likely where he'll end up," I agreed. "Where are you going now?"

She pulled her shoulders back and raised her head. "To the gun range, you aren't the only one around here that can shoot."

After a text to alert Maggie of what had happened, I called Susan Foster.

"Good to know he's still above ground," she said dryly.

"Why do you think he would show up at Angela's house?"

"Nostalgia? Word is Dinar is coming to Florida, probably to see how Gary is running his organization here."

"You really think Gary Jeffries is running this part of his operation?"

"I know he is. We busted a couple of his guys in Miami, running girls and drugs. They flipped on Gary, but they wouldn't say anything about Dinar. But remember Andy Gleason? He's been saying all along that Gary was one of Dinar's favorites, but I never bought it until recently."

"Maybe the whole thing about protecting the girls is bull. Maybe he was just looking for Gabriela."

"I told you how much I trust the Diablo, Slater. Andy tells me that he would do anything for Dinar. He says that the whole idea that Gary would kill him is an act. He said if Dinar told him to, Gary would have killed his brother without batting an eye."

"That's a stretch. Not saying he's wrong, but Andy Gleason isn't the most credible witness."

"Are you and Maggie moving soon?"

"That's on hold for a while, indefinitely now. Strength in numbers if they come after us. It's hard to believe Dinar would risk any more trouble than he already has."

"His oil interests aren't making him any money right now. The price is down and Maryanne Thatcher and a few others stopped doing business with him because of the rumors about his other activities. If he doesn't already know, he's going to put you and Maryanne together at some point. I doubt he even knows who Gabriela is, but you keep getting in the middle of things and sooner or later he's going to pay attention. You killed his assassin and took one of his girls. He might come after you for that."

"He killed Davey, Susan. The girls are with me on this, and it's not like we're going to give Gabriela back. We have to stop him, that's the only option. If it means killing him, that's what I'll do."

"I'm not supposed to agree with you, but I do. But whatever you do, don't trust Gary Jeffries. I'll keep talking to the locals here, Miami and Lauderdale, and keep pushing them to bust these scumbags that are pimping kids. If we can't arrest Dinar, maybe we can starve him out of the country."

We didn't know it then, but the vagaries of the Butterfly were turning their attentions to Rashad Dinar.

We met Susan Foster for coffee one afternoon about a week after Angela had seen Gary, and she had an interesting story to tell. Some she knew first hand, some she had pieced together from other sources.

One of the girls that Davey Templeton had on his list to be rescued from the brothel in the desert was a very young girl named Chrissy Michaels. Sandy Foster had bemoaned the fact that the thirteen-year old girl from Seattle had been kept away from the others and subjected to the attentions of the unknown proprietor of the Castle in the Sand, as she had called it.

We learned later that Chrissy had become Rashad's favorite, and as unsavory as the thought was, she had learned to relish the role, even excell at it. There came a time when the Master became the enslaved, imprisoned by his affections for the spoiled, temperamental child that had him twisted around her little finger. But as often happens when dealing with a madman, the relationship soured.

Normally, when Rashad grew tired of his captives, they could expect a swift and brutal end; but as much as it was in him, it seemed he had developed a real affection for Chrissy. Her tirades often centered around the fact that she wanted to return to the United States; not to see her parents or the rainy city of her origin, but to spend her time in New York or Washington DC. She had become a very devious and ambitious fourteen-year-old at this point in time, well aware of the value of power and money, and very interested in getting her share of both.

Always the businessman, Rashad made the most of the situation. He had a very good friend in the US Congress, a regular visitor at the Castle in the Sand that had noticed his young consort, and eagerly volunteered a place for her in his Washington penthouse. Dinar would be rid of her, and the Congressman could pass her off as his intern, a foreign exchange student that he had graciously allowed to stay with him should the wrong people become aware of her presence.

Chrissy Michaels, painfully wise to the ways of the world, had no illusions about what was expected of her in exchange for being returned to the United States. Unfortunately for the Congressman, his wife arrived unexpectedly while Chrissy was expressing her gratitude on the hardwood floor in the living room. The whole thing might have been swept under the proverbial rug had the Congressman's wife not been accompanied by a pair of journalists doing a human-interest story about her charity work, and instead walked in on the biggest story of their careers.

Chrissy's charity work wasn't appreciated by anyone, and within a week the Congressman was ousted from his marriage and his Congressional seat, as well as being investigated for a litany of financial indiscretions.

Chrissy Michaels was returned to Seattle to spend a few years on the therapist's couch. She would go on to write a best-selling book about her experiences as a captive. "The Castle in the Sand" was a catchy title that one of her fellow captors had coined. I hear they might be making it into a movie.

The Congressman knew better than to drag Rashad Dinar under the bus with him, but the press spared no expense digging up details about the man involved in the Congressman's downfall who had a suspicious link to the young girl in question. As more details were exposed concerning the Congressman's activities, the federal court prosecuting the case issued a subpoena for Dinar's testimony. That meant the days of coming and going to the US unfettered were over. His passport had been tagged, and he would be stopped by TSA should he try to leave or enter the country.

Susan Foster was ecstatic. "Do you know what this means, Slater?"

"That fourteen-year-old girls are a lot smarter than when I was in middle school?"

"Pig." Maggie hit me. "She's not responsible for anything that happened to her."

"I know, I'm just kidding. Any idea if he got into the country before this all happened?"

"No. He has his own plane, but according to flight records he isn't here. He might have snuck in on a commercial flight using a different name, but he'd risk being ID'd. My guess is that he's laying low in Dubai or Algiers right now, but I can't be sure. But it's the beginning of the end for him, at least in this country."

"Not good enough if we don't nail him for what he did to Davey and your sister, not to mention all those other girls."

"I'm not giving up on that, but at least we're making his life miserable. His oil numbers are way down and we've been stopping most of the trafficking. The good guys are winning for a change."

"You need to catch my uncle." Maggie sighed, picking up her coffee. "Maybe he'll testify if it looks like the whole organization is falling apart."

"I said I was done dealing with him, but if it means putting Dinar away, I would be willing to forget that I have a big scar on my left butt cheek." Susan smiled ruefully. "I don't know if it was Gary's idea or not, I'm just glad the officer came through it alright."

"You're the one who told me not to trust him," I reminded her. "If it wasn't his idea, I'm pretty sure he didn't discourage them. He wanted out."

"And don't forget, they killed those dogs." Maggie glanced at her phone. "Angela has news, something about Gabriela and trouble with a friend?"

"She just got a new cellphone so she probably has a bunch of new friends."

"This one needs help. Angela wants us to come home to talk about it."

"She gets a phone and the first thing she does is call Daytona?" I asked when we got to the Jeffries house. "Susan warned me about this."

"She didn't call her old manager, she called one of the women she worked with." Angela defended Gabriela.

"Manager? Is that what they're calling it now? Are you sure this isn't her being manipulated by that pimp?"

"No, it's her being worried about the other three women that he has working the streets for him. She called them to tell them she was alright, and to make sure they were still alive. And it isn't about them, it's about the new girl they brought in to replace Gabriela. Gabriela's friends said she isn't going to live through another beating."

"Are you going to take in another girl?" Maggie asked. "Are you sure you're ready for that?"

"No, I'm not, to either one. This girl has family in Miami. The three hookers Gabriela knows want to help her get away and get to her grandparents' house."

"Out of the goodness of their hearts." I rolled my eyes.

"Stop being so cynical," Maggie said. "We don't care about their motives, we can help a young girl get out of a bad situation."

"So why not just call the cops?" I suggested. "We just left Susan, this is what she does."

"We could do that, but I'm guessing there's an immigration issue. I have the resources to keep ICE from taking Gabriela, but not everyone has that luxury," Angela said.

"And how do we know it isn't a setup? I know Gabriela wouldn't send us into a trap, but we don't know what is going on with these other women. Maggie and I go down there and that pimp and his buddies jump us. I'm guessing he's still not very happy that we took Gabriela, and he would love to stick his knife in me. Sounds like a setup."

"Fine, then I can go myself," Angela said stubbornly. "I'll take my gun."

"You know we're not going to let you do that," I said.

"I was hoping you wouldn't." She laughed and winked at her sister.

"You two aren't fooling me, I know you're plotting against me. Just don't think this will work every time." I had to salvage something. "I want to talk to Gabriela, see if she thinks we can trust those women."

"Gabriela!" Angela called her. She came skipping down the stairs with Duchess at her heels. Angela tipped her head in my direction. "Show him the picture, la imagen."

"Si, Senor Slater, mira. Su nombre es Marie."

I was picking up a lot of Spanish. The girl named Marie might have been sixteen, and judging from the picture, had taken a good beating recently. Of course, if it were a trap, playing on our sympathies would be a part of the plan. That was a chance we would have to take.

"Fine, we need to know where we're taking her, and it needs to happen during the day. I'm not going to try to grab another girl off the street at night when they might know we're coming. Call that hooker and set something up, something in broad daylight where the chances of getting shot at are minimal."

"No worries, Slater." Maggie chuckled. "And we don't have to take your new truck, we'll borrow Angela's Escalade. The windows are tinted, so at least they won't be able to take our pictures again."

"It's the guy getting those pictures I'm worried about. If Dinar isn't already after us, we're sure as hell going to make him mad by taking another young girl away from him."

"Good! Maybe he'll get the message and get out of our country," Angela blustered.

"Not likely, but it would be nice," I agreed.

I skipped work the next day and Maggie and I drove to Daytona shortly after lunch. Most of the working girls were still asleep at that time of day and their pimps were just rolling out of bed for the first time, cursing their growing prostates before catching a few more winks. That was my hope, I couldn't pretend to know the particulars of that lifestyle.

I had always thought of it abstractly, people I didn't know participating in the world's oldest profession. Unfortunate, but a victimless crime. Except it wasn't. And not all the victims were the obvious ones like the fourteen-year old immigrants sold into slavery by some coyote, or the young women seduced into drug addiction by some fast talking pimp. Davey Templeton had worked at a modeling agency, telling young girls he could make them into stars. I was pretty sure that he had believed that, but when he realized his mistake, he had paid for it with his life.

Everyone agreed that the pimp on the corner was a reprehensible human being, and certainly men like Rashad Dinar and his buddy the Congressman were, but they were just part of a bigger culture. Maggie had said it, without customers, there would be no prostitutes, and maybe no Dinars. Maybe, if there were no college kids lined up to stuff dollar bills in her pants, Honey would go back to California, marry Derrick, and get a real job.

"Penny for your thoughts."

"About all they're worth. Actually, I was thinking about Honey. I kind of feel sorry for her. Must be because I'm forty now, I'm getting soft."

"You've always been soft, but that's what I like about you."

"Maybe it's because I was raised by a single mom, but I think you can appreciate the fairer sex without taking advantage of them, or beating them senseless."

"Some wise old man once told me that the world has an annoying habit of being what it is, not what we want it to be."

"Sounds like a pretty smart dude to me."

"Old, really old dude." She grinned at me. "But the world keeps changing, Slater, and all we can do is try to help it along. It would be nice if we could do it the easy way, but that's never going to work when you're dealing with people like Dinar."

"I'm guessing Gabriela's pimp isn't going to want to do it the easy way either. Hopefully we can grab the girl and slip away unnoticed."

It almost worked that way.

Vera, the woman that had been in contact with Gabriela, had talked with Maggie and formulated a plan of sorts. According to Vera and Susan Foster, the streets to the west of the White Sands bar and strip club were a popular spot for lonely men looking for "dates." Those same streets were also lined with seedy looking motels and two-story brick apartments that might have been hotels, back in the days when full service had meant something different than it did now.

Almost all of the hotels and apartments had signs out offering an hourly rate, which was a

349

pretty good indication of the clientele. After dark, these streets would be flooded with girls displaying their wares, while lines of cars crept by and negotiated with them. There were a few early birds, running to the store for cigarettes or eggs, talking and laughing with their friends and shaking off the gloom of the previous night. Most of them were girls, not women. Most were twenty or under, and many weren't old enough to buy the cancer sticks they had hanging from their mouths.

"Those girls will have lung cancer, you watch," I commented to Maggie.

"Slater, half these girls will overdose within a year, if they don't get murdered by some drunken John. Cigarettes are the least of their worries."

"A lot of them don't look old enough to be down here."

"They look eighteen, mostly. But there's one that can't be a day over sixteen." Maggie nodded at a tall redhead. "Give her a year, she'll pass for thirty."

"They made it seem so classy in Pretty Woman."

"They make everything seem classy in the movies, Slater. Keep your eyes peeled for a tall blonde with a black scarf. We're supposed to just circle the block and she said she'll flag us down."

"I see anything that doesn't look right, and we're out of here. I still say it's a setup."

"I don't think these women would be out here if it was a trap, they would have heard about it. Hookers talk amongst themselves."

"And you know this how?" I asked.

"They're women aren't they?"

"Now who's being sexist? Like I keep saying, I can't win."

"Then stop trying." Maggie dropped her window suddenly, put her fingers to her mouth, and whistled loudly. "That's her, and she has the girl with her."

"I didn't know you could whistle like that. I'm impressed."

"Pay attention, Slater, down the street!"

The tall woman named Vera came running across the street and opened the back door of the SUV, then pushed her companion in. "Ramone is coming, get the hell out of here!"

Ramone was the same pimp that had held Gabriela captive, and he wasn't happy. Also, this time he had a gun. He fired one shot in the air just to scatter the herd, then started running in our direction. There wasn't time to make a u turn and there were too many people in the way, although they were disappearing like gazelles when the lion gets hungry; which is to say, as fast as they could run. Ramone brought his gun down to shoot at us.

"Get down." I yelled and put the accelerator to the floor. We weren't more than a hundred feet from Ramone and he did get a couple shots off before I chased him onto the sidewalk with

351

Angela's Escalade. I wasn't really trying to hit him, but he stumbled over the curb and I had to pull hard on the steering wheel to keep from running over his legs. By the time he got to his feet, we were half a block away. I took the first turn up a side street before he could get a shot off. "Everybody alright?"

"Fine, let's just get the hell out of Daytona." Maggie glanced back at the girl behind her and spoke rapidly to her in Spanish, then looked grimly back at me. "She says Ramone will kill the woman that helped her get away, but she wouldn't come along."

"Hopefully that doesn't happen. He certainly was trying to kill us. Call the cops and tell them shots were fired."

"On my cell? They'll know it was me."

The girl in the backseat reached over Maggie's shoulder and gave her a phone. "Use mine," she said in very good English. "We can toss it in the canal when you're done."

"You speak English?" I asked, looking at her in the mirror.

"I attended a very good school in Venezuela, before the trouble. You will take me to my grandparents in Miami?"

"That's why we're here." I nodded. Maggie called the police and gave a remarkably vivid account of seeing a man that would match Ramone's description shooting at several women.

"The police will not come," the girl in the backseat said. "They are afraid of the man Ramone works for, but thank you for trying. Throw the phone away, please."

"Next bridge we cross," Maggie promised. "Sure you don't want to get the numbers from it first?"

She lowered her window and looked out at the water in the distance. "He will send me pictures of Vera after he is done with her. I cannot look at that."

It was a quiet ride to Miami. Marie sat stoically in the back seat, expressionless and wooden, showing no joy at having just been rescued from a brothel, or concern for the woman we had left behind. Maggie's attempts at sympathy and conversation were met with one-word answers and vacant stares. But as we neared Miami the sun cast long shadows across her face and I saw tears streaming down her cheeks.

Her grandparents lived on the north side of Miami in a simple single-story house that was well kept but far from extravagant. They didn't speak any English, and I never figured out how they had known of their granddaughter's plight. They hugged us and shook our hands and then cried and hugged us some more, while Marie stood watching solemnly and never said a word. Finally, when we climbed back in the Escalade and prepared to leave, she approached the window.

"I hope that this is the end of it, but the man who gives the orders, he will try to find me. He will try to find you too, so beware."

"We know the man you're talking about, Marie," Maggie explained. "We are going to see that he is in jail for the rest of his life."

It was the only time I ever saw her smile, and it was humorless. "I wish that were true, Senora. Godspeed."

"I say we drive back tonight if you're okay with that."

"You drive, I'll nap." Maggie leaned against me. "We did good, Slater. I hope Marie was wrong about Vera. What an awful life."

"One girl at a time is better than letting Dinar have his way."

"Dinar, or my uncle? And is there any difference?"

At about two in the morning, an hour from Jacksonville, my phone buzzed. Nothing good ever happens at that time of night. Maggie was asleep and I opened the message which included a video. It took a moment for me to realize that I was looking at my own house, poorly lit as it was by a streetlight. Two seconds into the clip there was a blinding flash and a cloud of smoke, followed by the sight of debris tumbling through the air and flaming boards landing close to the camera

354

operator. My house had just exploded. There was a simple, cryptic caption. *"Last chance."*

Maggie stirred beside me, and took the phone from my hand, replaying the clip. "They're getting serious. Good thing you have another place to live. Were there things in there, things of your mother's that had a lot of value?"

"Letters and a few pictures, but not a lot of things I can't replace easily. Not this time. Next time he might come after you or Angela."

"We stop when Rashad Dinar is in jail for what he did to my brother. In jail, or dead."

"Figured that's what you'd say."

"Wow, Slater, lucky you were shacked up with your girlfriend."

"Morning Jasmine. Always nice to see your smiling face."

We stood in my front yard, surveying the damage, which was total.

"Maryanne said to let her know if she can do anything. I came over to help you and Maggie clean up the mess."

"Maggie will be here in a bit. The insurance investigator was here yesterday, they figure it was a gas leak."

Jasmine kicked a board with her tiny foot. "Maggie said it was that Dinar asshole, because you took another one of his girls."

"She shouldn't have told you that. Don't ever repeat that to anyone," I said sharply.

"Jesus, sorry."

"I'm sorry, I didn't mean to snap at you, but this is serious, Jasmine. This guy plays for keeps. Don't even repeat his name. Maggie knows how dangerous he is."

"She's worried about you, and her uncle."

"Her uncle's a lot of things, but I don't think he would hurt her or Angela, or me for that matter."

"That's not what I mean, she's worried that Dinar is going to kill him like he did David."

"I don't think she cares what Dinar does to her uncle, she hates the guy."

"She hates her father too, but it's still kicking her ass that he's dead."

"Yeah, maybe I know what you mean." For seventeen, she was a smart kid. "Have you talked to your dad?"

"The sperm-donor?" She laughed at her own joke. "Maryanne is going to give him some money to go away. He doesn't want anything to do with me, he just wanted a handout."

"I know he's dense, but I think he figured out you're pretty special."

"Thanks Slater." She leaned against me and I put an arm around her for a moment.

"You can always pretend you're my kid."

"You're old enough." She turned serious suddenly. "Maryanne sent me over. She has a meeting overseas this week, and she plans to lean on some of the bigwigs."

"Surprised they let a woman be at those meetings."

"She's not like most women. Anyway, she's going to tell them what Dinar has been up to again, and explain the dollars and cents. She's going to go at it from the business side, bad public relations for everyone when a guy like that is whoring young girls all over the world. It's her new crusade."

"Could be the fact that her granddaughter was kidnapped and she knows how it feels."

Jasmine shrugged. "Sounds like my grandmother. Anyway, she wants to know what you think. She doesn't want him coming after you for something she does. Pretty obvious the guy doesn't like you."

"Tell her to go for it, anything we can do to get him. Maggie and I talked about it. Everybody at our house owns a gun now, we get a group rate at the range."

"We have two new security guards hanging around the house. Big, serious looking dudes, with guns." She grinned up at me. "One of them is young, and extremely cute."

I played my part. "I'll have to have a talk with that boy."

Rashad Dinar's fortunes were fading rapidly. That week one of the cable networks ran a story about him highlighting the fact that he was a self-made billionaire. But the story pointed out, there were things about the young, good-looking entrepreneur that didn't add up. They had uncovered connections to possible mob members, Russian oligarchs, and most recently a disgraced US Congressman. What was going on behind the scenes? Inquiring minds wanted to know.

"He is not going to be happy when he sees that story." Maggie muted the television then returned to her breakfast. "At the least, he's going to have to stop kidnapping kids for a while. Sooner or later they're going to drag him into court to explain what he knows about Congressman Douglas and that whole mess. Could be that little girl is covering his butt, she's probably afraid to testify against him."

"Susan's sister knew her." I added. "She said she was the youngest girl there, but she knew how to get her way. According to Susan, Dinar's whole operation is in trouble, but you couldn't prove that by me. He managed to blow up my house just hours after we took Marie back to her grandparents, that takes some reach."

"All the security is working, right?" Angela asked. "He wouldn't try to get Gabriela back, would he?" The girl had finished eating and was on the couch, chatting on her phone.

"I doubt it. He's going to have a bad week if Maryanne Thatcher convinces her contacts in the oil business that he's a liability. If he loses his cash stream overseas, he's going to have trouble keeping things going here, too. I'm guessing all those thugs he has working for him want to get paid on a regular basis."

"Where does Uncle Gary fit in? I get that he was involved with kidnapping girls, but is he running things here in Florida for this guy?"

"Nobody knows, but it seems like he is pretty high up in the organization." I wanted to tell her something positive about her uncle, but there wasn't much good to say. "He told me he's only waiting to get close to Dinar so he can kill him, but Susan Foster doesn't believe that. That's the thing, was he here the other day to check in on you, or was he trying to grab Gabriela to make Dinar happy? We may never know. If the feds manage to take Dinar into custody, Gary might just disappear forever."

"I thought Dinar had diplomatic immunity or something," Maggie said.

"The only immunity he had was Congressman Douglas and whoever else all that money bought him. After the fiasco with Douglas and Chrissy Michaels, all of Dinar's other friends in this country are busy covering their own asses. And I do mean that literally."

Chapter Twenty-Two

Total happiness for me has always been a fleeting thing. Not that I was an unhappy kid, but by the time I was a teenager I had convinced myself that making Angela Jeffries my girlfriend and the inevitable consummation that was to follow, would make me truly happy for all of time. I'll admit, back then I mostly thought about the consummation, not the rest of time. There were short-lived moments when that seemed within my grasp, but those times were few and far between. For too many of the years that followed, I held onto the hope that she would suddenly fall in love with me, and we would both live the happily ever after that I had created in my mind.

With the benefit of hindsight and forty years of life experience, I now realized that being happy is a lot more complicated than just getting what you want. But when I was young and obsessed with a girl with blond hair and blue eyes, I was taught that happiness never lasted long and you had to take what you could get. That had worked for me for a long time, and it had been the only reasonable way to approach my hopes that Angela and I would end up together, because in the back of my mind, I was pretty sure we wouldn't.

Now there was Maggie. Being happy with Maggie was easy, we fit together naturally without a lot of thought, and my relationship with Angela was what it always should have been, just two close friends that had shared a lot of history and cared about each other.

The days flew by, and Maggie and I decided to spend the summer at the Jeffries Estate before moving into the smaller house she now owned a short drive down the road. The summer heated up and we swam in the pool, taught Gabriela English, and spent some steamy nights in Frank Jeffries old bedroom. Being happy was easy for a while, and as the weeks slipped away, so did our caution. No one knew where Rashad Dinar was, and Susan Foster called to tell us that she thought he was in hiding in the deserts of his home country, far from our happiness. Turned out, she was wrong.

"I have some furniture in storage Slater, we should think about moving it over here one of these days." Maggie and I stood in the living room of her new house. She was calling it our house, which was nice of her.

"We can use the job trailer whenever you want and get Luis and the guys to help."

"When are you going to move?" Jasmine bounced down the wide staircase that led to the second floor. "I can commandeer McCade to help. He's supposed to be my personal bodyguard anyway, so if I tell him to come, he has to."

"How personal is this bodyguarding anyway?"

"I'm almost eighteen now Slater, you don't get to boss me around anymore."

"When did that ever work?" Maggie snickered.

"He keeps trying." Jasmine grinned at me, then spoke to Maggie. "Are you waiting to move until your mom gets back from her trip? I wonder how that's going to go, with Gabriela there?"

"Angela's house now, she'll have to get on board with it, or move out."

"Slater would love having the mother-in-law move in, right Slater?"

I ignored that. "Dinar is still out there. We're hoping someone will put him in jail soon. I don't like the idea of Angela and Gabriela being there alone."

"They're alone now," Jasmine pointed out.

I don't believe in premonitions, but the hair stood up on the back of my neck and I had a sick feeling suddenly. "Damn that Butterfly," I said aloud.

"You're making even less sense than normal, Slater," Jasmine commented.

"It's his personal superstition," Maggie explained. "Alright, we can go back to the house so you don't have to worry about them."

That didn't work out either.

As soon as we pulled in to the turnaround, it was clear that something was wrong. Jasmine's car was parked to the right side of the driveway, and one glance confirmed that all was not well. There were two small holes in the driver's side door and the windshield was gone save for a few shards of broken glass. The front door stood wide open and an alarm shrieked from inside.

I slid out of the driver seat and told Maggie and Jasmine to stay put. I thought at least Jasmine might listen, but they both burst through the door a half a step behind me. There was blood on the tile near the door and Angela's gun lay near it, slid up against the center island of the kitchen. From above I heard the crazed barking of a dog and we all tore up the steps as fast as we could.

There were two holes shattered in the oak door that led to Maggie's old room, Gabriela's now, and the shots had come from inside. Duchess must have heard us come to the door, because the dog slam against the door and continued barking and snarling like a crazed beast.

"Gabriela, it's Maggie! Don't shoot." The redhead called out loudly. Within seconds the door was ripped open and the small Latino rushed into Maggie's arms. Duchess barely glanced at us, then raced down the steps. I could hear his claws scrape across the tile floor as he lunged through the front door. Oddly, he started barking again, maniacally. This time I didn't say anything, I just ran after the dog.

There was a late model black Jeep Wrangler parked in the yard. The side windows were tinted, but I could see through the windshield. Gary

Jeffries sat behind the wheel, hands at ten and two, waiting patiently. I walked up to the vehicle with my gun pointed directly at him as Gabriela called Duchess back into the house. Within moments, Maggie and Jasmine were next to the truck with me, both screaming obscenities at Gary and pounding on his window. The glass came down an inch.

"I need to talk, Slater."

"You lousy piece of shit, where's Angela?" Maggie was beside herself, screaming irrationally, and Jasmine ran around the back of the Jeep, trying to see inside, then started pounding on the passenger door.

"Stop you two. Let him talk." I lowered my gun and stepped back. The girls stood beside me. After a couple of seconds, the window came down.

"Dinar has her. He came here for you, Slater. He blames you for most of his troubles, you and the Thatcher woman, and he figures you put her up to it. When he couldn't find you, he grabbed Angela. He has a house on the coast and a boat ready to make a run for it tonight. He said if I don't bring you to him within two hours, he'll leave pieces of Angela for us to find and feed the rest of her to the sharks. He'll kill her for sure if the cops show up."

"How many men?"

"There were six, but they're disappearing in a hurry. They know he's going to worry about his own ass and they're trying to save themselves.

Hard to say, but I'd guess by the time we get there it might be three, maybe four."

"You still planning to kill him?"

"I plan to try. If I bring you to him, he might slip up and give me that chance. He's been really paranoid lately. He always has a gun in his hand, and he's pretty good with it."

"You're not going with him?" Maggie asked. "You can't possibly trust him! Maybe he wants to save Angela, but he's not going to give a shit if you get shot."

"There's no choice, Maggie. Dinar will kill Angela without batting an eye, you know that. What are the odds of sneaking a gun in there?"

"I've got one, and none of the guys dare mess with me, but I'll have to strap your hands to make it look good. Hopefully I can sneak a gun to you when we get there. The guy at the gate will check you over, so no cellphone either."

"We can follow you, call the cops at the last minute," Maggie said frantically.

"Maggie, one thing looks wrong, and he might just shoot her out of spite. Gary gets an extra gun in there, maybe the two of us can kill that bastard."

"We have to go, he said two hours. It's only half an hour there, but God knows what he's doing to her," Gary pleaded.

"Maggie, it's the only way. Give Gary your gun, it's smaller and he can hide it easier. Here, take mine. If you don't hear anything within an hour, call the police."

"Gary, where are you going? How can I tell the cops where you are without knowing where you're going?" She started to cry.

"Sorry, but I don't want to lose two nieces today. I'll do everything I can to get Slater back to you Maggie, and your sister."

"I hate you," She screamed. "Don't promise me anything."

I handed her my gun. "Here, can I have yours?"

"Slater, no." She pulled me into a hug and I returned it briefly, then pushed her gently away.

"Maggie, we have to try this, it's Angela's only chance and we don't have much time." I ran around the Jeep and climbed in the passenger's seat. A quick glance in the mirror told me all three of the girls were in the yard watching us drive away.

There wasn't much of a plan. We had to get by the front gate and the guard there, then be escorted into the house where somehow, we had to dispense with however many men Dinar still had, free Angela, and kill Dinar. It might have seemed remotely possible if I had any faith in Gary Jeffries. With time, and Susan Foster's help, we might have been able to coordinate something, but we didn't have that luxury.

Dinar was reaching the point of desperation. He had watched his empire crumble in the last few months, his wealth disappear, and his iron grip on his empire began to fail. It had occurred to me, that should Rashad Dinar completely lose control of his business, the old Diablo Blanco might do well should he live through the coming conflict. If somehow Gary Jeffries managed to kill Dinar and I also fell victim to a stray bullet, there would be nothing stopping Gary Jeffries from returning to his former life. He could take over the trading of young girls in south Florida and rebuild the child trafficking operation that had taken us all down this dark path to start with. I didn't want to trust the Diablo, but until Angela was free, I had no choice.

"Why did Dinar come back? Once Douglas went down, I didn't think he would dare show his face in this country."

"He was already hiding here when that happened. He's not popular at home right now either. He's been skimming from his clients all over, and that doesn't play well in the Middle East. He'll be executed if they catch him. His only chance now is to make a run for Russia and hope his friends there will protect him."

"Why is he bothering with us?"

"He wants me to keep things going here, thinking he can turn it around somehow. You've been making him look bad. He has to kill you to warn everyone in the organization what will happen if they get out of line."

"He trusts you that much?"

"Not really, that's why he has Angela."

"He gives you Angela and kills me, then what?"

"Then I kill him."

"But if you get Angela and he gets away, you could go back to the old life, just disappear."

"I said I was done with that, Slater. If Dinar doesn't kill me, I'm going to kill him. Either way, I'm not going to be the one dragging kids into that life."

"You understand I don't trust you, not even a little bit."

He flashed a rare smile. "I'd think you were an idiot if you did. Unfortunately, before we get there, I'm going to have to zip your hands together and tie them to the grab bar. The guy at the gate is no rocket scientist, but he isn't going to believe you're my prisoner if you're not strapped."

"I figured as much, but at least I'll have my hands in front of me. How am I going to get the gun from you?"

"I'll have it in my belt, but we'll have to play it by ear. Rashad is good with that gun of his too."

"So you said, but if he gives me anything to shoot at, I can put him down."

As we neared the property, Gary pulled over and zip-tied my hands as we had discussed, then we continued on. We were still a good distance from the ocean when he turned down a small road that led north and we turned into a long driveway surrounded by sea-oats, then drove up a hill to a small gatehouse. The big house stood higher up on the hill. I could see the expanse of the inland waterway beyond it, but the property was set back away from the main body of water in a natural harbor. There was a large dock jetting out into the rushes and the boat tied there looked big enough to be seaworthy. I could see movement, at least one more person to deal with.

"Does Dinar think he'll be free and clear if he heads out to sea?" I asked.

"My guess is he plans to head south and catch a ride on something bigger, then find a place where he can't be extradited. So far, he hasn't been charged with a federal crime, but he does have that subpoena hanging over his head. If your friend Susan has her way, I know enough to put him away for a long time."

"Plenty of reason to put a bullet in you too," I advised.

"That's crossed my mind, but I'm here for the same reason you are, Angela. We could shoot our way in, but he'd kill her for sure."

We drove up to the gate and a short, stocky man in his thirties bent down to look inside the Jeep. He smiled at Gary. "This the guy?"

"Yeah, tell the boss I'm coming in." He unbuckled his seat belt and walked around to my side of the truck while the guard picked up his phone and spoke briefly into it, then pushed the button to open the gate. Gary opened the door on my side and pretended to fuss with the strap that held my hands to the grab bar. He glanced at the guard as he walked around behind the Jeep. "You got a knife? He isn't going to try anything between here and the house, just cut him loose from the bar so I can drag his ass out."

"Wouldn't want to be you, Dude." The man said as he leaned in and cut the zip tie with a quick flip of his wrist. He backed away and stood up just as Gary Jeffries lifted his gun. He hit the shorter man with a vicious swipe across the back of the head, grunting with the effort. If he lived, the guy would have a serious headache for a few days. Gary grabbed him by the collar and his belt and pulled him into the tall grass beside the gatehouse, then climbed back into the driver's seat.

He glanced at me and shrugged. "He was playing for the wrong team. That's one we won't have to worry about."

Gary pulled me out of the truck, gun in hand, and shoved me toward the front door just as it opened. A big man with an automatic rifle stood aside and motioned us in without comment. Another man, similarly armed, stood half way up an open staircase staring out a high window at the driveway. Fortunately, the road turned slightly and as tall as the grass was, I was sure he hadn't seen what had just transpired at the gate.

We were in a large entry with a table and a sofa. There was a second door in front of us, as well as another one down a short hall that led to the kitchen. Undoubtedly the room had been a formal dining room and the side door was for the wait staff to deliver food. It was a familiar layout, one I had seen a lot in the prosperous estates on Point Road. We heard a noise from the other side of the door, then a woman's voice crying out briefly in pain, followed by a resounding thud.

Gary started to rush forward, but the first guard grabbed at his arm. "I know she's your niece, but let me tell him your coming in. He hasn't hurt her yet, not badly."

Gary grabbed my arm and guided me up to the door. The guard stuck his head in the door, then opened it and let us in. He pulled it shut quickly behind us. With the gate guard down, that left three men and Dinar, counting the one at the dock. If I could put my hands on a gun, the shooting would be over before the third man reached the house, one way or the other. The door closed behind us and I got my first look at Rashad Dinar.

I was struck by how young he was, mid-thirties with a complexion darker than most of his descent, and the fact that he was strikingly handsome. He was dressed in typical Florida garb, a bright print shirt and light-colored Dockers that he might have grabbed off the rack at JC Penny's. There were traces of blood on his pants and when I got closer, I could see some red mixed in with the other colors of his shirt. I was sure it was Angela's blood.

371

She was lying close to his feet, holding one arm above her in a defensive position while the other one covered her face. The source of the blood was obvious, both her lips were cut open and continued to bleed. Rashad stood above her with a gun in his hand. He nodded to Gary, then stared at me. Suddenly he reached down and grabbed Angela by the hair, yanking her to her feet. He pulled her face close to his and leered at her as she sobbed.

"Come on, Honey, pay attention, would you? I don't want you to miss this."

Casually, like he was shooting at a tin can on a fence, he lifted his gun and put a bullet into my left leg. The pain was immediate and the impact of the shot took my feet out from under me. I went down hard.

"Damn it, I was trying for your kneecap!" He complained. The front door flew open and Dinar pointed his gun in the direction of the wide-eyed guard. "Get out." He yelled, and the man slammed the door quickly. Rashad grinned and pulled Angela's face closer. "But we have time, Sweetie, and I can have a go at his other kneecap. Mr. Slater, you two have a thing, right?" Angela muttered an explitive and Dinar cracked her on the side of the head with his gun. I looked to Gary, fighting the pain. Where was that second gun? Even with my hands zip-tied together, I would have a chance.

"You have Slater, Rashad." Gary spoke up. "You promised me you'd let me take her out of here. Do what you want with him, but she's my niece." He glanced at me. Maybe I saw some regret, but it was clear I wasn't going to get that gun.

"Not so fast, I think she should enjoy my company a little longer." Rashad leered at us. "Maybe on her knees, while her boyfriend watches."

Gary's gun came up and Rashad shifted his body slightly, using Angela for a shield. From the front room, or possibly from outside the front door, there was a shout and then the sudden static roar of automatic gun fire, followed by more individual shots. I knew the sound of that gun, I had heard it a lot lately at the range. I looked at Gary, pleading with my eyes, but he was concentrating on Dinar. "It's not too late, Rashad, let her go and make a run for it."

"Like hell. You set me up, didn't you?" He fired and hit Gary in the chest, throwing him back against the door, just as someone tried to open it. "Stay out!" Rashad screamed and put two more bullets into the heavy oak frame. Gary was hit, but he was a big man and Rashad would have been wiser to use those two bullets on him. He brought his gun up with one hand and tossed Maggie's gun to me with the other one. If I had been able to get to my feet, I might have risked a shot, but from the floor, I didn't dare.

Gary was sprawled against the door and when he started to lift his gun again, Dinar fired another shot. I wasn't sure where it hit, but I knew I was on my own. I pushed off the floor and managed to get to my knees, willing to risk a shot if he gave me just the smallest opening. Angela's eyes were wide and she was fighting him, but she went limp when he tightened the grip he had on her throat.

"Should I kill her first, or should I make her watch you die, Slater?" Dinar asked as he pointed his gun first at her head, then in my direction. I didn't dare shoot, there just wasn't enough of that twisted, evil face showing. Just when I thought he might pull the trigger he stopped suddenly. "Why, Slater, why the crusade to ruin me?"

I kept my gun on him, searching for a shot. "You ruined a lot of lives, Dinar, and killed how many young girls? But then you killed Davey Templeton, that's when we started after you."

"The little queer kid?" He mocked me, and I could see he was ready to shoot. "Aw, was he your special friend?"

The maid's door swung open suddenly and Maggie Jeffries stepped into the room as she raised her gun. My gun actually. "No Asshole, he was my brother."

She had a better angle, but Angela was right there and I had just a moment to be afraid for them both, then the 9mm roared and Rashad Dinar crumpled to the floor with a sizeable hole just below his left ear.

Angela, still dazed and unable to stand, crawled over to where Gary lay and tried to rouse him. Maggie ran to me, pulled her sweatshirt off, and began wrapping my leg.

I was feeling weak, but I managed a smile. "Kind of glad to see you. How'd you find us?"

"Jasmine and I got tracker apps on both our phones after the kidnapping. When Gary came to the house, she dropped her phone behind his spare tire. Then we called McCade and he came with me. No offense, but I think that kid might be a better shot than you are. He got hit too, so I need to check on him."

I managed a smile. "You're a better shot than me. I told you my gun wasn't too heavy for you."

"Men, you always have to be right." She pecked me on the forehead then ran out the side door.

In the distance I could hear the singsong shrill of an ambulance approaching. I knew Dinar didn't need one, and I was afraid Gary didn't either. I shifted my gaze to Angela, who was holding his hand and crying.

She looked over at me and smiled through a sob. "He's gone, but he smiled at me before he died. It counts that in the end he tried to be a good guy, doesn't it Slater?"

I wasn't sure if that was all there was to it, but I nodded. "Of course it does Angela."

"Is it really over now?" She asked pitifully.

"It's over." I sure hoped so.

Chapter Twenty-Three

Have I told you how much I love you?" I asked from my hospital bed. Dinar's bullet had fractured a bone and complicated my recovery. After several days in the hospital filled with expert opinions and consultations, the doctors finally decided to operate. It had gone well but I was still somewhat altered by the pain medication. Quite altered. The dreams were great, but it was difficult to wake up and make sense of the world.

"Slater, Maggie's right here and she can hear you," Jasmine said, and giggled.

"I don't care, she loves you too. That was pure genius, putting your phone behind the spare tire." I tried to sit up, but the room twisted and I fell back. "Why did you do that again?"

"My girl wanted to go to the party and you were trying to leave her out."

"But we got your boyfriend shot." I shook myself awake. There was a window near my bed that was open and a cool breeze whispered across my face, smelling faintly of someone's breakfast and the Saint Johns River. It was morning, the sun was warming my face, and I felt intensely happy to be alive. The drugs helped.

"He's tough, he'll be fine. I'm taking really good care of him."

"I can do without the details. If he and Maggie hadn't showed up when they did, I might not be here."

"Might?" Maggie asked as she sat down carefully beside me on the bed. "Face it, Slater, I saved your butt again."

"You did." I admitted. "We got the man that killed Davey, that feels good."

"Susan Foster is coming by to see you later, and she isn't thrilled that you got her star witness killed. There are still a lot of people she wants to prosecute."

"I have a feeling she's not going to be too upset. We rid of the world of Rashad Dinar and that'll make her happy. But I am sorry about your uncle."

Maggie shrugged. "My uncle died in a plane crash four years ago. The man that Dinar shot was the Diablo Blanco. He was the bastard that got my brother killed and sold those young girls into slavery. I know I have to put those two people together someday, but I'm just not ready to do that yet. He did help save my sister, so I owe him for that."

"Is Angela okay? She's probably going to need more therapy, or another dog."

"She's black and blue and has a few stitches in her lip, but mostly she's just exhausted. I checked on her this morning. She and Gabriela were wrapped up in a huge pile of blankets with the dog stretched across them both, dead to the world."

"That's what I need. I could sleep for a week." I closed my eyes, but Jasmine bumped my good leg before I could drift off.

"Tell him the other thing," she said impatiently.

Maggie laughed softly. "Our house is ready whenever you get out of here."

"Our house?" I remembered, but it was a phrase I'd never used in my forty years. "Is Angela okay with us leaving?"

"Mom will be back next week, and Gabriela will keep her busy. Andrew said he's going to try to be around more, so who knows where that'll go? Angela isn't that crazy, broken girl anymore, Slater. She can take care of herself."

I rubbed my eyes and shifted my leg away from accidental harm, trying to fight the drugs and stay awake. "I need to heal up and get back to helping Luis and the crew."

"Luis has been giving me a hand this week. I turned the front bedroom into our office, and now we have an outside door with one of those opaque glass panels like Davey had in Miami."

"Why the fancy door? All I need is a computer and a place to roll out blueprints."

"The glass panel is for the sign, Slater and Partners Investigations. I gave you top billing."

"I like that name," I mumbled as sleep won the battle. "Screw that butterfly."

My eyes slammed shut on their own, too heavy to hold open as reality twisted into a dream. That pesky butterfly floated away on the warm summer air and a boy with Angela Jeffries' beautiful blue eyes chased it down a white sand beach, laughing happily.

Maggie's face hovered above me suddenly, and I fought sleep again long enough to kiss her and ask the question I knew didn't need asking.

"Are you sure you want to keep doing this PI thing with me, Red?"

Vaguely, I heard her laughing as I drifted away.

"Slater, you and I are just getting started."

End

Free! Signup for a gift copy of the next Slater Mystery, to be released in October of 2019 at www.tjjonesbooks.com Everyone that signs up will receive a free copy.
(Your e-mail address will never be shared)

It would be wonderful if you could leave a review. A few words and a star rating help to sell books and improve my Amazon ranking. Thanks for reading.
T.J. Jones

Look for "Slater's Tempest" at the end of October 2019